Proud Empires

Austin Clarke

VIKING

For Loretta Anne Clarke, my Secondborn

VIKING

Published by the Penguin Group
Penguin Books Canada Ltd., 2801 John Street, Markham, Ontario,
Canada L3R 1B4
Penguin Books, 27 Wrights Lane, London W8 5TZ, England
Viking Penguin Inc., 40 West 23rd Street, New York 10010, USA
Penguin Books Australia Ltd., Ringwood, Victoria, Australia
Penguin Books (NZ) Ltd., 182–190 Wairau Road, Auckland 10, New
Zealand
Penguin Books Ltd., Registered Offices: Harmondsworth, Mid-
dlesex, England

First published in Great Britain by Victor Gollancz Ltd., 1986
First published in Canada by Penguin Books Canada Limited, 1988

Copyright © Austin Clarke, 1986

Canadian Cataloguing in Publication Data
Clarke, Austin, 1934–
Proud empires

ISBN 0-670-81756-2

I. Title.

PS8505.L36P76 1988   C813'.54   C87-094090-2
PR9199.3.C54P76 1988

Author's Note: .

All characters in this book are fictitious, and any resemblance to
actual persons, living or dead, is purely coincidental.

One

THE VILLAGE

I

It was really from the age of thirteen that Boy wanted to be a big man. He was born in a small country, an island, and he lived in a small country village.

Sugar-cane fields and the sea surrounded him: the sea on one side, and the green silent sugar cane, with blades sharp as the butcher's knife, on the other three sides. His home was made of wood and limestone. It had four rooms. It was surrounded by sea and canes, as if it was itself an island.

As he was growing up, all around him were always big men. Three of them, not counting in his father . . . in his village were the biggest.

The police sergeant was a big man. Everybody in the village called him a big man. He beat up many men and turned them into criminals from those beatings. Many of them were innocent. He broke their legs, sometimes; and after they came out of prison or gaol, from a long sentence with hard labour, or from a short term, the moment they saw him with his three shining silver stripes below the Imperial Crown, they would stand erect, as if at attention for the National Anthem, and address him as 'Skipper'. They would tip their cloth hats to him, and say, 'Good morning, Skipper. I could do anything for you? Like carry a message?'

The man who lived in the green-painted house on the biggest hill in the village which was described in the geography book as 'flat', in a house he christened 'Labour Bless', made of coral stone and hard woods that came from Demerara in South America, he too was a big man. 'Labour Bless' had an open verandah which ran on three sides. It was a rundown house now: decaying, and with its green paint peeling off like scabs from a wound. You had to look up the hill to see it. It stood like a reminder of its owner's large ego, and as a measurement of the villagers' own expectations. 'Labour Bless' was shaded by

7

luscious trees that bore breadfruits and hog-plums and sugar apples; and when you saw it, even from your lower vantage-point, you had to agree that it was indeed the biggest house in this small village.

And the tailor. He too was a big man. The tailor talked day and night about nothing but politics. The politics of the island, the politics of the entire Caribbean, the politics of England, and the politics of Amurca. Sometimes, when the men sat in his tailor shop, fresh from the rum shop next door, and with blurred, tired eyes reddened from the power of the rum which they drank in short strong 'snaps', they would gaze into the mellow soft light thrown against the unpainted wooden walls, and listen as the tailor talked about the politics of Russian socialism.

'The Russians is who invented socialism,' he said one day. 'So, don't let nobody fool you that it is they who invented *commonism*. Commonism is the invention of the English.' Nobody knew what he was talking about.

One day, in the afternoon, Boy was passing the tailor shop. The shop looked empty. Boy could not see a head amongst the shadows. But as soon as he drew abreast of the small unpainted shack, the tailor's voice came at him like a bucket of water. 'Have they taught you yet about commonism, at the College?'

The words have stuck in his memory. It was during the Christmas holidays, two years ago.

The tailor is fifty years old. And like the man in the biggest house, he has spent some time in Amurca, during the War. Towards the end of the War. He went there on a merchant ship which transported him along with men from other West Indian islands, destined for Florida, to pick oranges and cut sugar canes on a plantation. Every day of his life in the island, and before his passage to the orange groves and cane-fields of Florida, the older men say that the tailor became abusive whenever anybody said something bad about black people.

'The black race of Amurcans is the Jews of the new whirl,' he told Boy that day two Christmases ago. 'My life in Amurca and in Florida have teached me the politics of the black race. The black Jews of Amurca. When you hear people round here singing "Jerusalem My Happy Home", who you think they

8

mean? They mean the black race of Amurca. But you wouldn't know that, 'cause they don't teach modern politics at the College!'

Boy stood speechless. And furious.

'I have solve the reason why Barbadian men don't like to cut canes no more. The solution lies in the comparison between Russian socialism and English commonism. Amurca teached me all that. I love Amurca. I could talk about Amurca and Amurcan politics everyday. I love Amurcan cars, Amurcan women, Amurcan magazines and the Amurcan twang.'

Boy wished he was born in Amurca. The tailor was probably reading his thoughts, for he said, 'I shouldda been a goddamn born Amurcan!'

Politics and Amurca took up more of the tailor's time than did his tailoring. But the times were tough in the country, and he had time on his hands.

'Amurcans are the sweetest goddamn talkers in the whirl!'

'Haul your arse in here!'

Boy came to a full stop. The road was empty. It was hot.

'Your pee foaming now, so you can sit amongst men.' It was the tailor, smiling and beckoning him to enter the crowded tailor shop. The tailor's words ripped the College uniform off Boy's back, and dressed him instead in rags, torn shirt, torn short trousers, with the usual but mysterious L-shaped tear in the seat.

Boy knew what the welcome meant. He was being permitted to be in the company of men. He could stand in the doorway of the tailor shop, and listen to their talk.

'It is a point o' communal instincts that signal the way you change sudden-sudden so, from a boy and from your adolescences into the mould of a man. So we have decide that you is now a part o' we. We's now responsible for your *real* education. Let the blasted College tek-care of a certain portion. We don't mind that. Latin and Greek is great languages. But they dead. We in here, now want to learn you *something*.

'We going to teach you how to love women, how to foop them, and how to foop them without mekking them pregnant and with child. Now, who the arse at the College, going learn you these mysteries o' life?'

9

Boy sat on a bench that had no back. He was suddenly tired. He felt the heads of nails which had risen slightly from the flatness of the wooden bench.

'And in the process, you may even learn something concerning the history of this blasted village,' the tailor said. 'You may pick up something oral-wise, about the history o' where you living,' he added, using one of his favourite Amurcan terms, 'oral-wise'.

Boy did not know what it meant.

'We going-learn you the scandals, the successes, if they is any. . . .'

'The man on the hill is a success!' a man said. His voice was loud. He was less than three feet from the tailor and Boy.

'We learning this boy *comma*-sense,' the tailor said.

'And you wouldda think that a reputable place like the College wouldda done that!'

'I know this boy attending the leading and most pretigious school in the island,' another man said. 'Harrison College. And that they learning him the Classics. Latin and Greek.'

'Latin and Greek have not one shite to do with comma-sense, the comma-sense that the tailor could learn this boy!'

'We is the only ones who could teach you this.'

'What you know concerning the philosophy o' *commonism*?'

Boy didn't have a clue. The khaki College uniform was becoming damp from perspiration and he could feel the beads under his arms.

The village was heavily populated by children. There were children whose fathers were either unknown, or were away, in Amurca or in Panama or in Aruba. A few were in England, serving with the RAF or with the Commonwealth Army. There were numerous mothers in the village.

Now that he was with the men in the tailor shop, he would know the names of those children whose fathers' names were protected from public whispering, as if they were political secrets. He would know the names of those men who had children from women who were already married and living with their fathers. A shiver surged through his body, with this sweet anticipation of gossip. He felt his own stature grow. He could now trade secrets with young Lascelles, the son of the English solicitor. The knowledge of the gutter life of his village would make him belong to the village, and dig his toes in its soil.

'You's a son of the soil,' the tailor told him. The tailor admitted that he himself was a son of the soil.

Boy did not like these close ties of blood. The tailor had previously been talking about his journeys, real and imagined, around the world. He had just told them about 'night soil', an African thing.

'You's a son of the blasted soil, like all the rest o' us!'

But Boy knew that even his closeness to the men, which he preferred to call his new status, rather than his closeness to the soil; he knew that he would never learn the whole truth about those unmentioned fathers who were important men in the city, and whose names were kept from exposure just as secrets of crimes were kept long after they were committed, unspoken in the cupboards, with the skeletons of the village. Some of the women were from his village. But that is all he knew.

The boy had often heard some references to those names, made in whispers in the tailor shop. And he knew that he could never mention those names again.

It was Friday night. No homework. No polishing of his John White shoes. No memorizing of two hundred lines of Latin verse. No Greek tragic plays to remember, also by heart. It was Friday night.

Men are in the rum shop. Men are in the tailor shop. The woman at the corner of the main road is already sitting beside her coal-pot, close to the flames from the coals mixed with dried sugar canes and cow-dung, so close as if her face is frying in the flames, as she fries the steaks of dolphin and king fish in the iron pan.

Boys and girls of a certain age are already in for the night. Boys and girls of a certain age above that certain age are beginning to leave for close friends, near to their homes to talk and to listen to the Hit Parade on the Rediffusion radio system.

The entire Village is wet. The rain fell all week. The night is cool. The ground is soft. 'Boy, you had-better put on something on your two feet,' his mother said. 'Outside wet.' As a College boy, he would not walk around, even inside his village, barefooted. It was the wet, soft ground that reminded his mother about his status.

All week the rain had fallen, lashing the land like a mother scolding a child for some large misdeed; and in short intervals, or long pauses, depending upon where you were sheltering, and if the roof of your house did not leak out of the ordinary, the rain bathed the land, just as Boy's mother used to bathe him in the gigantic galvanized bucket, in the backyard; and the rain even tricked them all, and fell during a burst of sun from behind the black, purple, thick clouds, and this happened just as thunder rolled and lightning ripped the sky in quick haphazard pieces, the way silk tears in a brutal hand. Boy thought of timpani and triangle in a symphony orchestra. His mother thought of the end of the world.

'By Sin-Peter and by Sin-Paul,' she said, raising her head to the cobwebs in the ceiling. 'The devil and his wife fighting. Oh Lord.'

The lanes and paths where the people walked were like tracks of Dunlopillo. And when Boy walked to get to the tailor shop, this Friday night, his feet in the canvas pumps sank so deep that he thought the mud would cover his ankles. Beside his own prints were other feet, foot-prints that showed the heel and the five toes on each foot. Boy thought of Robinson Crusoe and of Friday.

Mosquitoes were out in full force. Every now and then, a man in the tailor shop would stop speaking, or stop drinking, would rest his snap glass on the wooden counter beside the tailor's cardboard patterns, and a sharp slap would strike against the sweaty forehead, or against the fat of an arm.

'Bastard!' a man has just said. He picked the dead insect off his flesh with thumb and index finger. In the semi-darkness, Boy could barely see the spot of blood that marked the mosquito's crucifixion.

One buzzed like a distant fire brigade siren round Boy's ears, moving away and darting back close, its cry almost as unsettling as the sting that would follow its landing. Boy located the mosquito's landing, and then, *slap!* To himself he said,

Bastard! The men smiled. 'Yuh get the bastard?' the tailor asked. He had missed.

'Somebody run next door,' the tailor said, 'and ask that blasted man to send back my newspaper.' He was referring to the owner of the rum shop. The tailor bought the daily newspaper every day; and he read it every day, and sometimes twice, quoting passages to anyone who would listen, and correcting the information of any story that dealt with politics.

A man, any man would do it; so, a man went next door for the newspaper. The newspaper was lent from door to door, from hand to hand, like a library book. Almost every man in the shop tonight had borrowed the tailor's newspaper.

'That is one o' the things that classify this blasted place to be so different from up in Amurca,' he said. 'In Amurca, a man buys two of the same newspapers per day. One for reading on the subways, and one for reading at home, in more leisure. And wunnah still want to know why I loves Amurca so much? In Amurca, people purchases five or six different newspapers per day. From all over Amurca not to mention the kiss-me-arse whirl. But down here, a rum-shop owner, a small businessman, as he would be known by and referred to up in Amurca, got to borrow a kiss-me-arse newspaper! In Amurca, people buys two o' the same edition. One to read 'pon the train. One to read in their den.'

'Not meaning to cross you,' said the man who had brought back the newspaper, 'but what does you mean by that term you just use, namely, "den"?'

'You fooping girls, yet?' the tailor asked Boy.

'Den is a place where you could find women,' a man said.

'If you fooping girls,' the tailor said, 'and you not fooping them right, you may have somebody girl-child knocking down your mother's front door asking for child support, and not only with the back of her hand!' Boy became scared. The tailor added, somewhat unnecessarily, 'Not only with the back of her hand, but with her big belly!'

'Den, den, den?' the same man said.

'I smell general elections,' the tailor said. Boy knew that would turn the talk to politics. Earlier this same Friday, the

13

Prime Minister read a speech on Rediffusion radio, saying that general elections may be called soon.

As far as the men were concerned, they were already called. The men began to talk about the candidates they liked and those they hated. They hated most.

'The black race of this island don't know the political power they have,' the tailor said. 'The stupid bastards you see around here, including present company which is not excepted, saving Boy here, all these stupid bastards round here, have the power to change the Guvvament.'

Boy was becoming confused. He knew that the tailor was a member of the Government party.

'If we had understand real Russian socialism, this Guvvament would fall just so. Just so!' He said this, in triumph, as he held up a dead mosquito he had just killed. One palm had exploded against his forehead, like small thunder. Boy saw the tailor's muscles shudder.

The tailor had recently joined the Government party, and was an unelected member of the Government, he had told Boy. He had probably not grown accustomed to his new status.

'Like how I just kill that blasted mosquito, or like how we does-kill a ground-dove in a downfall!'

Boy was becoming more uncomfortable. He was beginning to think that he was in no hurry to be a man. He winced at the violence in the language the tailor and the men used. All this violent speech peppered with abuse was so different from the sedate way they spoke at the College. And had it not been for the talk about politics, in which he was interested, he would have walked back to his house, in the thick slippery mud.

Elections were coming. He liked to listen to the politicians speaking for hours on platforms made out of the back of lorries; and he followed them throughout his village. The last general election was like yesterday in his memory.

He was at the back of the large crowd, propped against a clammy-cherry tree, close to the fringe of the multitude of people, most of whom were poor and undereducated. He looked up to the naked electric bulb placed over the chassis of the lorry, to see the politician's face bathed in light, in sweat and in lies. The politician was his own elected representative, who had reached the fifth standard in the village elementary school. Even with his classical education, Boy was carried away by the brimstones of promises in the words of Mr Alexander Bourne, MP.

'I is Alexander Bourne. Or in plain simple words, Mr the Honourable Alexander Bourne, Member o' Parlment. A poor man, a comma-man, representing the comma-man party, ladies and gentlemen.'

And now, with fervour of talk and tales as close on the horizon as was the sea from them, Boy was now drawn to the tailor who had some of this oratorical skill.

'In today's newspaper, whiching I have to refer to as the most authoritative authority round here, and taking into consideration the high standard o' the printed word in this island, I put it to you, that power lies in the hand of the comma-man, in this village, in this parish, and in this whole island. If yuh have eyes to *see!*'

The tailor was a member of the Workers Labour Party, the WLP as it was called. But he was not a sincere member. He joined, he said, because it was easier to get elected under the WLP banner. It was more through his skill with needle, thimble and scissors than through his ability as a platform speaker or a party organizer that caused the party executive to choose him as the candidate for Sin-James East, and the running mate of Mr the Honourable Alexander Bourne.

He won the nomination over the most important man in the village, the man who lived in the biggest house, on the hill.

Sin-James East comprised most of the village where the tailor lived. The seat he was nominated for was a safe seat. These promises did not come from the entire party executive, but only from Alexander Bourne, for whom the tailor had made many suits, at half-price.

But the moment the tailor was informed of his political importance, and the village understood this elevation in prestige only too well, his behaviour changed. He was kinder in his comments about the big men in the village. He was nastier and more vicious to all those whom he considered small men. And there were many of these.

Nevertheless, they flocked into his tailor shop, to be closer to power; idled away their time, borrowed a shilling the moment they saw a customer put a down-payment on a suit on the gnarled wooden counter and, with the money in hand, the men moved swiftly next door, to the rum shop.

'I have watch these bastards for years,' he said, 'and I know that these small-men and these unemploy and uneducated bastards going continue to live a life o' playing dominoes, and be-Christ, will remain small for the rest of their lives. Mark my word. And I going to tell you something. They going remain more smaller still, after I get elected.'

Boy could feel, in the way he was talking and behaving, that he was already a Member of Parliament. The talk about Russian socialism and about Amurcan politics increased. He became even more stentorian, and more dogmatic about the origins of 'commonism'.

'The pure causes of unemployment round here is that too many blasted poor people is without education. And by education I mean technical education, not the ability to say two-and-two, or spell "rat", whiching any arse could do. The race o' West Indian black man,' he said, working that actor's trick with his eyes, 'being as how he is an offshoot of the English man, like fooping more than working. He is a man who could work-up on a woman's belly more technically efficient than he can work on a job.'

The rain was harder now. And it seemed as if they were all cut off from the outside. They were in their own world of largeness and bigness and words. The tailor felt the power of the rain, hitting hard and unmusical on the galvanized roof. The thunder sounded in the distance: Boy didn't know whether it was in the north or the south; but it sounded like the blasting of stones in the nearby rock-quarry. And then the lightning. And with this as background, or simply because he was already caught up in his political calculation, the tailor made his most devastating political declaration.

'Any one o' you bastards in here right now, who refuse to support me in my campaign, and who don't support the WLP, be-Jesus-Christ, and who don't mark that X the right place, namely besides my name on voting day don't, do not expect me to sew-on a button for any o' you, hear?'

Boy left the tailor shop with a veneer of rawness on him. He imagined that it was a smell, a sensation, a sense of awe, almost like a new deep experience. The only thing he could equate it with was the night his mother made him sit with her in the Church of the Nazarene up the hill, when the deaconess led the rocking church-hall ten times in the singing of 'Rock of Ages Cleft For Me,' as if she was waiting like a whore, in the rain, for the first 'fare' to pick.

He was bareheaded. The light rain on his hair, thickened in Brilliantine, seemed to turn into thicker coconut oil, and ran down his temples, down into his neck, making the white sea-island cotton shirt, part of his College uniform, soiled.

In the short distance from the tailor shop to his home, a woman sat behind a hawker's tray. A flame from her snuff-bottle lamp made from an empty beer bottle that once contained Tennant's Stout, and with kerosene oil and a cloth wick in it, lashed about in the strong night air that followed the downpour.

She sat like a Samurai wrestler. From the distance, Boy could see her thighs. They looked like stumps of mahogany tree, exposed up to that part between her thighs, to that darker crevice, the apex, that the tailor called the 'hole'. Her thick legs were darker now that he was drawing nearer, and the light was weaker the closer he got to her. Her legs were shining. She had probably greased them in the afternoon, between a break in the rain, with coconut oil. A hat made from the cush-cush grass that grew wild in the village, and with flowers knitted around the brim, was planted firmly on her head. Her hat reached just above her eyes. She looked sinister. Her eyes were larger now that they could be seen in relation to her forehead.

Before he was in front of her, she struck her forehead. She then struck her arms, almost as large as her thighs. She struck her thighs. Each of these three times, the blow made a sound of different sharpness and determination. Boy wondered if she had killed all three mosquitoes. It was dark outside the arc of weak light thrown by her snuff-bottle lamp.

Men moved out of the shadows, like shades, as shadows in this rich velour of the night. One shadow moved in front of Boy, in front of the woman, still sitting like a strong, foreboding

17

guardian over her tray that contained sugar cakes, coconut bread and roasted peanuts. The shadow blocked her from Boy. She knew Boy. Although Boy had never, in all his life, stood before her tray to buy a one-cent sugar cake. The shadow continued to block her vision. Boy had not even looked up to see the face of the man. But then, he heard her voice.

'Brandford Nathaniel Cole, you stinking bitch, why you do not take your fucking nasty hand outta my kiss-me-arse tray? You hear me, Brandford Nathaniel Cole? I don't know what your hand touch before you come here. And to-besides, you don't see *decent people* about to make a small purchase from my tray? You don't see the black gentleman? Man, tek your fucking hand outta my tray!'

The flame from the lamp was seen again. Boy saw the shadow move from blocking the woman who continued to sit with her former untroubled patience, as if she was about to jump upon another opponent.

'You want me to serve you, now, young-gentleman?' she said.

Boy shuddered at the implication.

'Yes, my gentleman,' she said, 'what could I do for you?' Boy thought he saw a smile on her face. 'Some nuts? Or some sugar cake. Mine is the best in this village.'

Boy was born in an unpainted chattel house that had one roof, or gable. The villagers called it a 'one roof board-and-shingle'. The small house had no paling round it to protect its privacy. It stood on six limestone blocks drilled from the rock-quarry which belonged to the sugar plantation that owned all the tenantries. The blocks were drilled by his father's own hands. The six blocks were stolen.

The house was a small-scale imitation of the sturdy structure of the plantation house. And like the plantation house, Boy's house was perched among fruit trees, the most important of which was the breadfruit tree. The breadfruit tree with its luscious, green, filling fruits, provided all through the family's early poverty and straightened circumstances of birth, many meals which clogged the appetite and cloyed the belly. The value of the small house was tied up with the bearing of the breadfruit tree.

18

Boy would walk through the gully on his way up to the plantation house to buy tomatoes and eddoes cheap in season, and as he began the climb of rocky hills laden with fruit trees, he could see only a small part of the house in which the plantation owner lived. He could see the huge windows whose shutters were painted green, and his eyes would touch the pink wash of the coral stone out of which the plantation house had been built. And this small part that he could see corresponded to the entire size and architecture of the chattel house where he was born.

It seemed as if his father, out of envy or out of admiration, must have watched this same plantation house, day after day, and until his eyes became sore and bloodshot, and from a safe distance; and when the time came for him to provide shelter for his wife, he used the only model that he knew. The only model that existed.

It was as if, so the Boy argued, the similarity in appearance was an invisible and indelible bond which kept the inhabitants of all the chattel houses on the rocky and undulating land tied to the sugar plantation.

Life in those days was hard as the land on which Boy's father tried to make a living from a kitchen garden.

Two weeks before every Easter, he would hear his mother pestering his father to paint the one-roomed house.

'That is what Easter stands for,' his mother said. 'Newness.'

'For me,' his father answered, 'Easter stands for a lotta blasted hard times. Five years now, every Easter, every blasted Easter, beginning from Good Friday, you does-be in my arse to paint this blasted house. One o' these days I going-paint the blasted house *black*.'

'God going take care o' you, man. Mark my words. God going-judge you. If it is the day before you dead. And by the way, the right colour for Easter is white. Talking 'bout paint for the house, and the colour o' Easter.'

Two consecutive Easters ago, and many years ago, Boy's father threatened to paint the house red. He had had a close call with the deep watery grave during the first week he tried his hand at fishing. The land and the kitchen had remained intractable, and hard. But the very last time Boy remembered painting was ever mentioned, green was the colour he heard his

19

father suggest. Being a fisherman was putting money in his pocket.

But the house remained unpainted just as the tailor shop; and in time, both Boy and his father, seeing the wind and the rain and the sun take their toll on the wood and turn it like ash or like the skin of a flying fish, they consoled themselves that the house was now grey in colour; even if it had not been painted so, by the hands of man.

And suddenly, a stroke of luck delivered the family from this muddy lane, from this muddy house-spot, where Boy had lived happily in that mud along with the other agricultural workers. The family moved into the large house where they are now, on the front road of the village.

The village is the shape of a big-toothed comb. A 'horse comb'. The back of the comb represents the front road, as the people call the main road. And the two sides are the minor roads that lead off the front road. The teeth are the unpaved, dirt tracks that lead to the small unpainted houses, such as the one in which Boy lived, and which are near the hill on which the big man lives.

The hill is the boundary of the village. Paynes Bay is a fishing village. Men who can remember their grandfathers and great grandfathers, from the tales of fishermen, are now themselves the men who work in the sea, and are drowned in the sea, and have had limbs, a foot, an arm, sometimes two arms, torn off by sharks and swordfish, and sometimes too, by accidents in boats; and sometimes by miracles of waves or lost rudders.

So, the stroke of luck that happened to Boy's family threw him from amongst the teeth of the comb, and hurled him down the hill. It was an ironical descent of haughty ascendency and upward mobility. He was now squatting in a rented large house, at the intersection of the back of the comb and that side that pointed to the city.

And when boys at the College talked about their fathers and the amount of money their fathers had, and the size of their homes, Boy kept quiet on these matters. He never once mentioned his father. And he never talked about birth in the one-room board-and-shingle house. And even when the son of the big man on the hill, who liked 'Amerrica', as he pronounced it, more than he liked the island, and praised Amerrica and talked about the riches of Amerrica, and how a man from humble beginnings could rise to be president of Amerrica, like Abraham Lincoln, this foreign example of rising did not impress Boy.

'Only in Amerrica,' he told Boy. 'A man could be born in a log cabin, which in Amerrican terms is the same as a one-roof. And that man could rise and be President of Amerrica. That is what I call democracy!'

'Abraham Lincoln!' Boy asked. He knew the name, and from the tailor's informal history lessons, he knew the man. 'You mean Abraham Lincoln? It couldn't happen in Barbados.'

Because of the College and because of the island, Boy's earliest and most convenient recollection of his beginnings was the large house 'out the front road', as the neighbours referred to his place and status.

'Anybody at all. Anybody at all,' the tailor was telling Boy, repeating his words for effect, and looking directly into Boy's face, for corroboration, 'anybody at all who ever lived in England is a *born* commonist. Have to be. It is only logical. It is logical because England is one o' the most commonest places that I have ever set foot in. When I was sailing the high seas as a cook on a merchant ship, before the War break-out, and when I join-up with the Royal Air Force as a member of the ground-crew, I have seen this whole whirl. The whole blasted whirl. Panama Canal, all o' Africa, the Darnells, Amurca. . . .'

His voice drifted on as he named places which Boy had seen on maps and on the globe in geography classes at the College; places which had never left the pages of the textbooks until this evening when the tailor made them sound like places where human beings lived. Africa.

Boy had met Africa even in the pages of Latin texts, in a foreign dead language. The Africa he knew was *Africanus* and Hannibal, who crossed the Alps.

'. . . and I must have pass round the Horn o' Africa a hundred times whilst on that merchant ship. Putting in to ports in Africa, where we come from. Hommany o' you, not including Boy, because Boy would know this, but hommany of you *know* where we come from? We, and people like we? Where our ancestors come from? Have any of you, besides Boy, ever hear of the great Middle Passage? Boy, tell these stupid bastards where the Middle Passage is.'

Boy had never heard of the Middle Passage. And even if he had been taught about it at the College, after listening to the tailor, he was not eager to bear any ties of family with *those* men. Africans or slaves: men as black sweating bodies moving slowly in the thickness of jungle and of heat with packs on their heads, just as the women from the agricultural land above his new home came down through the gulley, into the valley on Saturday mornings laden with ground provisions.

Boy had seen those African bodies flitting across the silver screen of the Empire Theatre in the city. Every Saturday afternoon, he and his friends went to matinees to see Tarzan in trees and the apes, they the Africans on the thick, dense, wet and humid African land.

He listened now to the tailor, and wondered if the wet ground of his own village after the heavy rainy season was like that land he was hearing about? No, it was not. His village was not like Africa.

To take his mind off this uncomfortable association, Boy looked around the walls of the tailor shop, moving his eyes over the unpainted partitions, seeing the grain of the unpainted wood, the knots and the knot-holes where age and anger had knocked them out. The tailor drank every Saturday night and got drunk every Saturday night, and cuffed the walls of his shop and cried loudly and said, 'Jesus Christ, why you can't save the blasted unemploy bastards round here? Why you can't change this blasted guvvament that killing these unemploy bastards?'

'. . . travelling through Africa, and Amurca and coming back to this blasted small-arse country is what *drive* me to politics and to political life,' the tailor was saying.

Boy was looking meanwhile at the photographs and pictures torn from the local newspaper, and from magazines which he had himself seen Young Lascelles reading at the College: *Illustrated London News* and *Country Life*. The public library had these magazines too; but Boy could read them only in the reading-rooms. They could not be taken out. He wondered how the tailor got them.

'Sarge?' It was the woman sitting with her tray at the corner, who called out, recognizing the man on the bicycle. 'Man, goodnight, Sarge!' Her voice was high, and respectful. Sarge had arrested her twice last year, and then had dropped the charges. 'For a piece o' pussy,' the tailor told Boy.

The ticking of the black Raleigh bicycle grew louder. Boy could see the three silver and red-bordered stripes, with the Imperial Crown, on the black serge tunic.

'Sarge!' the tailor greeted him, as if he was relieved that the Law was present.

And Sarge emerged from the darkness, hopped off the gleaming bicycle, placed it against the side of the shop, and climbed the single coral stone step. Sarge was a silent man. He was powerfully built and almost the same complexion as his black night uniform. Two lines of sweat were running down his shiny face. He took a package of Trumpeter cigarettes from inside his tunic, and before he struck the match, he took off his black serge tunic. Boy saw his strong arms, and his large thick fingers. Sarge placed the thick, brown, shiny police truncheon attached to a thick, brown, shiny belt, placidly on the wooden bench beside him, as if it were made of rubber. The truncheon looked soft. Sarge looked violent. With his tunic off, Boy saw the thick grey flannel undershirt that all policemen wore. A large pool, like a stain of sweat, was in the middle of his chest. His chest was rising and falling in a movement like the waves. It was heavy with black hairs that showed through the neck line of the undershirt.

The two other men in the tailor shop did not work at any steady employment; and had no profession to boast about, not even as gamblers. These two men doffed their cloth hats, smiled and moved a little farther away from Sarge. One of them was Lionel. The best domino player in the country.

'Sarge,' Lionel said, respectfully.

'Lionel, you wukking yet?'

'But Sarge.' And a shrug completed the answer.

'A disgrace to this blasted country,' the tailor said. 'The number of unemploy, strong, young men.'

Lionel worked part time in the Westbury Cemetery burying coffins, the tailor said, when he wasn't playing dominoes in tournaments and representing his country at inter-island competitions. He also made money from odd jobs he picked up at the tourist hotels along the beach.

'And you still talking properganda?' Sarge told the tailor. The tailor laughed. And Sarge laughed too.

'I is a politician.'

Boy was now only a witness. He was not expected, even if he wished it, to contribute to this talk. So, he returned to the pictures on the walls. He saw Churchill and Stalin, Theodore Roosevelt and Hitler. Hitler's picture was the largest of the 'whirl-leaders'. Boy wondered why.

Behind Hitler were swastikas and flags and standards like those he had seen in Latin texts, and people with their hands raised, as if they were signalling a fast passenger bus to stop. Some of the men in the village who attended political meetings stood this way, too. And Hitler's mouth was wide open. Boy could easily imagine spittle spouting forth as the man talked. He tried to guess the colours of the flags and the swastikas and the standards. But he had seen them only in black and white in newsreels at the Empire Theatre, and in magazines.

He knew the colours of his own flag, the Union Jack. So, he used those colours, and painted them on to the German flag. Red, white and blue.

There was a photograph of a man, clipped from a magazine; an overweight man, black as his father, blacker than Sarge, and dressed in a uniform similar to the one the Governor of the island wore. The uniform was covered with medals and ribbons and regimental sash. On the man's head was a plumed helmet, similar to the Governor's, when he inspected scouts, girl-guides, policemen and the Volunteer Force, on the Garrison Pasture, on the same day each year when the country celebrated the King's Birthday, with ginger beer and hot-cross-buns and with gifts of a new shilling, with the King's face on it. The King did not smile on the shilling.

Was this black man a governor? Was he one of those African Kings the tailor talked about?

24

Boy looked closely at the photograph. Beneath it was the name, Marcus Garvey.

All the pictures and photographs were old and brown and brittle. But the tailor had clipped them with care, and had stuck them down when dog's-ears appeared. He used a paste made from flour and water, which he also used to stick cloth upon cloth; and when in season, and he had more sticking to do with the pictures and photographs, he used the juice from the clammy-cherry fruit.

Below Marcus Garvey was the American Declaration of Independence.

There were many pictures of bombers and Spitfires from the RAF, and fighter planes from the German Air Force, the Luftwaffe.

Boy felt he was in a museum. The wallpaper of history was all round him. He was facing Marcus Garvey, and the tailor was seated with Marcus Garvey as a backdrop. The tailor sat with the same dignity of Marcus Garvey, behind a sewing-machine operated by pedals, black with gold trim, and with the name SINGER in large fancy print, in gold.

Sometimes, the tailor pedalled as he talked. He could pedal and sew without looking at the calico or the khaki or the tweed. Tonight, he was just sitting and talking.

When he was pedalling his Singer and talking, Boy always thought of the organist of the Anglican Church up the hill playing Palestrina. The organist demonstrated the same cleverness and style. He could prance on the wooden pedals, with his feet crossing each other, just as a man who had St Vitus Dance would walk, if he could walk: without once looking below the organ stool, to see if his feet, dressed always in cracked two-tone John Whites, had touched the wrong pedal. The tailor was such a man of style.

The tailor placed a forty-ounce bottle of rum on the counter top he used for cutting cloth. Beside that bottle, he placed another one, the same size, with its label cleaned off. This one contained water. Four short glasses, thick and ugly and cloudier than crystal, were placed beside the bottles. He pushed the bottle of rum, with a gesture of privilege old as life itself, towards Sarge, after having pulled out the cork.

Sarge poured some water into his snap glass, shook it round, aimed for the small space between Boy and the door post, pelted the water into the road, as if it came from a pistol, and said, after the deed was done, 'Watch-out, Boy!'

He filled the snap glass to the brim. He closed his eyes. He tossed his head slightly backwards. He poured the dark liquid down his throat. He squeezed his eyes shut, tightly. The skin around his eyes became creases. And in this practised sightlessness, he reached for the bottle of water, filled the same snap glass, and with the same backward fling of his head, with his eyes still shut, he swallowed the water. He then poured a drop of rum into his glass, held it to his eyes, now open, and with his little finger and the one beside that finger cocked off, he said, 'Don't let we forget the spirits of our ancestors, man.' And so saying, he poured the drop of rum on to the floor.

Then and only then did he pass the bottle back to the tailor, who then passed it to Brandford Nathaniel Cole, who passed it to Lionel, who passed it to the fifth man present. Boy was ignored. It was as if he was not there.

'This guvvament that running this blasted country is keeping down poor people,' the tailor said. 'When I get elected, *all* that going-change.'

'Hear-hear!' all but Sarge and Boy said.

'If more of the people in this blasted country had-understand the pure meaning o' commonism, and would take a leaf outta England book, this whole country would be a more better place for the comma-man.'

'Hear-hear!'

'When I say *commonism*, I mean just that. Guvvament by the common-man, for the common-man and with the common-man. I is a common-man.'

'Hear-hear!' the same men said.

Sarge said, 'You talking *pure* shite! A blasted capitalist like you?'

It was as if he had just come awake, had resurrected himself from fatigue and also from the power of the rum. His snap glass was resting beside the thick, shining, brown belt attached to the truncheon. He filled his glass again.

26

'You should be a police, like me. You should have to face the blasted criminals they have 'bout here.'

Brandford Nathaniel Cole shifted his feet on the sand of the floor. They sounded like gigantic crabs scratching dried leaves on the beach.

'If you was a police officer like me, taking all the blasted night-dew that I takes in my chest, you won't utter all this blasted properganda and communist-talk. Especially not in the hearing of this boy. Have respects for the younger generation. All this properganda in the hearing o' Nathan's son.' He looked at Boy. Boy saw the red in his eyes, and smelled the steam on his breath. 'They is *pure* criminals,' he said, addressing Boy. 'They is *pure* criminals walking the streets o' this village, this parish, and this blasted country.'

Boy felt sentenced. He also felt the fruitlessness of giving evidence against Sarge in a trial. Sarge talked as if he was giving verdicts.

'They is *pure* criminals. The criminals *and* the politicians!'

'You is the Law,' the tailor said. 'And as the Law, you have power. But I is the legislative branch o' the Law.' He corrected himself, and said, 'I will be the legislative branch. And when I take my seat in the honourable, the honourable House o' Sembly, all kiss-me-arse parsites like you-so. . . .'

He paused, thinking probably that it was not wise, even with legislative power, to make such a threat to Sarge. He was learning fast about being a politician.

The men in the shop had sat and remained frozen when the threat was being made. Brandford Nathaniel Cole scraped his feet on the sand on the floor a second time. But when the threat was dropped, he and the other men relaxed. They held their snap glasses more easily now that the tailor had swallowed the threat with the snap of rum he drank.

Three of them had already tasted Sarge's enmity. Now, they laughed in short, tense, ejaculated sounds, like chuckles and coughs; and in this forced levity, they passed the rum bottle.

'All this blasted politics and political properganda going get one o' you killed,' Sarge said. 'It is *pure* violence, all this blasted politics. This country need the Law and the police. Not politics.'

All the men, except Sarge, were supporters of the government. They had lived under no other. The small island country had recently gained its first taste of semi-independence from the British.

'This is a country o' responsible guvvament,' the tailor announced. 'Responsible guvvament, the first stage to *pure* independent guvvament. But for the time being, the commonists up in England, give we responsible guvvament.'

'And what responsible guvvament mean?' Lionel asked him.

'How the arse I would know?'

'You think it could mean responsive guvvament?'

Every night now, when they met, they criticized the Government.

'It is the same as Latin-Amurca,' Sarge said. 'The same brand o' guvvament. The same brand o' dictatorship.'

'I never went there,' the tailor said.

'I thought you pass through the Panama Canal on the merchant ship?'

'Panama is *central*. South Amurca is south.'

'You ever been there, Sarge?'

'Not on your fucking bottom dollar! I is a law-and-order, man. The only thing I know 'bout Latin-Amurca is from the attitudes o' the politicians round here. They does-even-wear dark glasses, at night!'

'This guvvament more like Russia under Stalin,' a man said, remembering talk by the tailor.

'But when you say one thing, you got to say the next. This lil country is the best country in the world!' Sarge said.

'The political heritage of this country, small as she be, was bequeath to we, by Churchill. That is why we are call, Little England. Not referring to pure size, mind you. But referring to the greatness of association. And to the country that invented the principles o' commonism.'

Meantime, work was scarce. That is how Boy heard the men talk about unemployment. They never said, unemployment is high. But work scarce.

Sometimes, it was impossible to get. Boy's own father, Nathan, spent most of his life not working. And when he did, he worked as an independent man. He was helped along by the remittances which arrived every month from Boy's aunt, in Panama. So, Nathan caught a few fish in his one-mast fishing-boat, which he christened *Labour Blest*, to distinguish it from *Labour Bless*, the house on the hill. Boy spelled and painted the name on the hull of the leaky boat.

'I never know a time when work wasn't scarce,' Nathan would complain to his son. 'And when a man who have no job, and can't find none, and because of all the sameness o' scarcity that surround me, a man decide to refuse to look no more; and in these times o' giving up and not looking, *bram!* you could bet that they going call a general election. And the minute a general election call, the blasted Workers Labour Party swarming through this village, like bees. Everywhere you look, in two weeks' time, everywhere you go, you going see them, like pure bees and flies and insecks round a kerosene lamp.'

Nathan supported the WLP, because he had no choice.

Boy knew the time had come. Even before the general election was called, Mr the Honourable Alexander Bourne appeared in the village. He went straight to the tailor shop. He would go next to the rum shop. 'My supporters is found in these two important places,' he said.

Boy saw the power and the influence Mr Bourne had. It was reflected in the smiles of his supporters.

'We understand the plight of the unemploy man,' Alexander Bourne said. 'Work scarce. We understand the plight of the comma-man. But I promise each and every one o' you in here now, and those that are not in here, that we going put jobs in your hand, and money in your pocket. I mek these promises in here, and I intends to mek them on *any* political platform in this country.'

Boy saw how the men saw Alexander Bourne as a rescuer.

He pulled out a shilling and dropped it into Brandford Nathaniel Cole's hand. Then he pulled out a sovereign and gave it to Lionel. He gave Boy a dollar bill. And a two-dollar bill was placed in Boy's father's hand. He pushed his hand again into his deep trousers pocket, and it came out folded into a fist. This fist he placed, like a spy, into the hand of the rum shop owner.

'Man, give my friends two tins o' that Argentine *Fray Bentos* corn-beef, man!' The men around him drew closer to the counter. 'Put some rum on this table for my political friends, man!'

'Skipper! Skipper!' a man said.

'Hold on to this, man,' he told the man, whom no one had seen before. 'Hold on 'pon this, and buy yourself and the family a little something with it.'

No one knew how much he had given the man.

'I back you, Skipper. Skipper, you got my vote,' the man said.

The shilling or the sovereign or the dollar bill was now in the man's pocket. A smile came to his face. Boy could see that the money in the man's pocket had already wiped away the hardness and the bitterness of life they had been talking about, a minute before Alexander Bourne arrived.

Boy also knew that the moment Mr the Honourable Alexander Bourne left in his chauffeur-driven black Humber Hawk, the car of politicians and leading solicitors, the shilling and the sovereign, the dollar bill and the two-dollar bill would be placed flat and hard in the palm of the rum shop owner.

'Work scarce though, eh, Skipper?'

'I have give up trying,' a man said. 'I give up trying to get a job as yard-sweeper down at the hotel. They offered me one as a garbage collector, and I give up even thinking 'bout tekking that one.'

Mr the Honourable Alexander Bourne dropped another shilling into the man's hand.

'We taking care o' you, man.'

Boy saw how the gift of the second shilling took the man off the roll of complete penury.

'I back you in the last elections, Skipper. And be-Christ, I backing you in this coming one!'

At this point Sarge entered the rum shop.

'And you got my vote again, this time, too,' the man said superfluous in his praise and support. 'As man!'

'As man!' Alexander Bourne said. 'As man.' He was uncomfortable now that Sarge was so close to him. He seemed to remember, suddenly, a portion of the WLP's manifesto, and

30

he quoted it to the shop, saying, 'We intend, as a political party and as a political doctrine, to take care of the people. Our party is a small-man party.'

And with that, he left.

'Skipper! Skipper!' followed him to his gleaming black Humber Hawk.

The moment he sat in the back seat, first the new shining shilling, then the sovereign, and quickly afterwards, the dollar bill and the two-dollar bill hit the palms of the rum shop owner.

'A man going get *kill*,' Sarge said.

He took another snap glass of rum. Boy thought it was time to leave the rum shop. It was safer to be seen in the tailor shop. Sarge took another snap glass of rum, as Boy was stepping down on the lime-stone shop steps. He pulled a long chain of silver from his pocket. Attached to the chain was a large round gold watch.

'The time is here!'

Boy thought of political time and the time of day.

It was getting darker now. The road outside was filling up with villagers. Crickets were coming out, too. And more mosquitoes. Fire-flies lit up the islands of space in their almost invisible life-span, changed themselves into numerous small stars, and were seen no more.

The darkness inside the tailor shop was matching the darkness outside. The tailor removed the lampshade from the kerosene lamp, cleaned the previous night's soot from it, moving the dirty rag round the belly of the shade, and then blew his breath into it. His warm breath turned the shade to frost. Then it shone brightly and gave clear, perfect light.

Boy read 'Home Sweet Home' printed on the shade, in a cluster of white flowers.

People were moving in and out of the rum shop next door. From where he was sitting on a bench, Boy could see them in pieces, a leg here, a head there, through the spaces in the boards of the shop.

Through the only window that tailor shop had, Boy saw the woman next door, staring into the shop to see who was there, to report who was there. He saw her remove the stick that was the window-opener. She let the window fall in an expression of her

31

indignation at the tailor. They were neighbours who never spoke to each other.

Her name is Stella. Many nights, sometimes four times a night, Boy would hear her open her window, let it slam, and immediately listen with wonder, as she burst into song. She knew the hymn book by heart. But the song she sang on each occasion to express her hostility, was Hymn number 332 in *Hymns Ancient and Modern*. She sang with a trained contralto voice.

> *There is a green hill far away*
> *Without a city wall,*
> *Where the dear Lord was crucified,*
> *Who died to save us all.*

And she sang it too, like an accusing finger pointed at the tailor. And each time that Boy had the privilege to hear her, she broke into her own lamentations, and cried out, 'Bastard!'

'Bitch!' the tailor answered.

The tailor throws the dirty rag used to clean the lamp, into a corner, and it falls beside a box that contains scraps of cloth. The kerosene lamp glares like a giant's eye. And the shop jumps into joyfulness and light.

Boy is swallowed in the light, and drowning in the singing of the woman next door. Sarge seems lighter in complexion now that light is on his face. His face looks less square.

His thick fingers move agilely over the silver buttons on his black tunic, buttoning them up, as he shakes his head, hating to leave, and also shaking the rum out of his head. He buckles the heavy brown shiny leather belt with the truncheon, round his waist. A ring of fat, much larger than a bicycle tyre, appears above and below the shining leather.

'Abyssinia!' he tells the shop.

He roars with laughter at his own joke. The men laugh too. He has given them the story about the Italian army which marched through Abyssinia and 'licked it down', in two hours flat. The men roared with laughter then, and they roar with laughter now, as Sarge says, 'Abyssinia', to mean, 'I'll be seein' ya'.

He jumped on his three-speed bicycle and soon the ticking slow rhythm told them he was at the incline of the road, ready to turn in the direction of the police sub-station of which he was the Station-Sergeant. And then they heard the ratchet, as if he was back-pedalling; and then they knew he had kicked the well-oiled Raleigh into third speed.

'One of the most cruellest police in the history of this cruel country!' Lionel said.

'One of the most hated men by this guvvament,' the tailor said.

'One o' the meanest bastards!' Brandford Nathaniel Cole said.

'I have witness with my own two eyes, how one Saturday night, when Sarge drove a bull-pistle lash in a man's arse. And when that man tried to move, Godblummuh, he couldn't move a fucking inch! That man was bend-up in two. Like a hairpin. From one single lash.'

'One of the most cruellest men who ever walk this God's earth, and who was given three stripes and the Crown to wear on his blasted sleeve.'

'Did you notice that whilst Sarge was here, Lionel hardly take a drink?'

'Sarge say a man going get killed during these elections,' Lionel said, as if explaining his sudden non-imbibing.

'Propinquity!' Boy said. He wanted to say the word as the men would say it, if they knew the word. But it came out odd. And it was too loud.

'*Wha*?'

It was not one man's surprise. It was the surprise of the whole tailor shop. It came out in unison.

'Jesus Christ! This boy could talk!'

They slapped him on his back, and made him feel, by the pounding of their hard hands on his sea-island cotton shirt, that he was accepted.

'I got work to do,' the tailor said. 'Elections mean one thing. Tailoring work. I mekking a suit for Sarge, and I mekking one for Alexander Bourne.'

He pushed the rum bottle towards Lionel. He then placed some suit-lengths and trousers half-done on the counter, and some patterns, made of cardboard, beside them. 'Elections is money. Elections is tailoring-jobs. Take a drink, Lionel. I need your vote. I need your support. Forget Sarge, man. I will take care of you when I get elected. Well, take a double-shot, man!'

'As man, man,' Lionel said.

He poured one shot, tossed it back, poured a second one, tossed that back, too; and then he poured a third. When he held the snap-glass, you couldn't see any glass at all. Boy knew those hands. Those hands had held seven, large, ivory domino seeds as if they were seven common pins, hidden from the eyes of his opponents.

'This boy use a word just now. I don't know that word. But when I am near to Sarge, all I could think 'bout is a smell. A smell of iodine or Epsom Salts. Iodine and Epsoms mix-up in one. You know what I mean? Um is a smell like a stale smell, a powerful smell and a cruel smell. I don't know if I putting my words in the right way. This boy here, who is the only College boy round here, could maybe explain-um more better than me. But when Sarge is here, I does-always smell the smell o' cruelty. And I does think o' nothing but wounds, wemms, hospitals, graves and bull-pistles.'

'Association,' Boy told him.

'Well, Jesus Christ, then!'

He said it as if it was one word.

'When I get elected. When my party return back to power. We *intends* to fuck-up people like Sarge. I couldn't say it before. Not whilst he was here. 'Cause politics is like whoring, like picking fares. And politics is politics. And sport is sport. But Sarge will be taught a political lesson.' He looked into each face around him, as it expressed surprise at the threat. 'And I know, I have assurances from each and every one o' you, that what I just uttered in my shop, on my premises whiching I pays rent for, will remain right inside this blasted premises! As man?'

'As man!'

Boy saw him look a second time into the eyes of each of them, and pulled secrecy and conspiracy and confidence from each of them. That look sealed a threat they did not know would come to pass.

But Boy was thinking of other things. The scholarship examinations were on his mind. But the gallery of pictures and photographs was now lit well enough for him to see more. The Dionne Quintuplets were among them. All over his village, on doors and windows of shops, and on one shop in the city, he had seen this advertisement for Palmolive soap, with the five smiling faces. Nobody in his country had ever had five children from one woman, at one and the same time.

The Dionne Quintuplets were usually printed on sheets of tin. Now, their faces were two inches from his right hand. He wondered where they were born.

His attention was drawn next to a picture of Booker T. Washington. The writing beneath the brown, brittle picture said this man was born a slave. *Head, heart and hand* was written above. *Head, heart and hand* was written also in large wooden letters above the main door of an elementary school in the city.

Why these three parts of the human anatomy held so much significance for a former slave and a present headmaster, Boy wondered.

Stalin is in a soldier's uniform. Beside Stalin is a man named Rockefeller. To Rockefeller's left, is a colour photograph of the Pyramids.

All this new colour, all this knowledge and confrontation with persons and subjects began to unsettle him.

The colour and the knowledge and the confrontation sent him back to the classroom at the College and to ask himself the question: Are the men in this tailor shop wiser than he?

He could not face the answer. There could be terror in the answer, if it was yes.

One Saturday afternoon, some time before, as he got off the bus from his weekly visit to the public library, holding a book of Latin prose, *Caesar Gallic Wars*, the tailor came up to him.

'Lemme look inside that book.'

'You know Latin?' Boy asked.

'No. But I like Caesar.'

And now, it must be three or four years later, right here, on the wall of this tailor shop, Boy sees the page he had torn from his old copy of *Caesar Gallic War Book One* and given to the tailor.

Boy looks at the tailor covered with the light from the kerosene lamp that makes his high forehead more conspicuous, and he looks again at Caesar, thinks he sees some resemblance, and smiles.

'*Boy?*'

The voice of the woman calling is high and clear. It comes through the night along with the sound of dogs barking and children crying and men laughing. The voice is like a bullet meant only for him.

'Go and do your studies,' the tailor tells him. The loving concern in his voice is the same he would have for his own daughter. 'One o' these days, you will be a Barbados Scholar. And you will do Law, and be a barrister-at-Law. And save this kiss-me-arse backward country.'

He smiles, and raises his head from the Singer, and Boy can see no hair on his head.

'*Boy?*'

The voice coming through the dark night is more querulous now. It is reaching a pitch of uncontrollable anxiety. The single vowel in his name is drawn out to make the name seem longer.

'The Queen calling,' the tailor said.

'*Boy!*'

It is his mother's voice.

Four men prepare themselves for a game of dominoes. Goalie is the only one who does not frequent the tailor shop. They set themselves around a table. It is only four-thirty in the afternoon. The shade has reached the front of the tailor shop. These men do not work.

The surface of the wooden table is smooth and shiny from the constant pounding of the ivory dominoes, which the men call 'seeds'.

Lionel, the champion, puts his cloth hat under his seat for comfort. He knows that soon the pounding of the seeds will increase. And the slamming will get sharp. And his anger and anxiety will rise to fit his genius at the game, and his luck. He must be comfortable.

They are sitting just outside the door to the tailor shop.

A man who has just got off the bus enters the shop. He talks to the tailor about a suit he wants made for a wedding. He has to pass between the men playing dominoes. The tailor is pedalling his Singer, and talking to Boy about Amurca.

He is wearing his steel-rimmed spectacles, which he does only when he has to sew by hand. He raises his eyes, peering over the silver wire of the round frames and at the same time, he holds a needle in one hand, and the fly of a gentleman's trousers in the other. Elections are in the air; and he is busier than ever. He utters a sigh of disgust when he sees his customer having to squeeze between four *unemploy bastards* to get to his place of business, his premises.

He rose from his bench, went to the door, gripped the customer's hand to protect him from the contagion of the disease of unemployment he saw around him, and said, 'Let me tell the four of you! When I get my seat in the honourable the Honourable House o' Sembly, I intend to pass a law forbidding you unemployed bastards from slamming dominoes in broad daylight.' He ushered the customer up the step and into the dark shop. 'What you think this is? I carries on a professional business on this premises. And the four o' you representing me bad in the eyes of my customers?' He smiled with the customer and put him to sit down. 'I am tired telling those four bastards *don't* congest my premises. At four o'clock every evening, they already sitting down round a table matching blasted figures and numbers on a domino-seed, as if they're in kindergarden. What kind o' example the four o' you setting for the youths?'

The men ignored him.

The customer gave him the suit length of blue worsted and, after a few instructions, he left.

Before the man reached the corner, Lionel said, 'But Seabert Mascoll Marshall! As long's you been a tailor in this tailor shop, we been playing dominoes here, every evening at four o'clock! You have never said to-don't play in front your shop! Is this political talk? Or real talk?'

'Appearances, Lionel, boy. Pure appearances. I had to make the blasted customer think that my tailoring establishment is a serious place. He might be a voter.'

'Seabert, you is a real politician. But me? I is a scientist. A scientist at dominoes. I might be a small man in your eyes, being as how I unemploy. But I know one thing. I know the science o' dominoes.'

'I think the only science you know is the science of unemployment.'

'If this country was bigger, a man with my gifts would have had a higher living, more better recognition for my talents. I am where I am because of the mentality of people running this country.'

'People running this country? You referring to politicians? If you referring to politicians, you referring to me, Lionel, man.'

'I referring to people running this country.'

'Politics, Lionel, is the religion of life!'

'You say you lived in Amurca. You say you lived in England when you was in the RAF. You even say you know Russia and socialism. I know that in each and every one o' them countries, a man with my gift for dominoes would make a damn good living. I would at least have a guvvament job, such as guvvament coach.'

'This country, Lionel, and my party is built on hard labour. Poorly paid, but still hard labour, Lionel. *Work*. If people like you-so don't like work, how the hell will this blasted country progress and prosper. Offa dominoes and the science o' dominoes?'

Never had Seabert Mascoll Marshall, in all his years tailoring and talking politics to men whom he felt were beneath him in brains and social class, ever heard such argumentativeness from one of them. It startled him. It confused him to think that one of them held different views to the philosophy of socialism and 'commonism' he had been teaching them. It displeased him. He showed his resentment by continuing to sew the fly into the pair of khaki trousers, and not talking or looking at Lionel. But he was really not concentrating on the fly, he was trying to put Lionel's radicalism out of his mind.

The owner of the khaki trousers was a man who worked twelve hours a day. He was a man who pulled spiders that contained barrels of molasses. He did all this in the hot sun. He sweated blood. And he got peanuts for wages. This kind of man was responsible for building up the country. Not domino champions.

'He is a more better man than you!' Seabert Mascoll Marshall shouted.

The domino seeds were being shuffled. They made a deep sound as they were rubbed on the wooden table.

'Shuffle these seeds, good,' Lionel was saying.

The man who was coming for the pair of khaki trousers was a man who gave his labour. His labour was hard and stinging with sweat. He gave all this to his country, because he was taught to give it. It was from the rewards of this hard labour that he paid the tailor's fees.

The smells of the village, the fragrance of the mayflower trees, the burning of cush-cush grass, the high pungent stink of a pig pen, and the smell of a cow pen being washed out, and the frying of fish, all these smells mixed with the salty evening air from the sea nearby.

The sea was rough this evening.

Someone is playing a radio. It is loud. The owner of the radio hopes that each inhabitant of the village is listening. The wind from the sea carries patches of the rhythm and pieces of the words of the song in the direction of the tailor shop, and the four men playing dominoes sing along with the song.

Laughter erupts whenever a game is won. And each time this happens, Seabert Mascoll Marshall looks over his glasses, pauses in the hand-stitching of the khaki trousers, and enquires about the outcome.

The next song on the radio is 'Evening Shadows Make Me Blue'. Everybody in the village knows this song. They know the singer is Ella Fitzgerald. 'The coloured girl from Amurca,' Seabert Mascoll Marshall calls her. He told them he knew her when he lived in Amurca. He said he met her in Harlem at the Apollo Theatre.

The wind is stronger now. And the melody and most of the words reach the men playing dominoes. Seabert Mascoll Marshall picks up the melody and sings, 'Eve-ning shadows make me bluuuuuue. . . .'

'Six-love in your arse!' Lionel shouts. 'Six-love in your arse!' he shouts, flushed in his predictable full victory.

39

Boy sits alone at the round dining table covered with a white crocheted cloth, and listens to the voice of Ella Fitzgerald, as he studies the patterns in the white tablecloth. The cloth is old. The pattern is eaten out in places and is ripped by the points of knives and forks. He holds his head low over the white china plate with the blue border and eats the steamed vegetables. Dinner is pumpkin, yam, sweet potatoes and pulp-eddoes. There is a chunk of boiled, delicious, salted pig tail. In the centre of the plate is a steamed red snapper. Eyes in the head. The head a third of the size. The eyes large and grey and arrogant, keeping a secret of the deep.

Boy hates this kind of food. 'Dry food', the villagers call it. They call everything that is eaten, 'food'. He calls it dinner. He is the only living person in the village who calls 'food', dinner.

Seabert Mascoll Marshall comes into his mind. It is not often that he calls the tailor by his name; but now that he is a part of the 'man-company of the tailor shop', he thinks of the tailor by his full name.

The song that comes on now, is 'Perdido'. It has a Latin beat. It is played by Perez Prado's orchestra.

Did Seabert Mascoll Marshall really visit Latin America? Is he really one of the big men in the village? Is he really educated? Is he educated enough to be an elected member of the House of Assembly, to lead his country through the period of its present semi-independence to full independence? Is a tailor suitable? And why should he, a student at the best school in the country, respect a man who attended elementary school, and reached only fifth standard? Why must he have respect for a man who needed two more grades in school before he could even be qualified to be a gardener or an apprentice to a trade?

Boy's mother came into the room, and sat in a chair in a corner. She looked at Boy and smiled. She then held her hands down to the thickness of her dress which reached almost to the ankles. She sat with him each time he ate.

'Why you always listening to this ungodly music?'

She says this every evening, when the hit parade comes on. He never answers her. And she never demands an answer.

Boy knows she never sits with his father when he eats. It is as if she is content to be the servant in her own house. But Boy

40

feels she is close by, to make sure he eats all his food, all this 'dry food', all the time.

'You is not the same as them.'

Her voice came from a distance farther away than the corner of the room.

'And even although they take you in their man-company in the tailor shop, you is still different from them. You is a Thorne. And as a Thorne you have a big destiny before you.'

All Boy could see in his mother's words was the gallery of clippings and pictures and photographs in the tailor shop. No one at the College, even Young Lascelles, ever talked about international affairs, as reflected in the wonders he saw in Seabert Mascoll Marshall's tailor shop.

The collection was a commentary on black people. He knew that. But he was never called upon, either at the College, or among his friends, to think of himself as a black person.

'We Thornes didn't born here, not in the beginning,' his mother's voice said. 'We come from a land far from here. And not Africa, neither!' Was she reading his thoughts?

Boy felt that even if the tailor's collection dealt with development or with progress, even with plight, it was still too removed from his life to have meaning. It was too foreign. It was too loud. He was in a quiet, darkened room, eating on a white crocheted tablecloth. He ran his hands over the delicate material. And in some of the holes, he could feel the sturdy linoleum cloth beneath.

There is a photograph on the wall. It is an old colour print of an English countryside. A young woman with long reddish hair is walking beside a brook. The sky over her is not the colour of the sky he sees above him every day. And the colour of the grass on which she walks is not the same green thick tough fields of cush-cush grass.

Yesterday his 'dinner' was cou-cou and steamed kingfish. He liked that. Yesterday, his mother said, 'You different from *all* o' them.'

He was dreaming, and he placed himself beside the girl, beside the brook, and felt the same way as when he was walking beside the sea, across the front road; and the girl in the photograph had turned into his friend, Moo-Moo, who lived up the hill.

41

The voice was coming at him again. 'I been hearing that you goes into that tailor shop. I been hearing that you letting Seabert Marshall Mascoll, or Seabert Mascoll Marshall, whichever his name is, full-up your head with *ideas*. You is a College-boy. You come from decent family. My father's father and my mother's mother was decent people. I hardly know them, having never met them. But I know them. They were from Away. From Scotland. You have the blood of the Scottish people in you. You don't have none o' this village blood in you.'

He looked at the photograph on the wall, above his head, and he saw Scotland. The background shifted, and he saw the beach across the road, and he saw Moo-Moo.

'Those men play dominoes for more hours than your poor father spends in the sea, trying to make a living. Poor man. . . .'

Boy thought of the hours he had to spend studying for the scholarship examinations, and in that way put his mother's concern about his father completely out of his mind.

'Thou hast scattered thine enemies with thy strong arm,' the voice beside him said.

His mother rose, slowly, as if she was all cloth and no bones and no muscles. She rose like a cloud of white petticoats. But before she left the room, she said, 'I have something for you to read to me *after* you finish doing your studies.'

Boy realized he was still holding the knife in a tight fist round its silver handle, as if he was about to do something violent with it.

When she left, she left her perfume of Bournes Bay Rum behind her.

The violence in Boy's mind took him next to Sarge, buckling up his truncheon to its heavy brown shiny police belt. Sarge had challenged Seabert Mascoll Marshall. Sarge had challenged Mr the Honourable Alexander Bourne. Sarge had made seventh standard and had graduated to be a policeman. And Sarge had spent time in Amurca.

Seabert had said, 'The landing rites o' democracy is my political religion, and my political information.'

'It is only rights you talking about,' Sarge had said. 'It is rights that is lacking in this blasted country. Rights! And by rights, I mean the rights o' man, if yuh know what I mean!'

42

'What I want you to read for me, is a verse or two outta the Axe of the Postles, please. . . .'

The chimes of Big Ben thundered through the small, square speaker of the Rediffusion radio service. The chimes were clear as the bells of the Anglican church. They were more powerful. Boy used to sing along with the chimes.

'Big Ben, boy!' his mother said. 'Time to go.'

She moved silently through the dark house. It was eight o'clock in the morning.

'This is London calling. Here is the news, read by. . . .'

Boy held an oval-shaped tin of pomade, and dug deeply into its light-green paste. He plastered both palms and then plastered his head. His hair was short and tough. The pomade made it shine. He looked as if he had just emerged from a dive in the sea. Each time he pulled the fine-toothed, tortoise-shell comb through his hair, he eased its passage by closing his eyes and gritting his teeth. He drew a parting in the middle of his hair. He poured Bournes Bay Rum into his left palm, almost filling the palm, and spilling some; and then he slapped both armpits. The tin of talcum powder, oval in shape like the pomade, had a bouquet of flowers on both sides. He held it up and let the white dust fall into the same left palm. And when he had enough, he rubbed the palm around his neck, and then over his face. His face became lighter in complexion than the rest of his body. He felt clean and good. He wriggled about, passing his left hand over his right testicle over the white elastic jock-strap; and he did the same thing with his right hand and his right testicle. When he was 'fixed', as his mother called it, when he was tidy, he put on the long grey flannel trousers, the short-sleeved sea island cotton shirt, the brown socks and the brown shoes. They were all made in England. The trousers did not fit. Their design did not consider his narrow waist and his high-bottomed shape. The elastic in the waist had long lost its strength. He spent a lot of time pulling up his trousers. This became a style, a gesture, an indication that he was wearing English-made trousers. Barristers-at-law, doctors, politicians, solicitors, magistrates, and members of the clergy, all had this style, this gesture, this indication. They all wore Daks trousers, made in England.

43

Alternating stripes of maroon and gold was his school tie which he slipped over his neck. The knot was greasy. When he put on his College blazer, he shrugged his uniform into place, and fixed his jock strap a second time.

'You look like a real Thorne!'

Boy saw his mother's image in the oval looking glass.

'. . . *based upon reports that all the wrongs of the Mau Mau . . .*'

His book bag was decorated on both sides by blots of *Quink* ink. MWWT was penned on both sides of the book bag.

'. . . *the authorities regard this grave state of affairs . . .*'

He was in the kitchen now. The BBC news poured out onto his head. His mother had prepared his lunch. Sandwiches of cucumber and lettuce and yellow butter from Australia and made from white bread, with their edges trimmed. Two hard-boiled eggs, peeled and wrapped in grease-proof paper, lay at two corners of his lunch tin shaped like a coffin.

'. . . *and that is the end of the news from London.*'

Outside it was humid. The road was covered in pools of clear water. The road was crowded. School children, and some junior civil servants stood beside the bus stop. The children stood in a close knot. Moo-Moo saw Boy approaching, and said, 'The College boy, boy!' The other girls snickered.

'If I was one o' them Maw-Maws from Africa, you think I wouldn't kill anybody who stand in the way of my freedom?' a girl said.

'But the Maw-Maws only killing-off other Maw-Maws,' Moo-Moo said.

'You minding the BBC?'

The small knot of children nodded in unison. They heard the same news. All their homes contained the same ugly square box of the Rediffusion system.

'My father say we have to take up for the Maw-Maws against the English. They fighting for freedom. We have ours already.'

'If the Maw-Maws was really peaceable people like we, England would have give them their freedom.'

Boy reached their group. Moo-Moo nodded to him. Boy moved a few yards away from them. It was as if he was not waiting on the same school bus.

44

'My father say that the brightest man in this village, is Seabert the tailor. And that is why he running for a seat in the House o' Sembly.'

Moo-Moo laughed loudly.

'How could a common, ordinary tailor have brains? He didn't even go to high school!'

'Schools don't make you bright,' the girl said. No one believed her. And the argument petered away.

A large Black Humber Hawk changed gears, and appeared round the corner. They all turned and saw the gleaming black bug approaching them, and they rushed from the side of the road, into the gutter. Dead crappos with overturned yellow bellies were in the road. Some of the school children stepped into water, and on crappos.

'My blasted shoes!' Moo-Moo said.

'That blasted Limey!' a girl said.

The Humber Hawk stopped beside them. It had already splashed them.

The chauffeur was dressed in a khaki uniform, made by Seabert the tailor. He wore a peaked cap, its crown covered in white. He looked like the captain of a ship.

An Englishman dressed in a white drill suit, stepped out the rear door. They recognized Mr John Barrington Lascelles, King's Counsel.

'Come on, come,' he said.

No name was called, no finger was pointed in selection. But Boy walked towards the open door. He got into the Humber Hawk, and did not look back.

The car door was closed, and at that instant, the chauffeur drove off, sending the splattered children farther into the gutter, and leaving brown spots on their freshly pressed school uniforms.

'My blasted uniform!' Moo-Moo screamed.

'You see now, why I like the Maw-Maws?'

'You see now why I don't like those blasted English foreign people.'

2

Inside the black Humber Hawk was always sweet-smelling.
Boy smelled the powerful leather and crisp morning newspaper
and the after-shave lotion and the smoke of the cork-tipped
English cigarette. He always sat with Jeffrey Lascelles on his
right, and the father, Mr John Barrington Lascelles, OBE,
King's Counsel, on his left.

J. B. Lascelles was the leading solicitor in the island. His son,
Jeffrey, was one of Boy's two rivals for the single Scholarship in
Classics tenable either at Oxford or Cambridge University. His
other rival was the son of the man who lived on the hill.

The Humber Hawk was nearing a corner. The chauffeur put
the car into second gear. Boy could feel the animal purring
heavily as it reduced speed. His body was thrown against Mr
Lascelles', and the newspaper fell, no longer blocking his
vision. Boy could see an old man steering a donkey and cart out
of the road, as the Humber Hawk turned the corner. The
chauffeur changed gear. Behind them were left two sprays of
brown dirty water.

Boy saw the old man's lips curl. He read the old man's lips.

'Be-Jesus-Christ! You son of a bitch!'

When Boy turned round he saw a grin on Jeffrey Lascelles'
face.

'Will it be Oxford or Cambridge, Boy?' Mr Lascelles said.
'Jolly good competition between you and Jeffrey here. Jolly
good. May the best man win!'

Boy smelled the after-shave lotion. He imagined the sharpness of the razor blade. Gillette, obviously. Only the headmaster of the College smelled this way.

'Promised Jeffrey here, one hundred pounds if he beats you
in the Schol,' Mr Lascelles said.

Jeffrey nudged Boy, and grinned.

Inside the Humber Hawk was quiet again. Mr Lascelles

returned to his newspaper. All vision of the road was blocked for Boy.

Out of the corner of his eye, Boy could see men and women scampering out of the path of the car. Some of them made gestures of anger, of abuse and of defeat. And the voiceless words spat out. But all that passed, and he was back again as if he was inside a glass boat, beneath the sea, in the silence of the soft leather which chambered him from the noise outside the car.

The Humber Hawk is approaching a four-cross road. And as it gets near to the green, unwashed statue of Lord Horatio Nelson, a policeman directing traffic on an octagonal box, at the base of the statue, swings round and shows them his thick, pink palm. The chauffeur touches the brakes and the black monster comes to a stop.

The policeman steps like ginger off the black and white box, and approaches the Humber Hawk.

He stands like a matador one inch from the shining bumper, making up his mind: to dare the animal some more, or to kill it. And at this moment, the large morning newspaper is lowered, and the policeman sees and recognizes Mr John Barrington Lascelles, OBE, KC.

He taps the shining black thighs of the Humber Hawk. He salutes smartly. 'But you have the right o' way, Skipper,' he says. 'Morning.'

The policeman jumped back up on his box. He spun in three directions, ordering with the force of his pink right palm the long lines of traffic congested in three directions, to stop. And like a weather-vane, this same palm now became a saw, a blade of a windmill, revolved in the gesture of passage, of right of passage and safe right of way.

Mr John Barrington Lascelles tipped his hat as the car carried him in the direction of the College.

In Deo Fides. This is written, in bent wrought iron letters on the iron gates of the College. Each morning Boy travels through this gate, he curses his father for being poor.

The gates are like the statue of Lord Horatio Nelson. Green with age.

Boys in the path of the Humber Hawk move back like waves when the sea is calm. And Boy notices that when it comes to a stop, the deputy assistant head Porter steps forward like a cork floating back out to sea to meet it. He is dressed in khaki. Long khaki trousers and short-sleeved khaki shirt, felt hat, that was once brown, but now khaki, like the rest of his uniform. He is barefooted. This man extends his left hand, opens the door, bows his head and doffs his hat. His ten toes, shining from coconut oil are planted like ten stubby roots on the warm, black, friendly macadam of the quadrangle.

'Morning, sir. Morning, Master Lascills. Morning, Master Thorne.'

'Morning, Mr Lascills.'

He has now leaned farther inside the cool, brown leather of the back seat, and has met the grey eyes of the man who holds the large morning newspaper on his lap.

'Morning, Hands,' Mr Lascelles says.

'Good day, sir!'

Hands' association with the College is as old and solid as the sound of the door of the Humber Hawk he has just closed.

Hands stands relaxed, but still at attention, as the Humber Hawk circles the sandbox tree. His body is like wire. The sinews and veins in his arms and two in his neck, stand out as if at any minute, his blood will spurt through them. He stands like this until the car disappears round the ninety-degree corner.

'Best legal brains ever to come outta the United Kingdom,' he told Boy one afternoon, on the cricket field. 'Brilliant academic career at Eton, thence to Oxford, where he read Greats with a double first from Oxford, thenceforth, the Inns o' Court, Middle Temple, double-first again. The best legal brains ever to grace the shores o' this island!'

Boy looks at him this clear morning, and hates him because he is so much, even in stature, like his own father.

48

3

'London's bridge is falling down
Falling down,
Falling down,
London's bridge is falling down,
My fair lady. . . .'

Sis and Moo-Moo and Patricia and Sheila, school friends who lived in the village, were there. They were in the alleyway between Grace's house and Moo-Moo's house. This space was their playing ground. The mothers and aunts were sitting in the open front door, talking among themselves. They were eating roast-corn. Boy and Henry, the son of the man who lived in the house on the hill, John Moore-Adams, were the only boys present.

Henry was talking about, 'Amerrica, Amerrica is the biggest country in the world, Amerrica has the tallest buildings in the world, and my father is the only man in this village who knows Amerrica.'

They did not understand what he was talking about.

The girls played with him but they hated him. And Boy kept silent about the sizes of houses and the owners of these big houses.

'My father already paid my fees to go to study at Columbia University. That's in Amerrica!'

No one among them had ever heard of Columbia University, until he had called its name. And he had to show them picture postcards of Columbia before they would believe that such a place existed.

'You may be going to Columbia, wherever that is, and whatever that is,' Moo-Moo said, 'but Boy and me and all o' we are going to either Oxford or Cambridge.'

'You-all are damn colonials!'

'So, why did you have to come here to get educated?' Moo-Moo asked him.

They then laughed at him, and at his strange accent. But they did not forgive his blasphemy.

'Because my father *pays* for my education,' Henry said. 'And he pays for a lotta other things, too!'

Moo-Moo's father was a merchant seaman. He spent most of his life overseas. Boy saw him once. But Boy had heard of the places he visited, seas and lands he could barely find in an Atlas. Moo-Moo saw her father once a year. When he came off his ship, as they called it, he was laden down with gifts and money. He had already made arrangements for her education. She was the only girl in the village who attended the leading girls' school, Queen's College.

Boy liked Moo-Moo's mother. She was a beautiful, young woman who liked music and laughed very loudly. She was always laughing, especially at the dirty jokes she told.

Boy knew she liked him for her daughter. But she also liked Henry. Henry's father, John Moore-Adams, was her landlord. The people said bad things about the two of them.

'Moo-Moo's mother?' the tailor said one afternoon, while he was sewing a fly into a pair of khaki trousers. '*She?* Man, she does-pay her rent with pussy!'

Boy was smitten; felt dirty; felt very common by the tailor's sentence. He was wise enough however, to know that such a woman was practical enough to see some advantage in encouraging Henry for her daughter.

'She is the Yankee man's mistress!' Sarge said.

Boy was roused from these thoughts, as the other children prepared to play the game, 'London Bridge is Falling down'. He was too old to be playing these games, he knew, but he had played them with these same girls ever since he could remember. He liked to be with the girls too, because he could steal a peep at their panties. But he was more interested at looking at the outline of the hips and legs of the mothers and aunts of his friends. Their powerful legs beneath thin dresses which they always tucked above the knee, roused great passion and sin in his mind. He always wished he was older than seventeen. And immediately afterwards, he became ashamed of his thoughts, and would make the sign of the cross, although he knew that only Catholics did that.

As the others prepare, Boy looks at Moo-Moo's mother, and wonders why she never wears petticoats under her dress. He can smell her perfume in which she seems to bathe. He is close to her now, and he thinks only of the flower, Lady-of-the-Night. He feels a powerful protectiveness towards this older woman; decides that no woman in the village, not even his own mother at this same age, can touch her for her sensuality and her raw sexual style. He feels he is going too far, and when no one is looking, he makes the sign of the cross again. He defends her against the rumours of the village; and he hates all the men and women who whisper about the currency she uses to pay her rent.

'Mr John Moore-Adams, the Yankee, does-settle all matters including his accounts with her, in kind, my dear!' he heard a woman say. 'She spends her husband's hard-earn money that he risk his life for on ships, on nothing but pure perfumes and clothes. I swear to God, she does-bathe in perfume! Just like he! The Yankee bastard! Mr John Moore-Adams could knock-yuh-down with the smell of his aftershave lotion. He is a *real* Amurcan!'

'I'm tired playing "London Bridge",' Moo-Moo complained.

'Are you children behaving yourselves?'

Boy saw Moo-Moo's mother come full into the light which was behind her, and which worked like an X-ray camera on her dress and her body. The door was still open. And Boy listened to the story she was telling her friends.

'Be-Christ, the husband came home. Opened the door. And the first thing he see was another man on top o' his wife. In his bed. Christ! For a minute he couldn't move. But when he moved, he came back with a knife. And bram-bram! Off went the man's *two* balls! Both! And out went the wife' vagina! Clean-clean! Clean-clean! Clean-clean!'

Boy saw her laughing until tears came to her eyes. He shuddered.

'You children have *one* more hour! Then I sending-home everybody!' She laughed louder. And the women laughed louder.

' "Green-leaves", then?' Grace asked.

Nobody answered.

'What about "Hobbina-Bobbina"?'

'We're not *kindergardens!*' Moo-Moo said. 'We're big teen-agers.'

She felt Grace was her rival for Boy's affections.

'Because I'm not lucky-enough to be going to Queen's College, you think. . . .'

'I didn't make myself into a Queen's College girl! My father works hard to pay my school fees.'

'She didn't mean it that way,' Patricia said, trying to arbitrate. That was always her role. Patricia was the daughter of the tailor. 'So what?' she added, icily. 'I learning to be a dressmaker. I taking lessons in dressmaking and needlework. Does that make me a more lesser person?' She looked at Moo-Moo as she said this. 'You is what you are.'

Patricia visited the public library every Saturday morning, and returned with three books about adventure and the mysteries of caves in India. She read each book twice before the following Saturday, when she repeated the routine. At the present time, Boy knew she was reading *The Rifling of the Tombs of Pharaoh*.

'I may not be a Queen's College student,' Patricia said. 'But I am still a *person*.'

The argument was settled. It was always like this. The girls stuck together, came to their own conclusions, and the group was bound again.

'My mother and your mother,' Moo-Moo began, reciting the words of the game 'hide-and-hoop'. Everyone but the last would be eliminated. That person would become the 'catcher'. The 'catcher' had a limited time in which to catch them all.

The scent of the bougainvillaea touched him. He did not know exactly where he was standing. There was no moon. In the darkness, he could not tell how far he was from 'home'. The first song in the hit parade was playing. And out of the darkness, a hand touched him. He felt the soft hand on his face. And then he knew it was perfume he was smelling, and not the bougainvillaea.

'You want to kiss me?'

'Why not?'

'Well, kiss me then, you fool!'

He was still smelling the bougainvillaea. He was in the rose bush and the prickles were touching his skin. He did not recognize the voice, the perfume of the night was so strong.

'Well, kiss me, you fool.'

The light from the open front door could not reach the back of the house where they were.

'Do you need light to kiss a person?'

'I can't see.'

'Here.'

She put out her arms and caught him round his neck. She was wearing perfume. He closed his eyes. Her lips were soft like raw pork liver. But smelling better. She buried the length of her tongue in his mouth. He kept his eyes closed.

'*Catch-yuh!*'

It was Moo-Moo.

He had kissed Grace by mistake.

When they got back to the circle, everybody was laughing. Everybody already knew.

The hit parade programme was into its second song. The announcer spoke as if he had just returned from Harlem, Amurca, just like John Moore-Adams, in a smooth voice like foreign granulated white sugar. The announcer was as popular as a film star. Because of his voice. The children imitated his voice, and his foreign accent, and called him, 'The Voice'.

'He tries to talk like a black Yankee,' Henry informed them.

'An' now, members of the lis'nin' public, you-all out there in radio-land, here's the first lady of song, the one and only Miss Ella Fitzgerald, singing that most popular of all popular songs, the most requested, the most romantic, the most swingingest, sentimental song in the whirl, "Evening Shadows Make Me Blue" . . . so, take it away, Ella!'

'Oh-God! Oh-God-oh-God!'

The exclamation came from the house. It was a scream of appreciation. It was Moo-Moo's mother.

Fifty listeners in radioland had requested 'Evening Shadows'. The announcer called out each of the fifty names, mispronouncing many of them.

53

The night became all perfume. Boy could smell Moo-Moo again. He could smell Grace again. He could smell the Lady-of-the-Night flower and the bougainvillaea and the red roses. It was like black satin.

They all knew the words of the song by heart. Moo-Moo's mother was singing the loudest and the best of them all.

'Children! Time!'

'Good night, Henry.'

'Be seeing ya!'

'Good night, Moo-Moo.'

'Pat, good night.'

'Night, all. . . .'

Billy Eckstein was singing the second chorus of 'Blue Moon'. . . .

'Did you-all hear me say it's time?'

All of a sudden, there was a roar of men's voices that came clearly to them, from down the hill near the beach. Boy knew the shouting came from the rum shop. The men in the rum shop always made that loud noise on Friday nights. Rum and noise. Rum and politics. And more noise. Boy knew. And fights.

'You-all getting home safe?'

'Moo-Moo's mother's voice was almost as loud as the shouting down the hill. Boy always wondered why she never seemed able to talk in a normal voice. Everything she did, he felt, was extreme.

'Each one o' you-all have somebody to walk home with?'

She came into the doorway. Boy could see the thickness of her thighs beneath the thin cotton dress. She knew he was watching her. And she smiled. Boy hated Henry and Henry's father, all of a sudden, for having the most and the best of everything in the village. He hated them more because they were not even real Barbadians. He wished he could grow up within the space of this wonder, all of a sudden. He wondered how long it would really take him to grow up.

'Did you say goodnight to Boy?'

She was inquiring of her daughter; but it sounded more like a compelling order.

'Grace and Sheila are walking home with Henry, together,' Moo-Moo said.

Her mother knew that would be the arrangement. It had been the arrangement from the first time they began playing in her yard. But she always asked, to make certain that the same arrangements were carried out, each time.

'And the College-boy', Moo-Moo said, spitefully referring to Boy, 'is walking-home Patricia.'

She stealthily pinched Boy on his behind.

'Good!' her mother said.

The other women came to the doorway to see that everything was safe. 'Blue Moon' came to an end. The roar of the men in the rum shop could be heard again.

'Be careful passing that damn rum shop this time o' night, hear? Please. Those damn men have no regards for women. Hear? Christ, I-myself shivvers each time I passing that rum shop alone, at nights.'

The other women nodded their heads. They all knew the history of men troubling young girls.

'Every time you see elections in the air,' Moo-Moo's mother said, 'look-out for a lotta blasted crime. And woman-crime, at that!'

And then she laughed.

Boy and Patricia moved away.

At the end of the gravel road, they turned right, he and Patricia, travelling in the darker stretch of road, two hundred yards down the hill before they would see the next street lamp, before they could reach home. Her home was opposite the rum shop. Her father was the tailor, Seabert Mascoll Nathaniel Marshall. Seabert had shown Boy the campaign list, and this is how his name was printed on it.

Mr Seabert Mascoll Nathaniel Marshall.

His campaign was not going well. 'But I trying my luck,' he said. 'To make some money and to make something outta myself.'

Boy felt that since her father became a declared candidate, Patricia was putting on airs.

'My father say,' she began, 'that if he win a seat in the elections, our house will be fix up to look like Henry's father's house. With 'lectricity and running water. And that if he don't win, he leaving straight for Amurca.'

'My aunt lives in Amurca.'

'I know,' Patricia said. 'My father tell me so. My father say he would be a bigger tailor in Amurca. He say he may even change from being a common tailor, into being a designer of men's outfits. He say that all Amurcans like a lotta clothes. That's why the reputation of a tailor in Amurca is more better than here. But my father say that Amurca is not a place for a girl to grow up. He say he will send for me when it is time for me to look for a husband. Sarge say that when he was living in Amurca, a day didn't pass without a person killing another person. And a night didn't end without a girl losing her virtue. Sarge say he read all those things in the *New York Daily News*. Amurca must be a serious place to live, you don't think so?'

'I prefer England.'

'What about Canada?'

'I never heard of Canada. I only know it's a lot of red on the map of the world.'

'But where's Canada, though? Oh, I remember now. It's in Newfoundland.'

They walked on in silence. The road was like a dark valley. On both sides, the rock out of which the road itself had been hacked by prisoners doing hard labour, was four feet above their heads. On the embankment, on both sides, were fields of sugar cane. And fields of cush-cush grass. The houses on the embankment always seemed to Boy, as if the slightest wind would blow them into the road. Boy looked at them now, like silhouettes of tombs and sepulchres, and with no light in any of them. But he could hear people inside them, talking. A gramophone was playing one of the songs he had heard earlier on the hit parade.

They continued slowly down. On their left hand, the land was now at the level of their waists; and was sloping away towards the sea. They could see the hard stubby vegetation, like tough ghosts; and they could imagine the rocks and the boulders and the feet-worn paths across this land that they had travelled over so many times during the day time. The bigger boys played cricket there, on weekends. And the old women of the village, on their way to church, saw the boys playing cricket and pronounced Sodom and Gomorrah. 'Heathens!' the old women called the Sunday cricketers.

Boy could no longer see the sea from the falling incline of the road. But the sea was there. He could smell it and he could hear it breaking against the wall. He himself used to sit on this same wall, some afternoons, and watch the sunset. The sea was rough, but not so loud as the men in the rum shop they were approaching.

'You know that man who wears white from head to foot, white cork hat, with canvas shoes and white socks, and who's always walking in the middle of the road, in the city, when we're going to school? And after school, when we're coming home?'

'Who wears a grey woollen tie? And walks with a beat-up leather valise, every day?'

'Yeah! And who sits in the verandah of Goddards!'

'They say he can drink more rum than Sarge and. . . .'

He almost called her father's name. He checked his tongue, and added, 'We always laugh at him! Because he looks so funny!'

'My father say he is one o' the richest men in Barbados! And that he owns a plantation.'

They were getting near to Patricia's home.

'If my father don't win the elections, and before I go up to Amurca, I want to open a big big shop. And sell food. Goods, you know? Rice and sugar and salt-meat and salt-fish and sweet-bread and sugar-cakes and Limacol. But not rum. Nor anything strong so. And I hope that with profits and in time, I could turn that peddling shop into something big, something like a small store, or a supermarket. You know?'

Boy, who had seen a pushing out of the chest in Patricia's manner recently, was amazed that she was so mercenary and so much of a businesswoman. Patricia had many models in the village. From the time he was born, Boy had seen women as the most successful businesswomen, outstripping the men, including the tailor and the rum shop owner, many times over. It was not really strange for Patricia to be thinking about shops and small stores and little supermarkets. What was surprising to Boy was that she had made her plans so early, and with such clarity of ambition.

57

'And when I have the shop running good. You know? When the shop turning-over a lil profit, I intend to build a big big wall-house make outta coral-stone. And then I going look for a husband to married me. Maybe, even still go up to Amurca. You know? Or, stay here and enter politics like my father.'

Boy started to fall in love with Patricia. To him, she would make a solid wife.

'Being the first prime minister that is a woman is something to think about. You know? My father always say a woman could rule-over men. So, for me, it is a grocery shop, *or* politics. Or Amurca, if I fail.'

Boy was speechless: not in the sense of adoration and love; but by the way she knew what she wanted to be.

'You know? That man we was talking about, coming down the hill? The man that is always dress in the white suit? Do you know, he have a slight, a slight-slight resemblance to you?'

'You gotta be kidding!' Boy shouted. 'As Henry would say.'

'You have never ever ask me, in all the years we been going to school on the same school-bus, what I want to be, College-boy!'

'Really?'

'But I just give you the answer. Just in case. I could now ask you what you going to be, when you's a man? What you want to be, when you grow up, College-boy? You know?'

The domino 'seeds' were hitting the top of the wooden table, like bullets exploding. Four men were hunched in concentration round the table. The losing partners bought a round of drinks for the winners. The prize was rum. They drank it from snap glasses. One team of partners had already won four times.

The losing team were getting louder and angrier, and their eyes were red and they were losing their tempers.

The best domino players in the village and even in the country, were known to Boy. Reputations were built and were destroyed on the word of prowess in dominoes: or on the lack of prowess. Lionel, the champion domino player in the country, was in this game. He and his partner were the losing team.

The score was now five-love.

Sarge was inside the rum shop.

Henry and the other two girls had arrived home, a short time before.

Sarge had his black serge tunic unbuttoned, revealing his flannel shirt. The shirt had no collar. In places it was soaked in perspiration. On the back of the chair was his heavy shining, brown leather belt, and the truncheon, in its brown holster. The three stripes of his rank glimmered in the semi-darkness, as the silver buttons on the tunic were shining.

Beside him was Boy's father, Nathan. And beside Nathan, sitting on the third upright chair made of wood, was Patricia's father, Seabert the tailor, designer of men's clothes to-be, and member of parliament, to-be. These three big men were in the back room.

The back room was reserved for those of status: villagers and strangers. The politician who represented the village, Mr the Honourable Alexander Bourne, Esquire, MP, as he gave his full entitlements, sat with these men, in this back room, whenever he dropped by to pick up gossip and to listen to rumours, and to spread some, himself. And religiously, as was dictated by his exalted position, he bought the drinks, by the rum bottle.

Alexander Bourne talked only about politics and women. He had a reputation of rumoured prowess with three village women. 'They're my staunchiest supporters!' he always explained. Apart from politics and women, he talked about promises. But all his promises were political promises. 'I intends to repair every blasted road that criss-cross this village, and put in 'lectricity in every blasted chattel house in this blasted constituency o' mine! Mark my words!'

In his absence, the three big men of the village (the fourth never socialized with them) drank happily and talked about 'life'. And were happier.

Lionel and the three other men were still playing dominoes. He and his partner had lost the first set. It was becoming a national disgrace. To the three big men drinking rum and talking about 'life', it was becoming a disgrace. Domino players talked too much and laughed too loudly. But the domino players ignored the three big men. They sat in the kerosene-lamp light, in a corner of the shop, near the counter, in the short passageway that led to the back room. Regular customers buying goods for the weekend, were becoming angry. The four players were arguing about a seed that was incorrectly played.

The rum shop owner, Mr Manny Batson, a man who talked nothing but politics, or what he called 'the politics of politics, whiching is much difference from what the tailor believes in', was sitting now with the three big men, the three important customers in the back room. Before he sat down this night, to have a drink with them, he said what he always said, 'I am an unboughtable man. That's why I won't ever join no rass-hole political party. The politicians in both parties is nothing but blasted crooks. Kiss-me-arse crooks. I am unboughtable.'

A bottle of choice rum was on the table. Cigarettes and boxes of matches, with the Beefeater and sailor design, were beside the cigarettes. And a large rum bottle with its label torn off, filled with iced water. The rum shop owner had just placed a large plate of corn beef, taken straight from the Fray-Bentos tin, on the table. Chopped onions and generous portions of hot sauce were in the corn beef.

Every now and then he went outside into the common section of the shop, to keep an eye on things, and on the domino players. He hated them. But it was good business practice to stomach them in his shop on a Friday night.

'I gotta keep my eye on things,' he told the three men before he left. 'As a proprieter, I gotta be on the lookout.'

He said this each time he left to make his short inspection, and each time he returned from making it.

His wife was serving the women who were buying goods. She was serving them at the counter. In addition to rum, Mr Manny Batson sold canned meats, canned fish, flour, sugar and biscuits, salt beef and salt pork. Occasionally, he stocked salt fish.

'The shipments from Halifax too blasted stink and bony, anyway. Pure bone in the salt fish from Halifax.'

'I gotta keep my eye on things,' he said when he returned to the back room. 'As a proprieter, I gotta be on the lookout.'

He and the three big men in this back room were protected

from the eyes of the public by a blind made out of black cloth.
The blind was pulled together by a string made from herringbone cord. Flies by day, and bees by day and mosquitoes by
night hovered around the kerosene lamp. Fly-catching sticky
papers hang like long worms, long dead worms, from the
ceiling. Dead flies on the paper gave it a surrealistic appearance.

'My bicycle still in your backyard, Manny? You put it outta
sight?' Sarge asked, suddenly becoming concerned. He had
many enemies in the village.

'You have beat confessions outta at least two o' them
bastards playing dominoes in my shop,' Manny said. 'What
you expect?'

'Blasted snakes. Worse than politicians. Present company
not to be mentioned.'

Running down the side of his black serge trousers was a red
stripe. Miraculously, even on the darkest night, this red stripe
was spotted by the men when they had to run from Sarge,
when they were throwing dice. They had to get away fast from
Sarge, when they knew that Sarge 'wanted' them.

'They is nothing but *wanted* men! But I always catch them!'

Sarge never moved at night without his 'wompuh'. The
wompuh was a whip made from the penis of a bull-cow. He
had bent it into half. And when he hit a man with it, the man
was bent into half, in agony.

'This wompuh distributes what I calls private justice.'

There was a long secret pocket which Sarge had asked the
tailor to cut into his trousers. He kept his bull-pistle here.

'Men still talking 'bout the beating you gave Goalie,'
Nathan said. Goalie was one of the domino players. 'And the
way you treat Brandford for raping that girl! Sarge, you was
going kill Brandford?'

Sarge's face became full and pretty and proud as a full
moon. The sweat on his face made him look beautiful in his
cruelty.

'Nathan, I is not ashamed to tell you, since you yourself
bring up this matter o' Brandford and the raping of the girl.
When the bull-pistle landed the first time, Brandford burst in
tears. I-myself was sorry for the blasted crook. When the

second one touch-he, be-Christ, he start spitting blood. Seabert Marshall, you shouldda been there. Yuh see, Brandford take-up something to-wit, ravishment, that didn't belongst to him. It was more than petty larceny.'

Old women in the village, those who called the Sunday cricketers 'heathens', prayed every Sunday for Sarge; they prayed that he would keep his health; and when their grandchildren were disobedient, they quieted them and brought them back to discipline by saying, 'Don't make me call Sarge for you, you hear?'

'And when the third lash from the bull fall,' Sarge continued, 'oh my God! Brandford peed straight. Wet *and* shit his pants.'

Even Manny Batson, who bragged that he was the toughest man in the village, shuddered when Sarge talked about his bull-pistle.

'I know I amongst friends,' Sarge went on. 'Nathan is my friend. Manny, you is a friend o' mine, and so is Seabert Mascoll Marshall, never mind he is a blasted political viper. And to a less extent, I counts that Yankee-bastard up the hill, John Moore Hyphen Adams, 'mongst my friends. So, what I have to worry about? I am surrounded by friends.'

The three other men knew that everyone hated Sarge: perhaps, they themselves were included. And they knew, too, that the villagers waited like conspirators, to get even with him. That is why he had to hide his bicycle at night.

'This corn beef blasted good,' he said. He took two forksful into his mouth, and washed it down with a rum.

'From Australia?' Seabert asked. 'Or from the Argentine?'

'New shipment,' the rum owner told them. 'The big merchants in the city didn't want to sell none to the small retailers like me. But this is election time. And I pulled a few strings like hell, to get a piece o' that shipment. Whenever you see election-time come round, the blasted Guvvament always putting corn beef on the shortage list. The big wholesale merchants in the city making a hell of a profit, whilst the poor man like me, who trying to rub two pennies together, to mek a honest living, getting his two balls squeeze.'

'Every election time,' Nathan said, although he knew nothing about selling goods.

'I had to pull strings like hell, in the right places, to get a piece o' this shipment o' corn beef from the Argentine, to satisfy my customers. That is why I don't mix-up in no politics. Without corn beef, black people suffering. And the Guvvament know that.'

'Now that Seabert is a politician, we should get all the corn beef we want. Seabert going take care o' we. Eh, Seabert? With jobs and corn beef?'

Seabert didn't answer. He didn't even smile.

'But you have join the wrong party,' the rum shop owner said. 'You are 'sociating with a party that throughout the history of this land have stomp on, and kept-down the black man, and haven't done one blasted thing for the poor man.'

'A blasted traitor,' Sarge said. 'A traitor to mankind. Having all them pictures of great black men in his tailor shop, and still joining-in with *that* party?'

He ate some more corn beef. And he washed it down with a larger rum.

'Not only to mankind. But to *black* mankind. If yuh know what I mean?'

They knew that Sarge was getting drunk. They knew the discussion was becoming important. For when these two things happened, Sarge ended each statement with, 'If yuh know what I mean.' It was something he had picked up in Amurca.

'That political party to which you belongst is a brown-skin party. If you know what I mean?'

'This betrayal o' black people couldn't happen in the States, could it, Sarge? You lived in Amurca. You ever hear of a black man running for a white-man party?' the rum shop owner asked.

'But Seabert should be out there, in the byways and lie-ways o' political scampery, working for the comma-man, instead o' being in here, drinking rum and hiding from his constituents,' Sarge teased him.

'You mean buying votes!'

'Or thiefing votes!' Sarge said. He slapped Seabert on his back. Seabert fell on the counter. Sarge was a powerful man.

'My two eyes are not shut,' Seabert said. 'I am in this for *one* thing. My personal betterment. My family's betterment. My daughter's betterment. And my betterment. When I get elected

63

to the honourable, the Honourable House o' 'Sembly, *first thing*, I adding-on a' addition to the house, buying a motto-car, and opening a bank account.'

'A man, any man should have that freedom,' Nathan said. 'Not only a man in politics.'

He was thinking of his own life. The house in which he lived was being rented from John Moore-Adams, a man he did not like. He wished he could buy the house. He wished and he wished, and he did nothing about it. He did not even have the courage to talk to his wife about buying the house. So he continued, as poor men sometimes do, to wish.

'A man, any man, deserve the kind o' freedom that Seabert just talk about. That freedom to make politics pay. And pay *dear*, too.'

'Perhaps,' Sarge said, 'Nathan is just as bright as his own son, the Barbados Scholar to-be!'

'In the last elections, I voted for the party that loss,' Nathan said. 'This time, I just don't know. As I see it, a political party is a fucking party. And I am glad that Seabert here don't intend to walk-'bout this constituency that he running for, telling people a lotta blasted lies 'bout how he intend to fight for the comma-man. I was getting frighten that Seabert was that brand o' socialist, to talk about socialisms and forget to line his pocket!'

'You got my vote, though,' Sarge said. 'If yuh know what I mean?'

'Politics is for the betterment of the politician,' Seabert said. He was now awake and excited about his future. 'And I don't intend to change that basic philosophy.'

'Now, yuh making sense!' the rum shop owner said. He poured Seabert a double shot of rum. 'Yuh got yuh hat on, boy!'

'Self-betterment, first!'

'With this sensible talk that I hear coming from Seabert' mouth,' the rum shop owner said, 'I-myself might even join-in, and vote for Seabert.'

And he laughed, deep down, from the bottom of his belly. And they all laughed with him. He stood up, a bit unsteadily, raised his snap-glass full of rum and said, 'To the next

Honourable Gentleman, Member of His Majesty Parlment, Representative for Sin-James East, Mr the Honourable Seabert Mascoll Nathaniel Marshall, *Esquire!*'

Just then, before they could say, 'Hear-hear!', there was a roar from outside in the shop, where the domino players were. The anger and the argument which had been brewing, broke out.

'Godblindyou! You tek me for a fool? You just pass to fives! You passed to fives, a minute ago!'

'. . . Hear-hear!'

'I drink to that!'

'Mr S. M. N. Marshall, Esquire, MP!'

'You calling me a thief?'

'You's a blasted thief! You passed to *fives* just-now!'

'. . . and when you become a Member o' Parlment, a big man in this land, I hope that corn beef won't be scarce, no more. And I hope you would learn how to wear a three-piece suit. For the opening o' Parlment. Let we see you in the newspaper, wearing a three-piece, just like the Englishmens before your time always do, just like Mr John Barrington Lascills, the King's Counsel. Keep your two eyes on tradition, boy!'

'A fellow that I caught breaking and entering a store in town, hand-over a piece o' cloth to me, a nice blue piece o' material with a real pretty white pin-stripe,' Sarge said. 'For the longest time, I been thinking o' bringing that suit-length to you, to make-into a suit for me. I think I will wear it to the next wedding I get invited to. A police sergeant like me would look nice, wearing that pin-stripe to a nice wedding. Or even to a funeral. If yuh know what I mean?'

'Or to a christening,' Seabert said. Only he laughed.

'You think a man like *me*, would thief at a simple game like dominoes? Me? The hardest seed in the whole o' Sin-James East? Me, the domino-champion of this island?'

'You are a fucking thief. Not only at dominoes, neither. The fucking Transport Board had to fire you, for thiefing. Everybody knows that. You is a known thief. After the Transport Board, the only job you got is the one you have now. Digging fucking graves. For dead people! Well, why you think you're now digging graves and burying deads? And a big guvvament-supporter like you? Because you's a *thief*.'

Chairs and the table crashed on the wooden floor. Women getting their weekend groceries screamed. Glasses and bottles fell. Pieces of ice rattled and then rolled like clumsy marbles over the sand on the floor. The domino seeds were scattered.

'What the hell happening out there?' Manny Batson shouted. He swelled to his full two hundred and fifty pounds of proprietorship.

'Wait here! Wait here! I am going home. When I come back, lemme hear you call me a thief again. I bet you don't call me a thief, when I come back.'

'Whenever I meet you,' Goalie said, 'be it in church, or in chapel, you will always be a kiss-me-arse thief!'

Their voices were now clear in the back room. Loud and rasping and hoarse and powerful and cruel.

'Size-round,' the rum shop owner, Manny Batson, now more than two hundred and fifty pounds of self-importance and ferocity, said. 'Size-round, and lemme get out there and see what they doing to my establishment.'

'Blasted snakes! I didn't tell you they was nothing but blasted snakes?'

'Them is the kind o' mankind that you want to represent, Mr Member o' Parlment?'

'Who disrepecting my blasted premises? Who is the man? Who is the man that disrespecting my respectable premises?'

His wife was standing behind the counter, speechless. Her mouth was wide open, in astonishment. She was shaking. It was fear. She could not talk. She could not tell him who was disrespecting his respectable premises.

The other women were silent, too. They were standing, looking down at the mess of domino seeds, the chairs, the ice and glasses.

The partner of the man accused of stealing bent down and started to pick up the scattered domino seeds. He ignored the glasses. He picked up the seeds from amongst the sawdust and sand and cigarette butts and dead flies and bees.

The two women buying goods stood with arms folded, as if they were apart and above the spectacle.

66

The rum shop owner, swelled out now to his full two hundred and fifty pounds of respectable proprietorship, ripped the black cloth blind apart, opened his large blood-shot eyes wide, and demanded again, as if for the last time, '*Who* disrespecting my blasted premises? Who is the man?'

He was angrier than he looked. Only his wife knew this. She had seen him throw a man bigger than himself bodily out of the shop one Saturday night. And when the man landed in the gutter opposite, the sound he made was like that of a bag of brown raw sugar on hard rock stone. From that day, the man never was able to walk straight upright.

'Cripple for life. And the police, including Sarge, who was in the back room that very night, tekking his usual waters, when it happen, didn't lift a finger 'gainst Mr Manny Batson.' That was how Nathan described it to his son, Boy.

The rum shop owner was a powerful, big man in the village.

'I say, *who* is the blasted man?'

One of the remaining domino partners, Lionel, moved towards the door. He inched his way to the exit, just in case what he was going to say did not please Mr Batson.

'Well, this is the way it was, Skipper. We had them five-love for the second time tonight. We was playing the sixth game. We was about to beat them six-love. Give them a *sow*. We had them to beat, two times. And we had the pose in the sixth and final game, Skipper. Goalie was sitting 'pon my right hand, tekking seeds from me. Goalie send a four. My partner turn um two fours. Then Goalie pass. My partner send another four. I played four-tray. His partner lay-down, with double tray. Buddie here, put on six-tray. then Goalie put-on six-deuce. . . .'

He was fixing the domino seeds on the table, replaying each seed correctly from memory.

'Be-Christ!' the rum shop owner said, in awe and in appreciation, 'you can't make more better uses of your brain?'

Lionel was known as the best domino player in the country. Last year, the Government had sent him with an island team to Jamaica. He had helped Barbados to win the tournament, six-five over the Jamaicans. He was a kind of national hero. His heroic status lasted for one week after the tournament. And his Government was proud of him for one week following. It was

the representative of the village who had asked the Prime
Minister to make him an honorary Deputy Assistant Sports
Officer, to go through the country, to teach dominoes to the
youth. The position had no salary. So, Lionel refused.

Now, still with pride for Lionel's brains and recollection, Mr
Batson stood over him. Each time a seed was replayed, Mr
Batson sighed with pride. This was a legend. Of such inordinate
proportion, that some people called him, 'Seeds'.

Seeds, better known as Lionel, now conscious of his enlarged
and impressed audience, went on, 'Offa Goalie's deuce, my
partner put-on a *hard* five. I holding the last three fives, in my
hand. I holding double-five, six-five and five-tray. Goalie
passed to the first five. I see it with my-own two eyes, Skipper.
Then, I have the last seed in my hand to slam, and get out of the
six-love that we have them in. And then all of a sudden, Goalie
start screeling and calling me a thief, and. . . .'

Boy and Patricia were coming down the final stretch of the hill
when Goalie passed them. They could hardly recognize him.
He was running very fast. But Boy knew who he was. And he
ignored him. He had seen men run fast at night, for no reason
he knew. Some men, he did know, ran like that when they were
escaping from Sarge. Some men ran like that, from their
women. Some ran like that when they were exercising. Some
men ran like that because they liked running. And some men
ran at night, from the bus stop, right up to their doorstep,
because they were afraid of the dark.

It was dark tonight, particularly in this stretch of road.

They were now beside the rum shop. The road was crowded.
They had to walk at the side. Boy stepped on something soft. As
he lifted his foot, the smell of the substance rose to his nostrils.
Dog shit.

But they walked on, through the edge of the crowd.

Men were cursing. This was nothing new. Boy always heard
men cursing in the road, near the rum shop on Friday and
Saturday nights. Friday and Saturday nights were the two
nights when men got paid, or found themselves with money.

Boy heard a man say, 'No fucking wonder they fired him
from the Civil Service. And to look at that boy, today! You

68

won't imagine that once upon a time, he was a big civil servant. Albeit, selling postage stamps in the Post Office, in the city!'

'He attended high school, too.'

'Cawmere School for Boys, wasn't it, that he went to?'

'Not Cawmere, man. The Modern High School for Boys and Girls.'

'That's probably why he turn out, so!'

'The Modern is where he went. I think he did-even win a scholarship to a more better school. But the mother, being as how she had-just passed-away, and seeing as how Goalie's father had-already start-up with another woman, the boy was neglected. So . . .'

'I even hear he was a Latin fool! Bright-bright-bright in that dead-language. And stupid as arse, upstairs! Not much comma-sense to accuse him of!'

Boy felt the man's words like a sting of a whip. Like Sarge's bull-pistle. Patricia, who knew the judgement the villagers made on foolish children, walked silent, beside him.

'Not *Latin*,' another man said. 'You mixing-up Goalie with Nathan's son. Nathan, the fisherman, have a son, and the girl-child of the pretty woman up the hill, *them* is the only two living souls in this village who does-talk in pure Latin. Wasn't Latin, in Goalie's case, man. Goalie was talking in *German*.'

Boy and Patricia moved through the people at the edge of the crowd. They saw the last bus from the city stop and drop off a few passengers. Boy knew the men who got off were coming from the late cowboy movie at the Olympic Theatre. It was *Bad Man from Dead-end City*. He had seen the advertisement on the red brick of the Olympic that very afternoon.

Boy took Patricia right up to her door. He waited until she got inside.

'That man in the white suit,' she said, before she went in. 'Is that what they mean by an Albino?'

In the soft golden light from the kerosene lamp on the centre table in the middle of the small room of Patricia's small house, Boy could see her mother sitting in her chair. A vase of plastic flowers was beside the lamp. Patricia's mother was always in this chair. It was a rocking-chair, with a curved high back, and strong arms. Whenever he passed, she was in this chair. He thought she spent all her life waiting and sitting in this chair.

Boy walked the remaining twenty yards, thinking of Patricia's question about the man who always wore white. He could not understand her interest in this man, at whom he himself laughed, each time he saw the man sitting in the overhanging balcony of Goddards, with a glass in his hand. So, he began to think instead of Moo-Moo's mother, and the outline of her thighs, through the thin cotton dress.

There was little colour over the sea this Saturday. The evening had turned dark and quiet. The only noise was the invisible buzzing of the mosquitoes around his eyes and ears. Boy saw them only after he was able to lift them off his arms, only after they had stung, and had become bloated with his blood, and were too heavy to continue in their annoying manoeuvres, and escape.

'Jesus Christ!'

That was Nathan, his father. He swore always after he had killed a mosquito. He slapped his two palms together to kill them. He was as good at killing mosquitoes, as he was at catching sprats and red snappers.

'Good Christ!'

The palms thundered again. And then, there was the sound of rough hands rubbing khaki.

All of a sudden, the evening became noisy. The usual noise of the night now contained the noise of buses passing, cars blowing their horns and burning gas to accelerate round the sharp bend in the road where every other night there was a minor accident. A boy was killed there the previous Friday night.

Boy was in his bedroom. His aunt had sent the five Amurcan dollars in a money order, in the usual red and blue airmail envelope. And when he took the letter from the hands of the postman, he knew that it contained money. It always contained money. The money went towards the rent and towards the fees for his education at the College. He knew also, and this he did not relish, that he would have to write the letter of thanks to his aunt. The reply would not vary from all the others, countless letters of thanks, that he had been asked to write. He kept his bedroom window open, in spite of the mosquitoes. And he

70

continued to look out to sea. There was no difference between the colour of the sea, and the colour of the sky.

Boy's father and mother were sitting in the large sitting-room which they called the front-house. They sat there almost every night that he could remember. They sat and talked and worried in lowered voices about their lives and his own life, worries which he was not intended to know about.

A lorry came slowly along, and as it reached his window, he heard the words of the announcement.

'Come one! Come all! A mass-meeting in the Green, tonight! Eight o'clock, sharp! Come and hear why this Guvvament have to go! This Guvvament got to go! This Guvvament got . . .'

He had already memorized the message. The Latin verse he had studied earlier, was more difficult to retain. He thought of the tailor who was seeking a seat in Parliament, for the Government party, and he wondered whether he would win. . . .

The rocking of the mahogany Morris chair in the front-house was putting him to sleep. Its dull mournful movement over the uncarpeted floor was as monotonous as the ordered ticking of the grandfather clock in the room behind where they were sitting. His mother seemed to be rocking to the time in the house.

The rocking grew louder. Then, there was a pause. And in the pause, she was saying, 'Remind me before too long, to take Boy to let him meet his family in Sin-Joseph. . . .'

Boy was no longer interested in their conversation. He tried to draw a picture of his parents sitting in the front-house. The front-house was his favourite room in the house.

It ran the length of the verandah. It was one-third the size of the house. A high, round table made of mahogany, stood like a woman, hands akimbo, in the middle of the room. On this table were photographs of his family.

His father, laughing in front of the rum shop, bareheaded and barefooted, one trousers leg rolled slightly higher than the other, stood in the eye-closing sun. The one of his mother caught her in black and white, on her way to, or from church. She belonged to two church congregations: the Church of the Nazarene and the Anglican Church. This photograph was taken on her way to the Church of the Nazarene. She was in a good mood. She was dressed in a white dress that looked silver

71

in the glare of the sun; and her Bible was clutched under one arm. Boy's photograph showed him alone on the playing field of the College, dressed severely in his uniform of stiff khaki, and with the Hall as a backdrop. His eyes were squinting. The sun had been in the lens of the Brownie 127 box camera. John Moore-Adams' son, Henry, had taken this photograph. But apart from Henry's inexperience with the Brownie, the sun was not only photographed in all their portraits, the sun was everywhere in the village. The sun.

There was a group photo of his aunt, his father and his mother, taken on the Pier Head. A large Amurcan steamer was in the background. His aunt had five minutes before embarking, to be taken to another world, when this photograph was taken.

Boy always felt that the most priceless piece of furniture in the room was the cabinet. In this cabinet were all the family silver and chinaware and cut glass. These were used only at Christmas and on Easter.

On the wall near the door that led into the passageway, off which were the three bedrooms were two larger photographs, in brown oval frames. In one was a large man with a full beard. He was wearing a wing collar. In the other was a woman, dressed stiffly in ruffs, and with a chain dangling down her chest. On the chain was a large Maltese cross. Boy's mother now wore this cross. In the corners of both photographs were the pressed skeletons of insects and scorpions. Man and woman were both white. They were his grandparents. On his mother's side.

The rocking continued to creak. Boy could picture his mother sitting erect. At any moment, she would get up and go into the kitchen, to see that the chocolate-tea was not boiling out of the enamel kettle. He could picture his father remaining in the Morris chair, with his cigarette at a corner of his mouth, burning until the ash became almost the length of the cigarette itself, with one eye closed against the smoke. And if his mother was still sitting there, he could see her becoming nervous, and bringing her rocking-chair to a slower movement, waiting for the speck of ash to soil *her* floor.

Many secrets were discussed in this front-house. Sarge visited often. And one night, from his bedroom, he heard the three of them; and the rocking and talking and rattling of ice in glasses. But the glasses, he knew, would have been his father's and Sarge's. He never saw his mother drink alcohol.

That night, they had rocked and talked, and rattled ice until well past midnight.

His mother said, before she got up, 'Midnight should never catch a Christian-minded person out of his bed, not sleeping. I turning-in now, Sarge, boy.' She retired each night at nine o'clock. He heard her move, the rocking had stopped, and soon afterwards, he heard her bare feet walk out of the room, while she hummed 'The Day Thou Gavest Lord Is Ended'.

Sarge said, 'What a sister she had! Have. What a woman Ella was. Still is. If yuh know what I mean?' Sarge was speaking as if he knew someone else was listening. 'You remember what a sweet and lovely girl Ella was, Nathan? Ella was the most prettiest girl, before she went-away to Amurca. If you ask me, it is no blasted wonder that that Amurcan son-of-a-bitch up the hill . . .'

A lorry passed at that moment, and Boy could hear only the grinding of gears as the lorry prepared to take the sharp bend.

'. . . and I will tell you something now, Nathan. I telling you now, that if in them days, I was a man, if I had-already-make a man of myself, I would have propose, yes, man, I would have propose marriage to Ella. If you know what I mean? But in them days, Nathan, as you know, I was a man without a job. The same Guvvament we have-in now, we had-in, then. Was no blasted good for black people like me and you. And now that I is a sergeant of police, on the Force, if yuh know what I mean? Now, Nathan, look at life, eh. . . .'

From the time he could understand words, Boy has been receiving an oral history of his own life and that of the village by this means of eavesdropping. The partition which divided him from the front-house was nevertheless more than a secret listening chamber. It was a telescope. Things were explained and put into clear meaning. Perhaps, when he said he liked this front-house more than any other room in the large old house, he meant that this room brought him closer to things than he could have been brought by talking with his mother and his father.

And Boy had never heard his aunt's name mentioned so many times in all the years he had been writing letters of thanks to her, as he was hearing it recently. When he overheard what Sarge had to say about her, it made Sarge a softer, less cruel man.

But now, tonight, he heard his mother return to her rocking chair. Nathan had never moved from the Morris chair. He was saying 'Good Christ!' just after his palms clapped small thunder on the mosquitoes.

Boy knew Ella's name was called often when he was needed to write the monthly letter to her. The letter served two purposes: it gave thanks and it reminded the person being thanked to send the five Amurcan dollars, promptly, the following month.

Tonight, he sensed that something was wrong. In all his life, tonight was the first time he had heard his mother come back out from her bedroom so late. It was after ten o'clock. That hour too seemed to him to be ominous. There were other things about his parents' behaviour which caused Boy some alarm and concern. But he knew he could never enquire about them.

The iron custom of the rules of discipline, that he a child of theirs, in a fixed relationship, was never permitted to ask a question, was written in blood, in his mother's words, '*Dogs amongst doctors!*' He had to know his place. And he did.

His aunt, Ella, was a secret. He learned about her, by eavesdropping. And the recent rape of a young girl by a man named Brandford was a secret, until its knowledge, too evil and grown-up for his tender ears was leaked to his tender sensibilities through the partition that divided his bedroom from the front-house.

'Boy?' his mother called him.

He found her in the rocking-chair, sitting upright, enamel cup of chocolate-tea at her lips, inhaling loudly both the thick oily drink and a mouthful of her own breath to cool the drink. He did not look her in the eyes. He had seldom done so. She motioned like a school-mistress to the Morris chair beside the one on which his father was sitting, for him to take his place.

Even this late at night, in the soft light thrown by the naked bulb in the kitchen, the room still looked spartan and puritan and sparse. Its genteel dilapidation was rendered more charming than its natural harshness through the dimness of the light in which it was embraced.

Bats and moths hovered round the naked electric light bulb.

74

His father had just returned to the room. He held his cigarette jauntily at the same corner of his mouth. As he sat down, Boy could not help feeling his father looked slightly sheepish: he was like a student entering a class minutes after it had begun.

In the accommodating light of the room, Boy saw how handsome and black his father was. It was the first time he had allowed himself to have such emotional feelings.

From his father, he looked at his mother. She was small, diminutive even. She wore a white head-tie. Her thick black hair flowed on to the back of her neck. The blackness of the hair added colour to her pale features. Her eyes were large. Her eyes always looked as if she was expecting something or someone to intrude upon her private space; perhaps, something unknown; or one of those unknown, invisible men who stooped under windows in the dark of night, and listened to people's secrets. Her body was not quite concealed under the white blanket she had wrapped around her shoulders.

Boy found her body full and exciting and provocative. He was sorry he was thinking this way about his own mother. He always compared her body to Moo-Moo's mother's. But how could he be looking at his own mother in this lascivious way? How could he? It was his mother.

Boy felt it was more than the letter of thanks he was required to write. It had to be something else. It was late, and the next day was Sunday.

'A tragedy, ain't it?' his mother said to Nathan. 'A crying shame.'

Boy felt she could be talking about anything. And he knew he would get no more from his father.

'Election-time, Mother.'

'Why crime does-always get worse round election-time? You know why?'

'Politicians is crooks.'

'Sarge was saying the other day that even the postmens. Postmens thiefing money-orders from Amurca.'

Boy could see the grief in her face. This passion did not, however, make her look old. It freshened her complexion and this caused him to think again about her body. He passed over her body in his mind, when she was younger. He wondered how

75

she took it, when her sister Ella had to leave for a strange country.

'You finish studying, yet?'

'I wonder who going-win?'

'Election-time, Nathan, boy. Just like Christmas! The giving-way of corn beef and biscuits and bags o' rice. Just like Father Christmas at Christmas!'

'I wish I could buy this blasted house offa Mr Adams,' his father said.

He remembered his cigarette ash just in time.

'My sister not dead, man. If she were dead, I could understand you worrying so.'

'Amurca so far! I wonder if I will ever see that place.'

'Amurca is pure distance. And pure time from we. But we gotta wait, Nathan. It's in God's hands, now.'

'Get out the writing pad. The Quink ink. A envelope. And the fountain pen, Boy. The letter.'

'This blasted village so small! Everybody know everybody-else business!'

'Men are too vilent, Nathan.'

Nathan had just killed a mosquito. But she could not be referring to this.

'I works my fingers to the bone, fishing. Everything I owns, I works hard as shite for. And what the hell does I own?'

'Put down the day-de-month. The address. And the salutations. Meanwhile, I will catch my head in regards to what I want to tell your aunt.'

Boy saw his mother fix her face into a tight creased concentration. It expressed the seriousness she always adopted when she was faced by, or when she faced the written word. This determination to pierce the darkness of words and ideas which faced her always made Boy smile. His smile was his way of worshipping her ignorance of the word. And he loved her when she did it.

She was such a beautiful woman when she expressed this fear of the word.

He never heard his father once say that she was beautiful. But he felt that his father knew it, and was proud of it. His father assumed and accepted that she was beautiful.

'That blasted half o' Yankee, from who we renting this house.

76

They tell me he was *nothing*. Not one shite. Even whilst he was in Amurca. Now, he walking 'bout here with a hyphen betwixt his two names. John Moore Hyphen Adams! Jesus Christ! And still, he could have a housefull o' luxuries. Whilst I remain poor as a bird's arse. And I working my fingers to the bone!'

'Language, Nathan. You watch your language in the presence of my son.'

She closed her eyes, as if she was offering up a brief, but significant prayer.

'Watch your language in front the boy. If you have no respect for me, have some for this boy. This boy, our only son, will crown our head with glory, one day.'

Nathan lit another cigarette. He inhaled deeply. He then shot two white streams from his nostrils. It made him look like a walrus. He did this twice again, before he spoke.

'Year in and year out. And what have I 'cumulated in all that time? Four blasted fishing nets. And two fishing boats. I have to mend the blasted nets every blasted Sunday morning 'pon the beach, before I dare to brave the blasted sea, and. . . .'

'You should come-church with me. God would mend them nets for you.'

'. . . before I could throw them in the blasted sea, foreday Monday morning, the blasted nets break again. Can't catch one sprat. One fishing boat now leaking. And the next one not payoff for, yet. The roof in the bedroom leaking the first minute a blasted drop o' rain fall. And. . . .'

'Your bedroom? Or mine?'

And she laughed.

And Boy laughed. He always found it strange that they did not sleep in the same bedroom. And why not the same bed? Was it mystery and fate?

'The leaky roof leaking more than *Labour Blest*.'

'*Labour Blest* was such a lovely boat, in days gone by! A boat and a half, eh, Nathan?'

'*Labour Blest*. What a blasted boat, in she days! Win the annual fishing competition three years running, with she too!'

Boy knew the pride that the boat conjectured each time his father called its name. When he was younger, he himself thought of *Labour Blest* as a luxury liner. In his wild young imagination, it was no different from the resplendent, large, white painted ships which came into the harbour farther up the beach, and unloaded thousands of English tourists.

'Maw, I ready.'

'Do every boy at the College address his mother as *Maw?* The way you does? Boy, why you can't call your mother, *Mother?* Well, even *Mummy*, then!'

'I not *dead*, Nathan! I am no mummy – Why you burying me off, before I'm in the grave?'

'My dearest sister, Ella. I hope that the reaches of these few lines . . . would find you . . . in a perfect state of good health . . . as they leave me . . . feeling fairly well . . . at present. Am I going too fast?'

'No, Maw . . . Mother.'

He smiled. His mother smiled. And his father smiled.

But he was wondering who was the first person in the village, or in the world, to begin a letter with this opening?

'And . . . as I take up my pen in hand . . . this evening to write to you . . . these few lines . . . the whole family circle is all well . . . in the precious name of the Good Lord. . . .'

The letter had to be written on one page. Custom. Three-quarters of the page was for the salutations, the personal statement of health, plus a wish for Ella's good health. In the last few lines, Boy knew he had to make the request, or the appeal, or the reminder for more money.

The money was necessary for his fees at the College. He could not continue without it. Some of the money went to pay rent. John Moore-Adams their landlord was complaining everyday. He had begun to threaten them. And because of the competition between his own son and Boy, and young Lascelles, for the single Scholarship, John Moore-Adams was starting to make veiled threats about selling the house over their heads.

'Sometimes, I wonder what I killing myself for? Going in the blasted sea every foreday morning even before the dogs stop sleeping. Be-Christ, even the spar'-birds and wood-doves does look-down at me, outta the mahogany tree, and laugh, like shite! Even the birds! I risking my life every blasted day, except Sunday.'

'You know what you should be doing on a Sunday!'

She tugged the white blanket round her shoulders in a determined manner, to protect herself from the sinfulness in his complaints.

'Every man have a row to hoe. And if that man complains, he's doing nothing but talking-back to God.'

'To catch a few fish? And if it wasn't for Mr Lascills and the hotel people. When the tourisses come in. Fish is plentiful only when there is tourisses. You ever notice that, Mother? The hotels want to buy the fish wholesale. And I risking my blasted life to catch fish retail. . . .'

'I hope you are in good health . . . as usual . . . and that God hears your every wish . . . and prayer.'

She paused to allow Boy to catch up. Then she closed her eyes. Boy looked at the black waves of hair, and wondered how old she was. She never told him. The naked electric bulb painted golden fingers through her hair, from the edge of her widow's peak, high and majestic, on to her forehead.

His father was scratching his head, and cursing the sea and the hotels, and the principle of wholesale economics.

'How to put it?' she asked.

Boy assumed she was referring to the important question that was bothering them all evening. The letter was only a means of facing that question.

'I been thinking,' Nathan said.

'How to put it?'

'The more I think, the more I can't think.'

Nathan scratched his beard. He was stalling. He was really asking his wife for approval. He needed her opinion. And guidance. He made no decision without her approval.

'I been thinking of selling that piece o' land down by the beach. The piece my mother leff-back for me. Or even work it in sugar canes. If it wasn't so close to the hotel, though. But being close to the hotels, I could, maybe, get top-dollar. Maybe, to plant it up in canes is better. And stop risking my blasted life after a few fish. What you think?'

He scratched his beard some more. Boy wondered why his beard never grew.

'Put it plain to she. Put the question fair, and square.'

'Just so? Nathan, just so? Without any salutation? Or plea? Or nothing so?'

She waited to see what more he had to say. But he made no decision. And he suggested nothing more.

'I can't just make this letter of appeal look as if we are not sure. And don't know what our real intentions and desires is.'

'Hit the blasted nail on the blasted head, woman!'

The vulgarity in his words gave him more courage.

'Tell Ella we want help in buying this house offa that half-Yankee. As you know, Mother, we can't just march up the hill and face that Yankee man. Be-Christ, you must understand that the realness of my life, and the realness of our lives, won't allow me and you, two blasted big people, and Boy here, to face that blasted Yankee man. So, me and you have to siddown this late at night, in this blasted ungodly hour, and write to another semi-Yankee . . . not being disrespectful to your sister, my half-sister, or sister-in-law, and ask her to ask the blasted demi-semi Yankee up the hill, if we could. . . . Be-Jesus Christ, girl! Look! I going out for a minute. I need to drink a rum at Manny Batson rum shop.'

And he left.

'You would know how to make this letter into a letter of appeal? You would know how to make that request? By using decent, respectful and proper words?'

'Yes, Maw.'

'Well, son. After you make it, read it back to me. Put some saliva on the envelope. And address and leave it here on the centre table. Thank you, son.'

She watched him as the pen scratched the words on the delicate mysterious writing paper. She watched in awe at his ability to handle such difficult things. She marvelled at the ease with which he did it. And she seemed to be smiling within her heart, that he did not, like her, have to crease-up his forehead, and bring lines of tension and anxiety into his young life.

She could admit all this to herself, this tension over words. She faced the anxiety when she had to read her Bible.

But she wasn't going to permit him to read *her* Bible for her. That was between herself and God. And God himself would help her to untangle the difficult words. Her devoted presence in His church would unloose her tongue and enable it to pronounce his words of mercy.

She said a short prayer for her son. She said it aloud. And Boy became embarrassed.

'I am so glad that this boy have brains, and that I have somebody to lift the head o' my coffin, when you call me to my final judgement.'

'Lemme read this to you, Nathan,' Sarge said. 'Listen to this blasted *wirthlessness* and crime that only begin to take place in this blasted country since this Guvvament come to power. I blame this Guvvament for half the *wirthlessness* and crime that happening nowadays. Man, listen to this.'

Sarge cleared his throat.

'Brandford say to me, let she get a little further up the road and then we show she the runnings. When she passed we, Brandford and me get up and start to follow she. When we reach up with she, the two o' we hold she, and Brandford. . . .'

'Lower your voice.'

'I talking too loud.'

'The wife. And the boy. She not sleeping yet. And behind that partition there, the boy behind that. To-besides, I had Seabert read that part to me already.'

Nathan's wife's voice came sailing from the bedroom.

> '*As o'er each continunt and island*
> *The dawn leads on another day,*
> *The voice of da-da, da is silunt,*
> *Nor dies the strain of da, away.*'

'Hymn, four-seventy-seven.' Sarge said.

'Hymns, ancient and modern.'

'But listen to this piece, though. Nathan, just listen to this piece.'

'Not too loud, though.'

'All the time, Brandford had a long brown-handled kitchen knife holding upon she throat. After I finished, I take some money out of she bag, and cut she in she face.'

'The evil and damnation of these times! The evil and damnation of these last days!'

81

It was Nathan's wife. When they heard her voice, they both jumped up.

She was standing in the middle of the door of her bedroom. Her hands were akimbo. She was shaking her head from side to side. It was a heavy, sorrowful and stern movement. Her eyes were closed, they could see. She had tied her head with a white cloth. The long cotton nightgown had a fringe that reached her bare feet. Her feet were shining. She had already put coconut oil on them. And round her shoulders, and hiding the still luscious body, with which Nathan did not sleep in the same bed, breasts and cleavage and thighs, was a white blanket that looked like a shawl. It was this white blanket that she carried with her to the Church of the Nazarene, when the nights were chilly, when the nights 'had-in a touch o' chill'.

She moved one step into the front-house with them.

'Something terrible, something wicked, like the abomination of Sodom and Gomorrah, will surely visit this land.'

'I would like to tell you something for your own-own good and betterment,' the rum shop owner, Mr Manny Batson, was telling Lionel one night.

He had taken Lionel into the back room with the big men. Lionel knew what this meant.

This sudden rise and acknowledgement of status had Lionel nervous and confused. It was the first time he had ever been allowed into the back room.

'Siddown, man. Don't be ashamed to sit down amongst gentlemen. This is my premises. I sure Sarge don't mind. Sarge, you mind?'

'Take a pew, Lionel,' Sarge said.

'Seabert Mascoll N. Marshall, you take any objections to this man sitting down in here with we? Political-wise? Or otherwise?'

'Tell the constituent to siddown.'

'Nathan? You tekking umbrages 'gainst Lionel?'

'Copposessit!' Nathan said. He got that word from John Moore-Adams.

Only then, did Lionel sit down.

'You realize that Mr Seabert Mascoll Nathaniel Marshall

running for a seat in Parlment?'

Lionel nodded his head. He belonged to Seabert's party. He was a tireless campaigner for the Government.

'Want a snap?'

'If you don't mind, skipper.'

'When I was a young man like you, Lionel,' Sarge said, 'do you think I would be taking all this night-dew in my chest? If yuh know what I mean?' He paused. He handed a snap-glass to Lionel. 'You think you could ever catch me sitting down in somebody's rum shop slamming dominoes? Not that I have anything 'gainst the present proprietor of this establishment! But do you think you could catch me sitting down in a rum shop doorway, 'pon a Saturday night, playing dominoes? Man, I would be in some woman's bed! Or in my own. With a book.'

'With a book, Sarge?' Nathan said.

'That bed would have to be a married woman's four-poster,' Seabert said.

Lionel was beginning to feel more uneasy. He was hearing things that ordinary villagers had only guessed at.

'I heard you the other night out there, arguing with Goalie. A week have passed since. Are you going to let a mad-man like Goalie cause your wife and your children to grieve? Over a domino game? A *domino?*'

'But Lionel is the island champ, Sarge!'

'Champion of *dominoes?*'

A woman from the section of the shop that sold groceries, appeared at the door of the back room.

'Excuse me, gentlemens. Not meaning to interrupt. But Goalie out here. He out here, looking for Lionel. Not meaning to interrupt. But Goalie out here.'

'On my blasted premises!'

'And he got a cutlass in his hands.'

'Not on my premises!'

'What the hell is this? Crime?'

Sarge seemed disinterested a moment after he made the comment. He put another snap to his head, threw it down, and turned his face up into a sneer, against the sting in the rum.

'I off-duty. They could kill one another. If you know what I mean? I off duty.'

83

'You are not leffing this room, Lionel,' Seabert said. 'I need you to canvass for me.'

'I is the island champ of dominoes, Mr Marshall. I have to defend my honour.'

'Champion domino player? Is that what you is?'

'I am the champ, Sarge. I am the champ.'

'Well, champ, go out there, you blasted fool, and let that mad bastard kill you. You is the champ? Go out, champ, and die for a blasted domino, like a champ!'

People in the other section of the rum shop were screaming. They were encouraging Lionel to go out and meet Goalie. Goalie was shouting, calling Lionel outside, challenging him to come out.

'If you is any rass-hole man, come out!'

'Tell Lionel to come out!' a woman shrieked. 'Lionel, come out! Goalie challenge you to come out. Come outta there with the big shots!'

The woman clapped her hands in joy, anticipating the violence.

Inside the back room, Lionel could feel the challenge to his manhood, and to his honour. He was thinking only of that. His manhood and his honour. It was as if an opponent in a domino game was teasing him with a brilliant play.

'I going out. I have to go out.'

'Go out and be a blasted *arse!*'

'I gotta go. A man is challenging my reputation. I is the island champ.'

'*Lionel? Come out. Come out, if you is a man.*'

Sarge went back to his rum. He was off-duty. At any rate, he didn't think too kindly of anyone who supported the Government party.

Seabert took a handful of corn beef, and stuffed it into his mouth.

Nathan, who tried not to be involved, said only, 'Pass me that bottle, man.'

And Manny Batson, the rum shop owner, seemed all of a sudden, too tired, too resigned, to be concerned with Lionel's plight.

They made themselves comfortable as before, and were in the

process of having another snap of rum, and eating the corn beef, when Lionel parted the blinds, and went through them. They could see the herringbone cord where the blind had travelled over, to be open. They just sat and watched his back as it disappeared. He had a patch in his trousers. On the left side of the seat.

And then a roar went up. It was the kind of greeting a champion boxer receives when he enters the ring. A wild roar went up. In the light thrown from the spirit lamp inside the rum shop, the blade of Goalie's cutlass was shining.

Some women saw it, and screamed.

Lionel stood on the single step of the shop. The step was made of coral stone. He could feel his weight on the stone. He looked like a champion.

In the road, with the men and women was Goalie.

Then, all of a sudden, it seemed as if each wave in the sea could be heard, as the stillness of baited violence came down upon them, as if you could hear even the crabs scratching amongst the fallen grape leaves on the beach nearby. And the casuarina trees on the beach began to hum. And more than that, there seemed to be the scratching of the crabs on the dead grape leaves on the sand. The smell of the Lady-of-the-Night came up full and sensuous.

Across the road, somebody's Rediffusion radio was playing 'God Save the King', signing off for bed.

Lionel remained standing on the coral stone step. Goalie was in the middle of the road, cursing, challenging and beckoning.

The high beams of a car came round the corner from the front road. The lights blinded them for a moment. The driver blew his horn, and accelerated as he drew near the people. But the people were too many for the car. So, it had to slow down. They recognized the driver.

'The Yankee-man!'

'John Moore Hyphen! The 'Murcan-man!'

The large, shining Oldsmobile, the only Amurcan car in the village and beyond, inched its way through the people. LEFT HAND DRIV was written in uneven red tape on the front and rear bumpers. The E had fallen off months ago.

Through the thick crowd, the large, slow, foreign car edged its way like oil. As he passed the thickness of the people, and felt safe, John Moore-Adams hissed, '*Niggers!*'

They watched as the automobile climbed the hill, until its rear lights disappeared, like a boat sailing away. Only then, did the people reclaim the road. It was once more their ling.

'Call me a thief again, like you called me, last Friday night,' Lionel said.

It was said more tamely than challengingly.

'You is the same thief as last week.'

'Say so again.'

'I called you a thief once. And I will call you a thief two times. Twice. Thrice. Four times. . . .'

Goalie rushed at him. It seemed as if his words had become useless. A maniacal strength surged through his body. Lionel parried the first flash of silver lightning. And only Lionel knew that his hand was bleeding. He parried again. And Goalie moved in. The men and women moaned. Each time the shining blade flashed through the air, they moaned.

The night was close, and you could hardly breathe. It was like black velvet outside the arc of light thrown by the spirit lamp.

Lionel felt a taste of sickness in his stomach. The blade was coming too close, too often, to his face.

Lionel and Goalie moved into the middle of the road. Men and women created a ling for them. They moved fast. Each time the blade of silver lightning flashed, a moan went through the crowd.

And then, it seemed as if the entire sea, with all the fish and all the crabs and all the fishermen in it, had suddenly swept itself from the horizon, and had rolled inland. Just in this way, it seemed as if the sea had covered the land.

There was one loud cry.

And then nothing at all. There was one long exhaling of frustration, of venom, of strength, of power and of hate.

And then everything was quiet. And still. And was like death itself.

The blade had flashed. Fast and thin and keen. Lionel lay on the road among cigarette-butts and sticks of popsicles; amongst discarded walked-over cigarette and match-boxes; and the dried rotten leaves from the mahogany trees that were in the backyard of the rum shop; amongst the bits of sucked sugar cane from the last crop season; with the discarded French letters which the men used, and then threw into the road, as a

boast of masculinity and style, or of carelessness, in varying
stages of disintegration and stench; and dog shit.

His head was almost severed from his body.

Blood poured down the gutter. And the road was covered in
thick, rich, red molasses.

The people, men and women, shrieked. When they realized
what they had witnessed, and they knew that it was too heavy and
too telling a testimony to bear and be told, they disappeared.
Goalie was the last important witness.

He looked down at the blood and at the body, at the cause of his
great fury, and then he said, '*No* man talks to me, so!'

And then he ran off into the darkness, where the Oldsmobile
had travelled.

At that moment, Sarge appeared on the coral stone step. He
looked on the ground, saw the body, recognized Lionel's
panting, spluttering shirt and torn trousers; knew it would mean
lots of work for him investigating and asking the same questions
over and over, from the same people, and spat into the gutter.

Behind him, Nathan, Seabert and the rum shop owner, late
witnesses to all this, stood in a daze of shock. And all the time,
Sarge was shaking his head and realizing that this would have to
be explained.

But he could always say he was off-duty. He wished he had not
been interrupted from his snapping of rum. The three men
behind him probably felt that way, too.

He got on his bicycle, and holding it with one hand, he
buttoned up his policeman's tunic with the other; and all he
said, all he seemed able to say, to no one in particular, on the
lonely coral stone step, was 'Over a blasted domino! If you see
what I mean!'

And he rode off. . . .

4

People came from the neighbouring villages, and from as far as
the city, to visit the scene of the crime. The crime quickly
became a political killing.

The Government blamed the lawless members of the opposition party for the killing. The Prime Minister went on radio and said the country's police force was lawless, useless and infelicitous. He threatened to dismiss the Commissioner of Police. He accused the commissioner as a supporter of the opposition party.

The newspaper ran the story for weeks, in banner headlines, across the large shrieking page, with a headline in red type.

The people came from everywhere, saying they were witnessing history. And since the election campaign was almost in full swing, all the political meetings, those of the Government party and those of the opposition party, the Democratic Party, were well attended. The people were satisfied with speeches filled with blood and gore and rumour. Each speaker dealt with Lionel's death. And Goalie's fate.

'No more tricks!' the Democratic Party shouted.

'No more political murders, police brutality and injustice!' the Government party shouted.

The people enjoyed every minute of the speeches, until the pressure of words and sentiments and the keeping of loyalty was too much, and it exploded in fights. Bottles were thrown. Cars were smashed. Blood was spilt. The people loved it.

But in the village, the dwellers became overnight unenviable and notorious. But they carried their new nationwide importance with a stoical seriousness.

The old women prayed for the sins of the young. And they, above all others, resented the village's sudden popularity. These old women who had suffered and survived many hardships; who had been beaten by the sun and by the sea, agricultural workers and fishermen, in a long unbroken line of generations of hardships, and who had come to accept this life, 'this living', as the arrangement made for themselves even before they were born, these old women could not understand their sudden social and political propulsion into the living-rooms of the entire nation.

And to add to their importance, all the politicians, except the Prime Minister, were now crowding the tailor shop and the rum shop, and the homes of their supporters, with promises of electricity in each chattel house, of running water inside the paling of each backyard, the repairing of each road in the village,

88

no matter how small, and of course, there was the normal and generous distribution and consumption of corn beef and biscuits.

Rum flowed like the gutters during the rainy season.

'The end of the whirl is at hand,' Boy's mother cried. She said it during her nightly testimony in the Church of the Nazarene. She said it during her introduction of the sermon by the Anglican minister, on Sunday mornings. And she said it each night, at nine, on her bended knees, in her closed bedroom.

'The end of the whirl is at hand.'

Before Goalie stabbed Lionel, nobody from outside the village, not even the Member of Parliament who represented this area, had ever raised a finger to change the history of suffering.

'So, why now?' Boy's mother asked her large, hungry congregation. 'Why now, after such sinning and tribulation and damnation?'

In the afternoons, before Boy got home from the College, people would already be in the road. Many of them had copies of the newspaper in their hands, reading the latest treatment of the crime of the village. The newspaper carried the tragedy with pictures, and with historical and biographical sketches of the village. It carried articles on the principals in the tragedy, a table of the country's 'worst murders', and a biography of the three biggest men in the village.

Nathan was there. John Moore-Adams was there. Seabert, whose importance had risen with the village's infamy, was there.

Five of the 'top ten murders' were still unsolved.

Mr Manny Batson, proprietor of the rum shop, witnessed a hundred per cent rise in sales and in profits. And he did not mind that he was not included in the list of the big men of the village. 'I am unboughtable,' he insisted.

But the next week, the newspaper carried a feature story about his rum shop, and the road itself.

'What you think, girl?' he asked his wife. He had read the feature story more times than he could remember. 'What you say to my changing the name of this establishment? Something *big*. Something Amurcan. Something like The Sin-James Café and Restaurant?'

89

His wife just shook her head. She remembered the red night of thick blood too clearly.

A large red X, which marked the spot where Lionel fell, came out blurred and blown up on the front page story in the newspaper.

Boy picked up the newspaper from the verandah steps, and before he could read the latest instalment of what the newspaper was now calling *The Killing with a Political Twist*, his father appeared from inside the darkened front-house, and took it from his hand.

'Goalie isn't going spend one day in jail. Everybody knows that. Not for that murder. Perhaps the Chief Justice will throw-out the case. Or call it murder by aggravation. Or the Guvvament might have a Royal Commission. Because Goalie was a civil servant before he went off.'

He walked beside his son, his hand resting on the boy's shoulder, and into the gloomy front-house with its dead scorpions in the photographs of deceased mother and father. He glanced at them, and felt both nauseated and excited at the same time.

Lionel's murder had brought his sister-in-law to his mind. He glanced then at her photograph beside his wife's dead parents', just as the thought entered his mind. And just as quickly, he disregarded it.

His sister-in-law, Ella, was alive in Panama. She couldn't do that to me, he thought. She was to stay alive, until he got John Moore-Adams to agree to sell the house to him, for she was going to put up most of the money, if not all.

This was what was in his mind. His hand was still on his son's shoulder. He was getting strength from this source. He was getting strength also from the extension of this source, his family.

'What you learn at the College today, boy?'

'Oh, nothing, dad.'

'*Learn*. Learn for me, and for you.'

He sat in his Morris chair, and opened the newspaper. He threw its pages into the wind, as a woman would throw out a sheet before hanging it on a clothes-line.

His wife came in from the kitchen. She was wearing an apron.

'Didn't I tell you that nothing can't come to men who spend their time in a rum shop, but badness? Whether drinking or playing games? Or talking politics?'

Nathan grunted. Boy went into his bedroom.

'Only last week, I was asking the Lord to look after you and watch over you. It couldda been you that Goalie killed with that cutlash. Nathan, tears come to my two eyes, to think that you couldda left this boy, fatherless.'

Tears came to her eyes now.

'In the shop. Down 'pon the beach. In church. Everywhere. People talking 'bout nothing else. The Guvvament, if it was really a Guvvament, should have close-down *all* the rum shops in this country. Especially now, at election time.'

'And cause a riot? They would lose power, girl. Any Guvvament that tamper with a rum shop would lose votes.'

'They should try and see.'

'I may not be a church-going man, but the same God you got, does-be watching over me. How many times I have tell you about the rough seas I have seen and have sail through? And how many times I have come back to land? Alive. How many times I have fall overboard, in waves more higher than this house? Rolling over my back. Then, twisted-up by the next wave. Can't catch my breath. No kind o' how. And just as I am struggling to stay afloat, one of the biggest sharks in the whole Carbean, coming straight at me. How many times have I tell you 'bout them near misses and near disasters? It don't have to be God watching over me, then?'

She looked him steadily in the eye. And her eyes became watery. It was love. And admiration. And rejection of his tales of the sea.

He looked at her, and said with his eyes, what he had always found difficult, if not impossible, to say with words.

She knew the meaning of those silent stares, and the message in his eyes.

'Sarge and me have a meeting, in a couple of minutes.'

'Somebody tell me this afternoon, that the Prime Minister himself call in Sarge, and told him how to conduct the case concerning Goalie. Goalie still hiding out. You hear if he still hiding out in a cave near here?'

'Anything in this house to eat?'

She got up immediately. She was grumbling as she always grumbled on these occasions when she was given no notice about food. She went back into the kitchen. He could hear the preparations in the banged pots and collapsing cutlery, and in her grumbling which accompanied the noise of cooking. She started to sing 'The Day Thou Gavest Lord is Ended'.

As she cooked, she thought about the house, and of her secret scheme to purchase it from Mr Adams. Any day now, Mr John Barrington Lascelles, King's Counsel, would be calling her into his office, to sign the documents. This was her secret. Perhaps, some day, she would share it with Boy. But never with Nathan, her husband. She had prayed about it, and felt that God wanted it so.

She raised her voice, and a sweet, deep soprano filled the house. If Nathan knew about the secrets of the mind, he would have been able to detect that something great had happened to make her so happy.

Her words were distinct in the singing, until she came to a part she did not know. And here, she hummed the tune, until the words came back to her.

> 'So be it, Lord; Thy Throne shall never,
> Like earth's proud empires, pass away.'

John Moore-Adams wrote a letter to the Department of Education, in which he made veiled threats against the College and against the Government. He showed the letter to Sarge, now sweating more than ever over Brandford's rape case and Lionel's murder.

The letter ended with these words: '. . . *and as a citizen who spent time in Amerrica working for the prosperity of this country, I would not be denied my rights, my legal rights and my human rights, more of which I found in Amerrica.*'

'You sent this letter to the education department?'

'Goddamn! I born here. My son born in Amerrica. But no goddamn nigger in politics gonna take my rights from me! My son's born *here*, too! According to the rights of ancestry. Goddamn!'

Sarge left him and went straight to Nathan, to let him know about the letter.

'Goalie hiding in a cave.'

'Who tell you so?'

'I have contacks on the newspaper, these days!'

'I see. Since your photo was on the front page, you. . . .'

'How the case against Goalie coming? I hear the Prime Minister called you in.'

'Me and John Barrington Lassills is locking horns. In the rape case,' Sarge told him. 'Lissen to this blasted evidence.

' "Giving evidence, when Defence council Mr John Barrington Lascelles, King's Counsel, objected to the admission of a statement, was Police Sergeant, Joseph 'Sarge' Crawford. Sergeant Crawford read the statement which said:

' "This evening about five o'clock, I get a bus from the city and went down by the tailor shop near the front road where Seabert Mascoll live. When I get by Seabert tailor shop, Brandford tell me to wait outside until he come out. When Brandford come out, he tell me to come and go and sit down pon the bridge near the Front Road.

' "Me and he went by the bridge and sit down. While we did sitting down pon the bridge, Brandford tell me any woman or school girl that passed there looking good, we going rape she. While we did sitting pon the bridge, a schoolgirl get off a motorcycle.

' "Brandford say to me, let she get a little further up the road and then let we show she the runnings. . . ." '

'Haven't you read that passage to me, before?'

'This is sweet evidence, man. Lissen.'

' "When she past we, Brandford and me get up and start to follow she. When we catch up with she, the two o' we hold she and Brandford put a brown-handle. . . ." '

'Yes!' Nathan interrupted him. 'A brown-handle kitchen-knife to the girl's back. You read this passage already.'

' " . . . the two o' we hold she and Brandford put a brown-handle kitchen-knife to she back and tell she to-don't shout.

' "We drag she in the canes above the Front Road, in the back, in the gully. When we get she in the canes, I tek the knife from Brandford and stick she in she throat. Brandford take off she shirt, bodice, skirt and panties. I give she a cuff to tek she off me and she fall. Brandford tek off he pants and under-wears." '

'If that girl was *any* family to me, at all,' Nathan said, 'I would cut-out *both* his two balls!'

'But isn't that some sweet evidence, though?'

She was waiting for him. On him. Not for him, for she had hardly slept the night before. Her sister in Panama had been on her mind all night, and the problem with the house, and her husband's own inability to do anything about it, had kept her awake. Each lorry that passed, each car that screeched round the corner, even the waves building power and size, kept her awake and kept her company through the long, thinking night.

Before the man from Edwards Dairy put the pint bottle of milk on the step of the kitchen door, she was already dressed. She took up the bottle, a used Tennants stout-bottle, and smiled.

She had chosen a white cotton dress, immaculately white, and starched and ironed with each pleat and gather geometrically in place. The dress reached to the middle of her calves.

She was now sitting in a chair in Boy's 'study' in the cool verandah, and drumming her eight fingers on the arms of the Berbice chair, in which she had watched him sit, and study for so many hours of so many interminable days. The chair was comfortable. Perhaps, that was why he could sit so long.

Her drumming was her own anxious counting of the minutes she would give him to get dressed; and also, it was her own enumeration of the things she wanted to do in the city, before the sun got too hot.

The bodice of her dress was buttoned to the neck. It had long sleeves which were buttoned at the wrists. On her head was a white headcloth, itself equally starched, equally stiff as the dress and the bodice of the dress.

She was barefooted. But in her plaited cane basket, which lay beside her, were her canvas shoes, 'pumps', as she called them. She walked barefooted everywhere, except when she was going to church. But when she went to the city, she carried her 'pumps' in her basket, just in case.

Her feet were greased with coconut oil. They shone, were clean, and looked as if she had just stepped out of the sea.

She was looking forward to this trip with her son.

A thread appeared on her left sleeve, near the wrist. And she wet her fingers, rubbed them around the thread, twirling it into a ball, and when she had the correct smallness she desired, she bit it off with her teeth.

A silver brooch of flowers on a stem, whose name had remained unknown to her in all the years since the brooch had been given to her by her grandmother, was on her left breast. And the silver Maltese cross, without its chain, was pinned just above her heart by a gold safety-pin. The pin of the Mothers' Union which she had earned from the Anglican Church was on her right breast.

She moved the Mothers' Union pin to her left side, just above the silver Maltese cross, and as she was about to wet her third finger, and clean the corners of her eyes, Boy appeared.

He was dressed in white shorts, white short-sleeved sea-island cotton shirt, white socks and white 'pumps'. In his hand were four library books about Ancient Rome and Ancient Greece, which he was returning.

'Wait!' she said, moving her eyes over his body. From his hair, over the parting he always wore in the middle of his head, around that part of his neck she could see, and down over his clothes.

'Where you think you going? Dress like that? I don't see why I should walk out on the public-road with you dress like that! I not going playing tennis with you.'

She expressed her disapproval of his dress always in this manner, as if she were talking to herself. And when he moved away to change his clothes, without protest, she was still talking.

'I don't see why I should leave this house with him dress that way, as if me and him going on a field to lick-'bout some tennis ball! I want him to dress proper. He could put on that silk shirt I buy for him last Easter, and his school tie, with his grey flannel trousers, his new socks, the ones with the arrow in them pointing upwards, and his brown shoes.'

He was already in his bedroom, trying to find reason in her regulations of dress.

'On top of that, please put on your school blazer for me. People must see you the way you is. People must *know* you is a Thorne!'

He did not hear her. But he was changing. He didn't even

argue that she was barefooted, while she was disapproving of his dress. He wished he didn't have to walk beside her. He wished and hoped that none of his friends would look at her feet, and see the long uncut toenails on her big toes, and the cracked nails on her two little toes; that none of them would be going to the public library on the same bus as she and he. . . . 'Christ!' . . . that she would not insist upon accompanying him to the library, and sit on the top step outside the entrance to the adults section, and wait, perhaps in all that time, buy a stick of sugar cane and peel it with her bare teeth. . . 'Christ!' . . . and he could not even say he was not going with her; could not invent a belly-ache; could not suddenly drop dead, but had to obey her, because she is his mother, even though. . . 'Oh Christ!' . . . the blazer was already making him sweat.

He had seen the big men of the city, barristers-at-law, solicitors, doctors and senior civil servants, wearing three-piece worsted suits in the middle of the hot steamy afternoons, and *none* of them ever released one drop of sweat, either under their arms, or from their foreheads. Perhaps, his mother was teaching him something. . . .

'Your father is a fisherman. A man who works with his hands. But you is my child. A Thorne. From the parish o' Sin-Joseph. And the Thornes is *people*. So, even if he's a fisherman, and poor, he's honest.' And I want you to understand that you is *people*, too.'

When he came in dressed to suit her taste, she looked at him, still muttering, '*Now* you look like a Thorne. *Good!*'

The morning was already humid. The street was filled with people, most of whom were heading in the direction of the city. Saturday mornings were for shopping, for selling, and for buying.

And the moment she walked down the short path of cement slabs from the verandah and stood beside the dilapidated wooden fence that needed painting she appeared taller and larger. The fence was latticed. Respectable, but breaking down.

By the time Boy reached the gate, the humidity had already wrapped him in a close embrace, and perspiration formed on his face and under his arms.

He had slapped his underarms twice, with Bournes Bay

Rum. The smell under his arm would not rise as the temper-
ature would rise. He had put Brilliantine on his head, and his
hair looked as if it was melting, with bubbles all over it. But the
bus would be cool. He would feel the breeze from the sea
blowing through its unenclosed seats. And if the bus driver was
speeding, the bus would seem as if it had air conditioning.

At the bottom of the gate, he turned right, to walk to the bus
stop. But his mother touched him gently on the hot blazer
sleeve, and without saying a word, without too much pressure
on the sleeve, she pointed him in the direction of the city. It did
not occur to him then what was in her mind, for there was a bus
stop further up the road, where passengers would get off and
where there would be a better chance of getting a seat.

'Walk on the side of the traffics. A gentleman escorting a
lady, is to always walk on the side of the traffics.'

She put the cane basket in her other hand, then placed her
arm through its single handle and with her free hand she settled
the pair of 'pumps' which she had cleaned at daybreak with
Blanco, at the bottom of the basket. She laid her pocketbook
beside it, and covered them neatly with a white tablecloth made
from a flour bag. The flour bag with the origin and name of its
contents, had been bleached for months on stones in the
backyard, to get out the red and blue trademarks that said it
came from Canada.

She started out fast.

'You with me, now. You gotta look your best. Your father is a
man who can't make up his mind. But that don't kill. Every
man have his place. In life and in death. Death. I thinks of my
poor sister every night. Every night. You bring-along the
letter? Yes, boy. That letter in your pocket is your life. And
your future. Your father happen to be a fisherman, as I say. But
you isn't a fisherman-son. You know what I mean? Of course,
you know. You is this College-boy. They say you is one of the
brightest boys at the College. So, with your knowledge o'
knowledge and brains, you must know. Knowledge and brains
going-transform you into something. Death. I worries from
night to night. From night to night, worrying if my sister will
ever see the place she was born. You getting to be a man now.
There is certain things. Things you is man-enough now to

97

know. 'Cause your head have-in knowledge. Things concerning my sister. Your aunt was a lady. Is. Even from when she was young. Growing up in Sin-Joseph. Ella could do *anything*. Needlework. Make paper roses. Knitting and crochet. But she grow too fast. And that fastness brought freshness to her. And became her downfall. Men would pass and cut their eye at Ella. And Ella was only ten. When she was sixteen, she was a woman in all but age. And that is when it happen. I was six-seven years more older than Ella. Well, boy, you shouldda hear the grief Ella brought on her family. Nights and nights my mother, God rest her soul, didn't sleep. And it was Gran who came to Ella rescue. 'Cause everybody, every person, every dog deserve a helping-hand. There is things 'bout Gran and what Gran do, *had* to do to Ella, that a mother can't utter to a child. Nevermind that the child is almost a young gentleman.

'Years and years ago. More years than my poor brain could count. Years ago when this place was like a garden. Before the politicians came. Years gone by, when Barbados was a Barbados, my family came to this place. People from Away. I remember Gran saying the country o' birth and origin was some place call Scotland. But do I know Scotland? Do I know anything 'bout Scotland? I knows only Barbados. Anyhow, you got to know where you come from. And it is Scotland. So, when I tell you that to-don't mind your father is a fisherman, and that you is not a fisherman-son, now you know what I mean! Whoever hear of a man from Scotland, wherever the hell Scotland is, making a living from catching a few sprats and dolphins?

'Last night, flat on my back, God gave me the words. Words from God does-come during the dead o' night. In the darkness. But even in the darkness, the light o' God shines. And look now! Look now, in the bright daylight, boy, and I can't remember *one* iota of the testimony God put in my mouth.

'The man from which we renting the house. None other than John Moore Adams. Plain and simple. Before he join-up his name to hide his ancestry. Just came back from Amurca. Gold teeth in his mouth. Gold watch brekking-down his two hands. And a gold ring 'pon every finger. Smelling sweet as a flower, a bougainvillaea, he came to my mother house, God rest her poor soul. And what he do, he did. What that 'Murcan-man did, he

98

do. All the goodness that he playing he doing now for we, could never wipe-way that act. So, don't tell me 'bout goodness. Don't tell me 'bout goodness that come after badness. It is his mind. His mind hurting him. And me, a Thorne from Sin-Joseph, now find myself at the mercies of his kindness? Your aunt, my sister, was put in the. . . '

Just then, the black Humber Hawk roared by. Her voice was drowned in the dust of speed it left behind. Then, the car stopped in a screech of more dust, and reversed and stopped beside them.

'Mistress? Why are you walking?'

It was John Barrington Lascelles, King's Counsel.

Boy was saved. The accumulating embarrassment would end. He had listened to very little of what his mother had been telling him. And it was only when she began to talk about John Moore-Adams that he became interested. He had heard pieces of guarded conversations before, and he wanted to know the truth about his aunt's sudden disappearance. He did not care so much for her plight. But he wanted to know. He wanted to know the patchwork of his 'family-history', to spread it out in one clean pattern.

'Mistress, let me give you a lift into town. You are heading to town, aren't you?'

She put the cane basket on the ground, in a slow, deliberate and arrogant way, stood straight, so straight that she looked taller than her five feet five inches; and with her hands akimbo, she told him, 'Thanks, Mr Lassills. Me and the boy walking.'

'In this hot sun?'

'It can't kill him!'

She smiled, and the contagion and self-determination took Mr Lascelles into their hands, and he smiled too. It was the first time Boy had seen him smile, the first time he had any inkling that his mother knew Mr Lascelles so intimately.

'A lil walking can't touch this big man I have here 'side o' me.'

'If you reach town before I leave the office, I hope you'll come in, and let's discuss that matter.'

'You going-see me, Mr Lassills. You seeing me, this afternoon.'

The large shining black car moved away from them, and she took up her basket and continued, as if there had been no interruption.

She was walking slower now. And it reflected in her speech. Boy submerged his resentment into his legs, and allowed them to carry him along beside her, with willing and automatic lethargy. All the time, he pretended that he was invisible.

He was sweating under the arms. And this discomfiture put more hostility into his face, and made his features malevolent. He wanted to be invisible beside this woman in her white peasant dress, who looked so much like a maid, or a fish-seller, and barefooted, looking so much like the family maid by whom he was being taken on an errand. He wanted her to look this way. But his mother did not pay attention to any of his antics, although she knew he would be uncomfortable beside her.

'How many years now, eh? How long it is since that Amurcan-man, John plain-and-simple Adams, had the gumption to present himself at my father's house, saying he asking for my sister's hand in marriage? It was a long time ago. And I can still remember how he come up the front steps, with all his pretty clothes that didn't fit him, and shoes shining like dog's stones in the moonlight, cap in hand, that's right! John Moore Adams had his cap in hand in the presence of my family! He had just come off a merchant ship where he was working as a engine-room something, a helper perhaps. Appears that the merchant ship had touch-in in Panama, in the Canal Zone and he happen to see my sister, and he come back to Barbados, pretending that after what he do to she, that he still wanted permission to married to Ella. When my two eyes rested on that John Moore Adams, I could not believe I was seeing right, 'cause in Sin-Joseph there wasn't tummany men of his complexion who could dress in that fashion. Rings and gold teeth and wrist watch and shoes shining like a dog's. . . .'

A woman across the road hailed her. With a waving hand that was like a windshield wiper the woman moved her hand fast, as if it was on a wet piece of glass. The woman was about his mother's age. She was tall and black and elegant. She wore a blue dress that had white dots in it. On her head was a large straw hat with fruits and green leaves worked into the brim, in coloured string.

The woman came down three steps of concrete, from the entrance of the shop which was crowded with housewives, and she stood there, still waving.

'Sister Thorne, how?'

'How?'

'Living.'

'Thank God.'

'In the name o' the Lord, child.'

'Well, how, then?'

And she moved on.

'Sister Christopher,' she told Boy. 'From my church. A lady, if there was one. And a Christian-minded person, to-boot! And you would not believe, that it was only a few years before, when the same John Moore Adams, who everybody uses to call Johnny, 'cause nobody ever thought he had a real name, he was Johnny to everybody in Sin-Joseph. But this man dress-off in his 'Murcan clothes, and you can't tell from clothes only. No. Yuh can't. But this person who made money and get riches and wealth in Amurca was the same man who used to sweep-up Pappy's yard. And before he went on the merchant boats. And before he store-way and lived in Amurca. Why am I telling you all this? I only telling you this to show you, as I said, that in the morning, you could be flourishing like a lily of the valley, and at dusk, you are *nothing* but a withered-up plant, praise the Lord.'

A passenger bus passed them. From the back seat, Boy saw two of his College friends. They waved at him, in the same windshield manner. They called out his name, and smiled, and continued smiling until the bus turned the corner by Eagle Hall Road. Boy did not wave back. His underarms were wet now.

'I don't mean to tell you that we was high-and-mighty and was looking down on poor people, like poor Johnny. Or that it was because we was a family of complexion and colour. And that Johnny was the same colour as Nathan, your father. Or that we, that my father chased him from the house. 'Cause God knows I is a person who don't carry grieviances and grudges. But after we find-out that it was John Moore Adams who did that terrible thing to a member of our own-own family, well, I ask you in all fairness, I ask you, hummuch can a simple Christian-minded person bear? It was a sin above all sins. Indecency of indecencies. A girl's honour. A girl's only precious gift. I talking about a times when a man courted a young lady for years, visiting her home, and sometimes in them two or three years, that young gentleman could not cross the threshold of that girl's father's home. Fatherless, to say he bringing *wirthlessness* to her! Of a times, when decency was decency. When a man knew his place. Whatever that place maybe. When things was in order. And nothing could be out of order. In them times, boy, a man who was a man, make-sure he had a roof from the lumberyard, or at least a roof in mind, to provide his betrothed with, *before* he come talking 'bout the sins of the flesh. All that, all that brand of life this semi-Amurcan, John Moore Adams, contrabanded. Contrabanded. And now, for me, a Thorne from Sin-Joseph to see that man passing in front the house in his Amurcan car, and in his Amurcan clothes, and me, to be renting a house from *him* who contrabanded our entire family, boy, in all fairness, it is more than a Christian can take. But. Where there's a will, there's a way. I am glad enough at the way you growing-up, the way you learning your lessons, and the chances you have in life. And I prays every night, that you will do the right thing. Namely, leave this damn place. The first chance you get. I do not know tummuch about learning. And particular, the learning I understand you are learning at the College. But I understand you stand a chance for good things. Mr Lassills who pass a minute ago, been telling me about your prowess and progress, whiching has made me proud-enough that you probably take-after your forebears, on the Thorne's side, who were people from Scotland, and places over there. And I *hope.* . . .'

She stopped. She just stood up; stopped walking. And Boy, caught unawares, continued to walk on. Then, seeing his mother standing up, with the basket at her feet, and wiping the perspiration from her face with a large white handkerchief, he too stood up, and waited for her to catch up.

'You hungry?'

'No, Mother.'

'Why you don't say you hungry, if you hungry?'

'No, Mother.'

'You sure?'

'Yes, Mother.'

' 'Cause the shop cross the road, over there, is a nice decent place. It is one place where you don't find no drunken mens, and the owner keeps fresh sand and sawdust on the floor at all times, and the glasses he gives you to drink out of are always washed with clean water that have-in lime-peth, and he never serves you a drink from a glass that he didn't himself run a lime-peth over the mouth.'

'No, Mother.'

'Come, anyhow.'

The Harlem Restaurant & Bar, James W. W. Clarke proprieter, was filled with customers. It was always full. Whenever Boy passed in the school bus, *The Harlem Restaurant & Bar* was always crowded. And only once did he see, about three-thirty one afternoon, a man stumble on legs of rubber from the rum, down the four steps.

'But Mistress! I thought you wasn't passing today, yuh!'

The proprietor, Mr James W. W. Clarke, was a wrestler of a man. Big thighs. Big arms. Big body. And very handsome. One front tooth was capped in gold. He was always sweating. He was dressed in white, from head to foot.

'I says to myself, when I see the hands o' this clock approaching noon and twelve o'clock, and the Mistress didn't put in an appearance, I says to myself, James-Clarke, the Mistress like she letting you down today, yuh!'

'But, Clarkey! You *know* me!'

'How Nathan? I just send-down some twine that I get from a fellow offa a ship, for Nathan, 'cause Nathan did-telling me the fishing nets mash-up. Nathan drinking close to home, these days, 'cause I can't rest my two eyes on that man!'

'This is my young gentleman. I taking him to town. He not accustom walking with me. Yuh know this young generation! And he tell me he don't want a sweet-drink, not even a rock-cake outta your glass case, Clarkey, boy. He not too pleased walking 'side o' his old mother. But what to do, eh, Clarkey, boy?'

'*This* is the brains, Mistress? This is the *brains* that everybody in Barbados talking 'bout? Boy, you should be proud you got such a nice lady as a mother! Mistress, but you must be damn proud o' this boy! This boy is *pure* brains, I hear. The one I got, I don't know if he dead or he living. But, anyhow. Man, only last night, a fellow from down by you, who was in here, was telling me over a bottle o' rum, that the 'Murcan-man, Johnny Adams, have a son in your boy's class, but that he can't touch this boy, for brains. The fellow say that Johnny Adams not too pleased. His son coming second all the time. And this boy coming first, all the time! But, Mistress, you ever hear anything so? We who know Johnny, know Johnny not to be nothing, at all. A blasted 'Murcan-man like him, going-come here and tell decent people like we, how to do things? Excuse my French, boy.'

'*Everything* in the hands o' the Lord, Clarkey, boy.'

'But how you mean? And to think that I hear the same blasted 'Murcan-man, pardon my French, young fellow. I hear from Sarge that that blasted 'Murcan-man telling people not to vote for Seabert the tailor-fellow, and that they must vote for the oppositioners, 'cause the oppositioners promise to give the Scholarship to his son. I hear the boy didn't even born here!'

'A Tennants stout for this boy, Clarkey, boy. His brain so active with Classics that a stout won't do him no harm.'

Boy couldn't imagine that his mother knew such a thing as a bottle of stout.

'The usual, Mistress?'

Boy wondered what her usual was.

Mr James W. W. Clarke selected a water-coconut from a bin. He held it high in the air, as if he was inspecting its rich green skin, or if to make sure it was green enough. From somewhere beside him, he held up a cutlass. And with three of the prettiest waves of his right hand, using more wrist than brute force, which his body suggested he was capable of, three pieces of the top of the coconut dropped on the sand and sawdust on the floor. With one other flick, as if this action was a full-stop, or better still, an exclamation mark put to a sentence, a hole appeared at the top of the coconut. He placed the coconut over the mouth of a tall glass that contained chipped ice. He poured the rich, clear, almost white juice into the pint tumbler. Boy's mouth was watering as he watched.

'And Clarkey, boy, seeing as how she so hot, and I walking, would you mind please dropping two times the amount o' brandy in the glass? Please?'

'But how you mean, Mistress!'

Mr Clarke poured more than two full jiggers into the glass. The colour swirled, and the drink became a translucent honey colour.

'Don't stannup out here with these ruffians, Mistress. Take your place, in my Private Quarters.'

He then placed the coconut water and the stout on a tin tray. The tray had a Tennants bottle painted in its centre.

'Don't stannup out here! Come round in my Private Quarters, where decent people does-drink. You is one of my special respected customers. So my Private Quarters is yours! And the boy-own, too.'

Boy was moving over sawdust and sand, as a man in a dream of crumbling confidence would walk. He was in a strange land.

The sensation of a feather on sensitive skin came from the pit of his arm, his left arm, in the soft skin there, and ran almost straight, but slowly, down his left side, and stopped tickling him when it reached the vicinity of his heart. The humidity was almost deadening.

The road they were taking to the city was now full of people, going in two directions; and they all seemed as if they were carrying the sum total of their belongings or their recent purchases, in their hands and on their heads. Boy had to walk perilously close to the fast moving cars and lorries. The donkey carts moved slower. And all the time he had to move out of the way of pedestrians coming towards him, as if he was invisible. 'John Barrymore Adams, that play-play Amurcan, would do *anything*, anything at all, legal and illegal, to get we outta that house. He would even poison the three o' we with ground-up glass-bottle. And only because, as I been hearing from that white gentleman, Mr Lassills, he feels that you will beat his son for the Barbados Scholarship. He uses to live in Amurca, that ungodly place. And because he lived in Amurca, he want to own everybody in the village. He wants to own the village. He wants to be the boss-man in the village. He must be a damn plantation-owner! What he say, everybody must do. Only because he is a man who have lived in Amurca. But God put brains inside your head. And if God didn't put the same equivalents of brain inside his son head too, who is this John Moore Adams, alias Johnny, to kick against the pricks of God's wisdom?'

They had reached the outskirts of the city, at last. A narrow road, without sidewalks, packed with people, tight; just as his mother would pack the ingredients for making black pudding into the fragile tubes of pig-belly, people walking body to body, hips to hips, touching legs and arses in the two directions travelling, orderly within this strained space, moved like ants near their nests, in an ever-changing but unchanged pattern. It was a complicated quilt that shimmered in the sun.

Indian men stood beside their doors, in front of the darkness and mysteriousness of the inside that was always smelling of incense. Some of these same Indian men came through his village on Sunday afternoons, on bicycles, selling cloth in small pieces, for large deposits and larger instalment payments from the poor villagers.

'Blasted ungodly nicodemons!'

There were no Indian boys at the College. There were no Indians in the civil service. They were as unplentiful, in higher social circles of the country, as turtles in the sea.

'I have to stop at Weatherheads Drug Store, to get some tonic wine. I am on the last bottle o' Wincarnis I bought last month. You know something? Wincarnis and communion wine come out of the same bottle. Sarge was telling me the other day, that you should see how the reverend at the Anglican church does-drink the leavings of communion wine, when Communion over. Sarge is a real sinner! Imagine a reverend, a man o' God, drinking like a drunkard. But how would Sarge know that? He don't even go church.'

On this narrow street, with the Indian merchants, were many rum shops, already filling up with men and a few women. They were talking loudly, and laughing; and some stood at the entrance, encouraging others to come in, and 'fire one, man'. These men and women were already finished working, because

Saturday was a half day. But some of them were on their lunch hour, which on Saturdays, lasted two hours, or three hours.

The men and women on this street are poor. Their clothes tell you so. Boy knows that they patronized this area of the city because prices were lower than on the main street, where his mother is taking him.

A few women with trays laden with fruits and vegetables sat on low stools, legs wide open, and with their aprons and dresses tucked severely betwixt their heavy black beautiful legs. Boy felt they sat this way to torment the wandering eye, and also to prevent that same lascivious eye from travelling too far into regions that could only be obtained and enjoyed if the women were willing.

Boy stared at one woman's legs, and felt himself buried alive in the strength of her thighs. And he remained strangled by his lust, until the woman's eyes caught his. She stared his mannishness down into shame and embarrassment. She mouthed an obscene phrase, held her head back, and then laughed. He could hear her laughter, and see her legs, all the way to the main street.

It was less crowded here. Men wore suits and walked slower than on the narrow street with the Indian merchants. And the women were well-dressed in frocks of light-weight cotton with patterns of flowers and of circles and other designs he could not identify. Some wore chiffon, in all the heat. And they wore straw hats. And all of them wore shoes with heels, shoes without heels, sandals and pumps.

A group of boys from the College was walking with a group of girls whom he knew were from Queen's College. He slackened his pace. And he hoped his mother would, too. For at any moment, the boys might look back, to see the progress the girls were making, and spot him. For he was conspicuous in his College uniform. No one else was dressed that way.

But his mother did not slow down.

'Hold on for a second, boy.'

It took him a while to hear her, for he was planning his excuse in case his friends looked back. He saw her standing beside a doorpost of a store, trying to balance herself on one leg, and trying to get her left-foot 'pump' on. Her feet had swollen from the long distance on the hot tar road.

107

'We in the city now, boy. And friends o' yours might be all about here. And I won't feel right to see you embarrass by walking beside a barefoot old woman like me. But these damn pumps behaving as if they got more smaller since we left home! If I could only balance myself for a sec more better, and get-on this, this, damn shoe!'

Boy moved to his mother's side, and held her arm. It was soft. He remembered how soft the legs of the woman selling fruits were.

She got one 'pump' on, and he held her other arm, and balanced her. She got that one on, too.

'First thing! Something to eat!'

When she moved off, Boy was still standing, watching her. This well-shaped woman, his mother, of unknown age, because she had never told him, and never showed her birth certificate to him, if she had one, since also, he had been brought up never to ask, was a queen in his eyes.

Her age was one of the innumerable questions and secrets of family life that was never answered.

Her legs were at least as large and as beautiful as the woman's who sat in the squatting position behind her tray of mangoes and plums and sweetmeats; her complexion lighter than his, and reddened in the sun, and flushed red immediately after she had drunk the Hennessey brandy in the coconut water, and flaring red, when she was angry with his father; dressed from head to toe in white, stern and starched and stiff, with a gait similar to that of the Governor's wife, but more feminine: how old is she, really? Forty, yet? Fifty-five and looking forty? And if he subtracted his seventeen years, and assumed that she was twenty when she got him, it would make her younger than forty. She looked like a nurse, or like a nun.

'Thanks, boy.'

She was smiling, as she wiped the perspiration from her face.

The group of boys came towards them.

'Your school chums, ain't they?'

'Hello, MWWT!'

The four of them greeted him, in different cheerfulness, one of them slapping him on the back, the others nodding and smiling. And then they walked on.

'Is that the way they calls you at school? By your initials?'

'Yes, mother.'

'And you don't mind?'

He shook his head.

'I suppose it is more better than calling you by no name at all!'

She led him across the street, to the ground floor of a large and imposing store, Goddards. He passed this store every day on the way to the College. It was here, on the second-floor balcony, that he had seen the man dressed in white, and about whom he and Sheila had talked and laughed. There were always men holding over the balcony, looking down at the people. These men were merchants, bankers, solicitors, barristers-at-law, plantation owners and managers, and other men who were so wealthy that they didn't have to work.

Boy got to know most of them by seeing them holding over the balcony. He knew them also by reputation. They were all white. The same complexion as his mother.

One afternoon, he saw Mr Lascelles holding over the balcony. In his hand was a glass. In the glass was a drink the colour of clear lemonade. In the drink were pieces of ice. He was rattling the ice in the glass. He tried to imagine, that afternoon, what the inside of Goddards was like. He concluded that the inside would have to be English.

'We English bring our customs with us,' young Lascelles said.

She was leading him up the dark stairs, carpeted in green, past the shaded light bulbs which recorded the climb by their position on the wall, right up to the head of the stairs at which a black man sat at a desk with a light similar to those on the stairs. Before him was a book which looked like those in which payments were recorded.

'Good afternoon, Mistress,' the man said.

From the desk, Boy could see tables with white linen cloths on them. The tables seemed set for appetites that would consume the fish and the pork chops he could smell, each time another black man, dressed in black trousers and white shirt and black tie, came through the swinging door on his right hand. And as the door opened, like a too-large mouth, he got a glimpse of pots and pans and other kitchen utensils, shining

109

like silver and bronze, and whose opened mouths were breathing like dragons filled with steam. Each time the door opened, a smell of rich Bajan-stew hit his nostrils.

There were oil paintings of famous men on the walls on his left, on his right, and on the wall facing him. He recognized the King of England, the Governor of Barbados, the headmaster of his College and Winston Churchill.

'Tell Mr Thorne that May Thorne here.'

'Yes, ma'am.'

The man checked his book, and nodded.

'Mistress, why you don't tek a seat, right here?'

She put Boy to sit, while she remained standing.

'And outside so hot, and in here more cooler. I could get you a drink whilst you waiting?'

She shook her head. The man disappeared into the larger dining-room, where there was a loud rattle of knives and forks talking to the china plates, and where Boy could hear the rattling pieces of ice in glasses.

'But Ma, I didn't know that. . . .'

'Rest yourself, boy. Enjoy yourself. You leaving home soon, and I just wanted to give you something. I wanted to show you your place, before it's too late. Rest yourself. You too young to be worrying your head over things.'

To Boy, she looked as if she was born to this gloomy vestibule; to these gloomy and rich surroundings. She looked as if she was at home, in the large dim front-house; in her rocking chair, bare-footed, with her Bible in her hand, and with her eyes closed, sleeping, or else worrying about the spelling and the meaning of the small-print words. Boy always thought that the pages of the Bible were too fragile and pliable for her mind.

He continued to look at her in these surroundings which he himself had only heard about. But he had had a good picture of their grandeur. They were English. Now, he stared at the vast mahogany staircases that came down from a third floor to where they were standing. The staircase was like two giant polished arms of an unnamable monster. On the stairs was a thick carpet of royal blue. At the head of the stairs was the large colour photograph of His Majesty the King, in a gold-painted, embossed frame. The Union Jack and the Royal Standard were folded and crossed, pinned to the wall beneath the photograph.

A slender built man, skin blotched by red spots, complexion the colour of a white person who forgot, and fell asleep in the sun, dressed in a white suit with a white waistcoat, all of cotton drill, and sparkling from the ironing it had been given that very morning, white shirt, white leather shoes and white socks, for his trousers were slightly above the ankle, and wearing a blue tie with white stripes, like a university tie, and a large silver chain that came from the button on the lapel of his jacket and ended in the pocket on that side, this man came towards them.

Boy had seen this man many times. Dressed in the uniform of plantation power and aristocracy. When he wasn't walking the main street of the city, he was being driven in the back seat of an old black Bentley car. He was always wearing a white cork hat that had green undersides. The cork hat was always blancoed so heavily in white, that sometimes Boy thought he saw small clouds of white dust fall off, whenever the man doffed his hat to a lady.

It was the same man he and Sheila had laughed about.

'Ch'ist, May Thorne! Ch'ist, I thought you wasn't coming. I already had three rum-and-waters whilst waiting on you! How, boy? I hear you is a pure *brain*. Well, come! Ch'ist, May Thorne, I hungry as shite. We kin-talk whilst eating. You must-be-hungry-too, boy.'

'Tell your uncle, how–d.'

'How do you do, sir?'

'That is how they does-teach-you-to-say "afternoon" at the College?'

He gripped Boy's hand, and the pain from the handshake made him shiver.

'Call me, Delbert. I name Delbert. I is your blasted uncle, boy. So, you don't have to ask me how-do-you-do. I not English. We is plain people. We Thornes from up in Sin-Joseph is plain people. Your mother didn't tell you?'

'No, sir. I mean, yes, sir.'

'You does-fire grog? What I asking you? Ch'ist, I-myself been pelting-back grogs even before I hit the third form at

College. If you is a real Thorne, you kin-handle yuh liquors. Man, let we go up here with these blasted poor-arse English big shots!'

He put his arm round Boy's neck, and led the way into the dining-room where men sat large and comfortable, round square tables covered with white linen cloths, their seams still prominent from the ironing, where black men in black trousers and white jackets moved silently and reverentially through the laneways of the table-placings, where the smell of food was high and delicious, and the two whirring but silent fans in the ceiling cooled the luxurious comfort, where everywhere was collar and tie, mainly white cotton suits and ties with emblems and mottos and thick blue-and-white slashes running veritical, and comfortable over the rich fabric, this man no longer strange and laughable, and Boy, right up to a table in the corner, beside a window that looked down on the street, down on the people in the street who were dressed mainly in khaki. Some of the people Boy was now looking down on were bare-footed. All of them were sweating under the savage sun.

And when Boy looked back inside the dining-room, on one table in particular, where two Englishmen were having lunch, he saw two huge chunks of beef that had the rawness of a life-sore. They were as thick as the muscles in his own thighs, and red as blood. A pool of blood surrounded each steak, like the sea around his island. He was shocked. He could think no more. He could not understand. He just stood and stared. And it was his uncle's arm on his own arm which broke the reverie, and led him to the reserved table for the three of them.

'May, I have to fire a stiff one. Gimme a double-rum, on ice, please. And some water. Them two stinking bitches that just get off offa a blasted boat from England, come talking up in my face, 'bout we is still colonials! Pardon my French, boy. You still drinking brandy and coconut water, May, girl? Mek that a double-brandy and coconut water. Mek the coconut water a single. For my sister, here. Wha' to order for this boy, now, nuh? Look, man, give this boy a rum-and-ginger. Not too strong, though. He still going-school. And his pee not foaming yet.'

And when the waiter left, Boy's uncle took out a package of

local cigarettes, chose one, tapped it against the box which had a man on a horse with a trumpet, and he lit it with a box of matches that had a Beefeater and a sailor on its advertisement. He inhaled deeply as if his lungs were going to burst, as if he wanted them to burst, and when he exhaled, a long, thin arrow of smoke was shot in the direction of the two Englishmen whose backs were turned towards him.

'Them two stinking bitches! They come to this country in khaki short-pants, right offa the boat. And in two-twos, they getting-on great, because they wearing a cheap suit, and working in a store selling cloth. The only difference between them and the blasted Indians out in Swan Street, is that the Indians does-stay by themselves out in Swan Street. Them stinking bitches come in here, and because they got this funny accent, they think they could walk-over people like *me?* Good. Thanks, man.'

The drinks had come.

'Now. To get down to brass-tacks. I had a lil talk with Lassills, yesterday morning in his chambers. And I sign-over the papers in your name, May. Ch'ist, Lassills is the only Englishman that have manners, and know his place, in this blasted place. Lassills say the best thing is to buy the blasted house in your blasted name, or in the boy's name. Not that he don't trust Nathan. Nathan is the man you went and married. Ch'ist, you know I don't have no love for Nathan. But you married to him. Not *me!* It's only that Lassills feel you would be in a more better position, in case, if the house in your name. Now, seeing as how the boy stand a chance to go to university overseas, and yuh could never tell what might happen in England when he get there, Lassills say that is a next reason to give you title. Lassills say this boy have a real chance at the Scholarship. I didn't know you was so blasted bright? You certainly didn't tek-after Nathan! And be-Ch'ist, you had to tek-after the Thornes. May, but why you never change your name to Nathan's surname? You don't love your husband? Thorne may, or may not, be such a nice name, yuh. But to get back to brass-tacks. Lassills already write to Ella. And Ella surrender her share in the property and agree to cross-out her name outta the will. 'Cause um don't look as if she coming back to her home and birth-place, to dead. She is a real Amurcan these days. So, when you leff here, all you got to do, is go-down to Lassills chambers, and sign the blasted papers. Lassills waiting.'

'We meet Mr Lassills on the way up. But we didn't take the lift he offered. I wanted to show the boy a few things. Learn him a few things.'

'You and your walking! I don't understand how my sister, your mother, won't spend a blasted cent to see the world go round! People would think that May Thorne born poor. But yuh got money now, May. Spend something, nuh. Boy, your mother is almost a millionaire now. The Old Man dead and leff-back summuch property and land up in Sin-Joseph! So, we just sell-off a piece to fix-up May with the purchase o' the house you living in. You don't think you mother is a pretty millionaire-woman? Man, look at she! Ain't she pretty? If I wasn't your brother by blood, and if I was a more younger man, I-myself would ask you a question, and hold-on 'pon you, and foop you, and married-you-off, yuh!'

'Don't mind you.'

Boy saw his mother smile, and saw how the smile covered the blush.

'Be-Ch'ist, if they have a law concerning incess, this boy here would be my blasted nephew and son, at one and the same time, yuh!'

'Don't listen to your uncle, hear?'

'And foop yuh sweet, too, May!'

'You not 'shamed?'

'Foop yuh, like shite!'

'Look, Delbert, mind your language in front my son! What you doing, spoiling my son?'

'You start fooping girls, yet, boy?'

'Delbert!'

'Getting back to brass-tacks. I talk to the manager o' Wilkinson & Haynes, the lumber people. And they assure me that they going-give you a few shingles and a few pieces o' lumber to repair the house with. 'Pon credit. 'Cause I agree with you. Um don't look good to see a big Barbados Scholar living-in a house that brekking-down. So, after we eat, you is to

114

go there and open the account. I think that is all you need me
for. But yuh looking *good*, though, May! They have any boys at
the College who does-foop their sisters?'

'Watch your mouth!'

'Your mother don't look good to you? Answer me, boy. You
is to call me uncle. You have to obey me. I ask you a question.
Don't your mother look good-good-good, like something to
eat?'

'*Don't* you open you mouth!'

'And *raw*, to-boot?'

She smiled with her son. Boy lowered his head, and moved
the glass, and made another ring on the immacultely white
tablecloth.

'It take me and Lassills, and a couple o' merchants from who
that son of a bitch Johnny Adams does-trust, and where he have
credit, and at the bank where he owe money, to put a lil
pressure in his arse. The uppity son of a bitch! So, you don't
have to worry about Adams, no more. He as good as dead! So,
let we eat this steam-fish and lobster-soup that Goddards does-
sell!'

5

There was a knocking on the back door. A knocking soft
enough to be barely heard, but just loud enough. It sounded
like a code. Nathan jumped. His wife stopped rocking.

'Who you think that could be, at this hour, Nathan?'

'Where my blasted stick?'

Nathan found the stick. And without making a noise, he
crept to the back door.

'Careful,' his wife whispered. 'This is election time, so
careful.'

She made the sign of the cross on her bosom twice. Her
fingers seemed to sink into the white blanket about her body.

'This thing have everybody jumpy. The 'lectricity been cut

off for four days now.'

Boy realized how jumpy she was. Everything was going wrong. The Government told the villagers they were repairing something. Until the electricity came back on, Boy had to study with a kerosene lamp.

The wind from the sea came through the shutters. And just as the knocking stopped, the flames of the lamp jumped, became brighter, and then died. The front-house was in darkness.

'Careful, Nathan.'

The floorboards creaked the softer Nathan tried to walk to reach the back door. He was walking as Boy had seen cats do. He stopped, waited for the floorboards to die, and when he thought they were firm beneath his frightened weight, he moved again.

He rushed to the door, and flung it open.

'Who there?'

His voice was a shout, an angry shout, loud enough to frighten away the intruder.

A torchlight was shining in his face.

'Be-Jesus-Christ!'

He was scared now, too frightened to move.

'Shhh!'

'Sarge? Sarge! What the arse? You is a thief?'

Inside the front-house, Boy and his mother heard Sarge's voice. And they relaxed.

'Sarge? When Sarge started taking back-doors?'

'Cat-piss and pepper!'

Sarge was talking as if he was short of breath. His words came out as an exhalation.

'Cat-piss and pepper, Nathan!'

'When you start taking back-doors, Sarge? You can't come through the front? Somebody after you? The Guvvament?'

'Worse than that, Mistress! Worse than that. Pure cat-piss and pepper! Pardon my French, Mistress.'

Nathan took the jimmy-john of over-proof rum from the larder and poured a large shot for Sarge. Sarge liked this rum. Nathan had cured it in prunes and currants. Sarge even commented on the jimmy-john. It had 'Home Sweet Home' in white lettering above a bouquet of flowers, marked on it.

Nathan's wife left them in the kitchen, after she had greeted Sarge. They were sitting round the kitchen table.

Nathan cleaned the brightly coloured oilcloth tablecloth with his palms, collected dried bits of food into the cup of one hand, and threw them on the floor.

'Ahhh!'

Sarge liked the rum.

'Nathan, I don't know where I stand. I was up for a promotion. And they turn-over that. Nathan, I was going-to-be the *first* black man in the history of the Force of this country to make inspector-rank. They turn-over that. All because of a blasted yard-fowl who couldn't do nothing more than slam a blasted domino. And get kill. Nathan, I know I am a man with bad luck. It was my bad luck to be in that rum shop the night Lionel get kill. It was my bad luck that Lionel get kill during an election campaign. All this bad luck I having don't make sense. Cat-piss and pepper, Nathan! The Commissioner o' Police send for me. He have orders from upstairs to take me off the case. I must not prosecute Goalie as a murderer. They want Goalie to go free.'

Sarge patted the jimmy-john. Nathan poured him another rum.

'Nathan, you was there that night. Seabert was there. And Manny Batson was there.'

'Now, wait a minute, Sarge. I was there. But I wasn't a witness before the fact. Or even after the fact. I happen only to be in the vicinity of the incidence.'

'I not implicating you, Nathan. I merely stating, from a *primer-facial* point, that Goalie is a blasted murderer. If you see what I mean?'

He helped himself to the rum.

'The Commissioner also tell me, that from next week, he putting me on the traffic beat in the city. Nathan, I will be on a black-and-white round box, in the middle o' the city, near the statue o' Lord Nelson, directing traffics, like a blasted mock-man! Me? A crown-sergeant?'

'Why you don't take your case to a politician?'

'I talk to Seabert. And Seabert say the order come from upstairs. Seabert can't save me. Nathan, they demote me to lance-corporal! Nathan, *acting* lance-corporal, at that! Seabert can't help me, now. I went to a lawyer. And the lawyer tell me, he won't touch my case with a ten-foot pole. Nathan, it is sheer cat-piss and pepper! When neither Seabert nor the lawyer could bail-me-out, I approach John Moore-Adams. I figure that John Moore-Adams would assist me, seeing as how he have connections in the Guvvament, and how I fix-up some traffic tickets for him, and a little accident he had when he lick-down a girl with the car. I also helped him get his son's citizenship papers. . . .'

'So, the boy wasn't born here?'

'The boy is a blasted Yankee!'

Sarge held the jimmy-john through its handle, which was barely large enough to fit his index finger. He tilted the pottery jar, and filled his glass. Nathan poured himself a small shot.

'Last Friday night when I get home, and before I unbuckle my bull-pistle, I get a call from Lone Star Supermarket. I been dealing with them, on a credit basis, for ten years. The manager call and tell me, my account close. I takes milk, as you do, from Edwards Dairy. Edwards Dairy tell me I not getting no more milk. Even if I pay cash. Yesterday, after standing up five hours 'pon a blasted black-and-white round box directing traffics, and as I jump-on 'pon my bicycle, all two of my bicycle tires flat flat flat as a bake. You think somebody telling me something? The man who represents me in the House o' Sembly, Alexander Bourne, passed round by my house last night. Me and he sit down and drink rum for three hours. And just as he stepping in the back seat of his car, he turn round and tell me, "Sarge, if I was you, I would tek a vacation. Why not try Trinidad? Or Jamaica or even Amurca? The party will take care o' you". Cat-piss, Nathan, and pepper!'

'Have a snap, Sarge.'

'The stigma of this murder case goes more deeper, Nathan, than a mere murder. This is a political murder. The Guvvament could fall over this murder. But to me, as a crown-sergeant, this is nothing more than a civil-servant who kill a domino-player. It isn't as serious as Brandford who raped the girl.'

'What can I tell you?'

'I have something to tell you, though. Nathan, there is some nasty sons o' bitches living in this village. I don't rightly know how to say this to you. But since it involve Boy, I better say it straight. I hear that John Moore-Adams and some other people are doing all they could to mek-sure that Boy don't win that Scholarship.'

'That can't happen. The exam is a' English exam. It have to go up to England to be corrected. The people in England is fair people. They believe in justice. Boy will win, if there is English justice.'

'It don't happen so, Nathan.'

'You mean Boy could come first, and still somebody could say he come second?'

'If yuh see what I mean!'

'You mean what I think you mean?'

'Nathan, we is ordinary people. We don't really know how things work. We don't really understand how the system works. We is therefore a race o' people with no connection to the system. And I have to advise you, due to the circumstances that are now bursting your arse and my arse, to get a Godfather. And make-sure that that Godfather is a white man.'

'I don't know none.'

Nathan poured himself a shot of rum that was larger than any of the portions Sarge had served himself.

'My Christ! And Sarge, I trying to buy this house offa John Moore-Adams! Who to trust, these days?'

'I have a favour to ask you, Nathan. This is why I come. Now, listen good. I have a list. I have a notebook.'

He took the book from his tunic pocket. It was the first time Nathan saw the single stripe, signifying Sarge's demotion to lance-corporal. Sarge put the book on the table.

'This notebook have-in every name of every big shot in this country who have something to hide. I don't think I should keep it on my person. You think you could hold-on 'pon this book, for safe-keeping? Till things clear up?'

'But Sarge!'

Nathan put his glass down. For a while he did not look Sarge in the eyes.

'But Sarge? With a wife and a son, a man like me, a

119

fisherman, trying to buy this house, you expect me to take-on a big responsibility like that?'

Boy was waiting at the bus stop. He was late for an appointment with his uncle at Goddards.

'Don't keep me waiting like how your mother had me waiting last time! Ch'ist, I don't know why black people can't keep time.'

Boy was sweating from the tension. And then, he heard the car.

Seabert Mascoll Marshall, Candidate, reversed his brand-new Morris Minor from beside his house, straight across the road from Manny Batson's rum shop, with the headlights on, for he was not accustomed to cars, or to this new respectability in status. Beside him was his daughter, Patricia, on her way to the public library, with four books now, of adventure and mystery about Indian treasures and Egyptian mummies.

Seabert slipped the car into drive by mistake and almost knocked down the carpenter who was putting an addition on to his house. His daughter became frightened and screamed.

'Daddy?'

Seabert ignored her.

'This blasted gear!'

He eventually got the car in the right gear, and he made the tyres screech and he turned on the high beams, although it was midday. And then the car stalled.

'This blasted car!'

But Seabert Mascoll Nathaniel Marshall was a determined man. He saw Boy, and not wanting to stop the car and start it up again, he applied the brakes and allowed the car to move just slowly enough for Boy to jump in. Boy sat beside him. Patricia was in the back seat.

Boy knew that Seabert was a determined man, more determined now that he was a Candidate.

He had entered politics, Boy knew now, determined to reap the financial and monetary benefits of his decision.

He blew the car horn by mistake, and all the people in Manny Batson's rum shop looked out, and seeing him jerking the car to the corner, where he picked up Boy, they cheered him loudly.

'Skipper! Don't mash-it-up!'

He turned left, to head for the city, to attend an important political meeting at party headquarters.

'Alexander Bourne ask me to a important meeting,' he told Boy.

But he was nervous. The party had given him this new car. The party had helped him to get credit with a lumber company, to put the addition on his house.

He had lived in a one-roofed house, with a shed-roof all his life. And now, all of a sudden, credit accounts with the largest merchants in the city were opening a vista beyond his wildest former radical and democratic beliefs.

'When this is all finish,' he told Boy, out of the corner of his mouth, and without turning his head, because he had to keep his eyes on the road, 'When this done, I must have a house with three roofs, some wall for the verandah, electric lights, *and* running water.'

'And Daddy will purchase a brand-new Singer sewing machine, for me.'

Boy realized that Patricia would practise what she had been talking about.

Seabert got the car into first gear and was turning a corner when it refused to go into second gear. He was sweating. He never understood how Englishmen could wear suits made of material more suited to the frigid zone, with cork hat, collar and tie, and never sweat.

'And walking 'bout in the blasted hot sun! Boy, you think it have something to do with breeding? Or with ancestries?'

He would have to get accustomed to wearing suits, and not sweating up the suits, and destroying the silken material with which he had lined his suits. And he thought of his perspiration. This politics business, he was thinking, as he drove slowly, not because he was being careful, but through ignorance of the gear-system; this politics business he was thinking of, and how suddenly his life had been changed by it.

He glanced quickly at his daughter in the back seat, and saw her sitting more comfortably, as if she was born there, on the smelly leather seat, than his three days' ownership of the car warranted. He wondered how her life would change.

These thoughts followed him as he reached the imposing Roman-columned building of the public library, where he dropped her off. Boy decided it was safer to get off here, too.

Patricia took her four books, put them under her arm, closed the door too hard; he must teach her how to close the doors; and walked with a new pride, which Boy did not notice before, up the marble steps, and then stood, and waved, and attracted some attention, before she went inside, and before Seabert could get the car to move. Boy stood a safe distance from the car.

Seabert could not move, because the first gear refused to engage. He needed practice. And in more than driving, he knew he had a lot to learn. For instance, this emergency meeting to which he had been summoned by the party.

'Something big came up,' Alexander Bourne had told him. 'Get here by two.'

And the telephone was dropped unceremoniously in Seabert's ears. He had stood for a long time, looking at the black instrument, recently installed on the orders of the party, wanting desperately to play with it a little, and call all his friends, to let them know that he 'had-in telephone now, man'. But he had been forced by the new urgency of his importance to regard the telephone as an instrument of tension and short, curt messages.

Seabert moves now like a novice driver, through the thick streets, people and donkey-carts and bicycles and other cars, and lorries which seemed, even when he was a mere pedestrian, to have been built for larger, bigger roads, and bigger countries. If he had not been a party man, he knew he would have to drive this car with a large red L, attached to the front and rear bumpers, indicating that he had no operator's licence.

'But how would it look, Seabert,' Manny Batson told him, 'that you, a big politician, and a prospected Member o' Parlment, driving-'bout the blasted public road with a pair o' L's?'

Seabert did not, however, throw caution to the wind, as his position in society had thrown regulations to the wind. He was driving in first gear, for the last mile.

He parked the car in front of the party headquarters. He took the long staircase at the side of the building. It was an open, outdoor staircase which went straight from the ground floor to the second floor. A bulb shone. He could see no light that it gave. A bee buzzed around the bulb. And he tried to remember the hour of his appointment. For the staircase was dark.

The party headquarters was on the second floor of the building which was built in the late eighteenth century. It was made of wood, and it had an enclosed verandah of shuttered windows. These windows were opened by long sticks. They looked like the lids of eyes, on the point of sleep.

The Workers Labour Party was written on a sign board. This name ran the length of the building. On the street level, was a shop which sold rum and goods, such as rice, meal, salt fish, pigs' feet, everything needed to make the working man strong. And at the side of the shop was a bar which catered to party members of a lower status than those members who were ushered upstairs, into the back room.

Yesterday, Seabert would have stood on the sand on the floor, and leaned on the wet counter made of dealboard: today, he was being greeted and ushered into the dark back room – or he felt he would be – where the sand was cleaner, where the lights were just as dim, but where the flies were fewer.

As he mounted the stairs, he heard voices. And chairs scraping the wooden floor. At the top of the stairs, the door was closed. *Members Only* was written at the top.

He paused, mopped his face, his neck, and after a glance down the stairs, he pulled off his jacket, and ran the large white handkerchief under his arms.

'This blasted heat! This blasted hot weather and these heavy clothes!'

He rapped softly on the door.

Immediately, it swung inwards from him, and he was exposed to a large room with chairs scattered throughout randomly, as if a meeting had been hurriedly concluded. The room looked like a ballroom. At one end, the darker end, was a makeshift bar; and behind the bar was one of the party members, doubling as a barman. He was mixing drinks.

A few tables that men played bridge and poker on were haphazardly placed in the room. At these some men sat. They were all dressed in three-piece suits. And they were not sweating. A revolving fan in the ceiling was not spinning.

'Come in, Brother Marshall. Come in, man,' one of the men said.

Seabert did not recognize him.

'Come in, Brother.'

Seabert stood just inside the door. All round him, men were talking and ignoring him. Photographs of former party leaders and one former Prime Minister were on the walls. He recognized all these important men, for he was a student of history. Political slogans, including the one being used in the present campaign, UPLIFTNG THE COMMON MAN, and many others which bragged about 'self-betterment', and the 'last days of colonialism: the beginning of free times'; and a small desk at which an older man, also dressed in a three-piece suit, and not sweating, sat in a straight-back chair. There was an office at the other end of the room, overlooking the road. Its door was closed. On the door was written *The Leader*. From this office, in spite of the noise of passing traffic below, and the loud voices of hawkers and men talking loud in the road, and the hum of conversation in the room, and the noise of glasses and of pieces of ice dropped into the glasses, Seabert could hear three voices. He recognized one of them as the Prime Minister's.

The representative of his village, Mr Alexander Bourne, who summoned him to the meeting, had been sitting almost in front of Seabert all this time. Seabert had not recognized him earlier. Mr Alexander Bourne was bending over, and whispering like a conspirator, like a man talking very important secrets, to two other men.

'Over here, Seabert,' he said.

The speaker of the Rediffusion radio system was placed high on a wall, near the road. The voice of the BBC announcer was saying, 'And that is the end of the news from London'.

The barman brought a tray of drinks for the table where Seabert was heading. Mr Alexander Bourne pushed a double-shot of whisky before Seabert. How did he know? How did the representative know that Seabert had stopped drinking rum, and had turned to whisky from the night following Lionel's

murder, when he was in Manny Batson's rum shop? Seabert felt
very uneasy in this room.

'Siddown here, Seabert.'

Mr Alexander Bourne said it, although Seabert was already
sitting down. He seemed to have so many important things on
his mind, and the atmosphere in the party headquarters was so
businesslike, and important, almost as important as the
atmosphere in the House of Assembly, that Seabert easily
forgave him.

'How your campaign going? People turning out at your
meetings? You giving-out enough money? Corn beef and
biscuits and things? And how the women treating you, Seabert
boy? Yuh know, women is who does-win elections! Spare the
rod, and spoil the vote!'

And he roared at his own joke. And the men with him roared,
too.

'The life of a politician is a hard thing,' a man said.

'I don't know the last time I slept in my wife bed!'

Mr Alexander Bourne hardly finished this confession before
he was roaring again. The others joined him.

'Yuh can't get elected in Barbados unless you make-up your
mind to sleep with five women a night! I-myself now taking iron
pills and Wincarnis Tonic Wine to give me more energy to face
the beating I does-take!'

'No politician in Barbados,' another man said, 'or for that
matter, in the whole blasted Wessindies, could ever get elect
Prime Minister, unless he decide, and not only decide, but is
capable to pelt some wood. Regular wood. And good wood, too!
Politics in this part of the whirl is pure pussy-politics.'

'How you know so good?' the other man challenged him.

'Wait! You didn't hear? That this son of a bitch already
hanging-round Lionel's woman's house? Almost every night?'

'If you know what is good for you, and for your political
future in this honourable party,' Mr Alexander Bourne said,
this time not laughing, 'and if I can give you a piece o' advice,
the PM already have eyes for Lionel woman, yuh.'

'Well, in that case. . . .'

Seabert tasted the refreshing bubbles in the Scotch whisky
and soda. He shuddered slightly at the first taste. But he soon

settled to its new sensation, with the feeling that this was the life his political career had marked out for him. And he might as well enjoy it. He noticed too that, except for Mr Alexander Bourne, and the two men with him, the other six men, party members almost certainly, although he had not been introduced to them, were white. These six white men sat apart and talked as if they were not associated with the others in the room.

'Oh!' Alexander Bourne said, as if he was reading Seabert's mind. 'This is the representative for Westbury North. And this is the representative for Westbury South.'

'Seabert,' Seabert said.

'No, man!' Mr Alexander Bourne corrected him. 'Say, "I is the candidate". Seabert, you is a candidate now. No more ordinary comma-man. You is a important man. Important as any son of a bitch in here. Including them six over there! But except the Prime Minister. Who, incidentally, want a word with you. Seabert, you got to learn to live *big*. Big like a politician. It don't make no blasted sense to me if, as a candidate, you can't begin to live big, and think big. 'Cause who knows, in a month or two, you may be representing big people in the House o' Sembly.'

'I am the representative. . . .'

Seabert saw his mistake.

'You's not *that*, yet!'

'I mean, the candidate for Sin-James East.'

'Now, yuh talking like a politician!'

Voices inside the office became louder. Seabert tried to listen to what the Members were telling him and at the same time his instincts told him to keep one ear on the conversation coming from that office.

'We was just discussing your friend, Sarge. And we decide, Seabert, that seeing as how you know Sarge more better than any other political strategist the party have, that maybe, you could get to Sarge before Sarge do more harm to the party. And to we.'

Mr Alexander Bourne's voice had such a cold calculation in it, it hit like ice water. But Seabert did not hear what was being said. He was hearing the voice of the Prime Minister's, on the telephone.

'Well, Lord Bishop! How? Good! You hear about Lionel. . . .'

126

'. . . now, we not too sure of your other friend, Nathan, who have a son name Boy, at the college. . . .'

'. . . the same boy who I hear will win the Scholarship from all reports. . . .'

'. . . the fisherman-fellow, with the light-skin wife from Sin-Joseph, is who I mean! He and Sarge are thick thick as peas in a pod, so. . . .'

'I want you to read the Eulogy at Lionel's funeral. . . . What you say? You in bed? Sick?' There was an abrupt banging of the telephone into its cradle. And then Seabert heard, 'That son of a bitch! He doesn't remember who made him Lord Bishop? Get somebody to check and see if the bitch is really sick. If I hear he's not sick, well. . . .'

'. . . and at your next political meeting, I want you to get some fellows, about half-dozen or so, and when you come to the part concerning Lionel, I want them fellows to start pelting some big-rocks at you, and brek-up your meeting. So, duck like shite, Seabert! I want you to run for cover. Scream. Run like hell. We going-have some photographers and reporters at the scene. Run like shite! Bawl for murder! Scream for blue-murder! Cry assassination! Do anything. Think of how that going-look the next day, in the papers. Comma-sense, boy. Political savvy.'

'Venerable? How? Good! I hope you not sick, too. And that you not too busy these days. How the women, Dean? But Venerable. You know and I know that you have a certain lady whose husband is overseas on a course. . . . Exactly! The Lord Bishop indisposed. But of course! I'm waiting on that son of a bitch, as you say. If we win-back the Guvvament, and who's to say we not winning-it-back? Naturally, a man in your position could become anything. Even Lord Bishop . . . it is a promise, and not a political promise, Dean. I giving you my word. . . .'

And then, Seabert heard the Prime Minister laugh, just as how he and Sarge and Manny Batson and Nathan; and Lionel, before he was dead, would laugh when Nathan told dirty jokes. Seabert never expected a Prime Minister would laugh that way. And he never expected he would have the privilege of hearing this explosion of hearty laughter.

He had been, for so long, tentacled to a small dilapidated shop, with pieces of cloth, ends of suit material, a shop whose walls were covered with pictures and photographs of great men, most of whom he had never seen in the flesh; and now, in such a short time, through the assistance of Mr Alexander Bourne who urged him to get into politics, his entire life was changed.

He was now amongst big men. Men who ran the country. Men who, until two months ago, ran the country without even knowing of his existence. And his nearness to these big men, his good fortune to be in the same room with them, while they made decisions for the people of the country, was like the sweet, short, total shiver the Scotch whisky had sent through his body. It was a blessing.

'And Seabert,' Mr Alexander Bourne was saying, 'we don't expect you to go on being friends with certain persons, who in the past, and outta custom, or even through friendships, you use to 'sociate with.'

He cleared his throat, for effect. And he took a sip of his whisky. He held the glass daintily, with big thumb and index finger. He allowed the other fingers to cock themselves off, thereby giving more daintiness and a bit of graciousness to his style. Seabert observed this. And there and then, he decided that in future, at meetings like this, this would be the way he himself would hold his glass. He was amongst big men. And he had to behave like one.

'So, Seabert. It don't mean that because you know certain persons all your life, that they is naturally your friends. In politics, as I learn, they isn't many friends that a politician can count on. Saving the women in his constituency. . . .'

'But, Mr Bourne, I grew up with Nathan and Sarge! We went-school together. I know that neither Nathan nor Sarge belong to a political party. But even so, I don't see them as natural enemies. I don't understand how I could drink with them two fellows yesterday, and sudden-so, today, I must pass them at a bus stop, and not give them a lift in my car, whiching I can hardly drive, or change from second gear to third gear!'

'In the *car* we give you?'

Mr Alexander Bourne turned purple with resentment. He spluttered. Some small pieces of ice and whisky spurted from his mouth.

'You are willing to ruin your political career by picking up those two bastards in we car? In our car?'

He then looked Seabert full in the eye. His own eyes were closing in a glare of both disbelief and distrust. He tried by that stare to discover how this startling party disloyalty could have come to the surface which he thought he had prepared with such care and with his usual brilliant political savvy.

'Seabert! It is I who bring you in this party. I, me, your humble servant, Alexander Bourne. Is me who stand-up 'gainst odds in your behalfs. Axe any one of my two colleagues sitting down here with we. Axe them. Axe them if I didn't fight like hell, to get you nominated? And now, you questioning my political judgement? Seabert! If you want the situation on a platter, well, here it is. I going-give it to you on a platter. If you want to really know, why I call you up here to headquarters, I going-level with you. If you want to know the long-and-short of the situation, Seabert, you getting it plain plain plain, from me!'

Mr Alexander Bourne knew he needed some nourishment. He needed some punch and purpose to his words. And he sought to obtain these from the glass of whisky and soda before him. Seabert had seen him revert to this kind of nourishment, in this kind of way, many times before, when he was making a political point with a man who was proving difficult to convince. Seabert watched him now, as he lifted the glass with big thumb and index finger. The other three fingers were allowed to cock off, this time in a stiff vengeful manner. They looked like three fish hooks.

'Seabert! We facing defeat. Political disaster. Political annilation, then! We, the whole Guvvament. The whole leadership. The whole entire blasted infrafractures of this whole blasted country facing complete, total, thorough disaster. You know what that mean, Seabert? I will tell you. It don't only mean that from the day after voting, that I is no longer a blasted Member o' Parlment. It don't only mean that my motto-car take-way. And that I have to revert-back to taking bus, and hopping-on 'pon a lorry to get from point A to point B. It don't only mean and connote that I got to find money to meet my house-payments, and other payments, like paying-off debts that I get-in to help me live the way a politician have to live. It don't only mean that from the day the votes cast, I is no longer, the Honourable Mr Alexander Bourne, Esquire, Member of the fucking Parlment. Seabert, it mean that *anybody*, anybody out there in the street, any little kiss-me-arse barrister-at-law could start asking questions. Seabert! It mean scandal. And secrets leaking-out. It mean the end, Seabert. Doom. Destruction. Disaster. And all I asking you, as one o' we, is to keep a eye on Nathan and Sarge. I asking you this little favour. And you have the guts not to understand what I saying to you?'

He had to pause. He whipped out a large white handkerchief, and ran it over his face. While he did this, there was no face to be seen. He then took a sip of whisky.

'I did-thought that you was a believer in justice. I did-thought that you did at least look at and study some o' them pictures and photographs you have in your tailor shop. I did-thought that you was a believer in the justice of the comma-man. I did-thought all them things. But I see that I did-thought *wrong*.'

Mr Alexander Bourne, apparently exhausted by this declaration of political disaster, slumped slightly into the straight-back chair, took the large white handkerchief again from his breast pocket, and mopped the beads of anger and of frustration from his large sweating face. The more he mopped, the more the sweat seemed to exude through the large pores of his face.

'Listen to wisdom, Seabert,' one of the men said.

'Listen to what Bourne telling you,' the other man said.

They were equally morose. Their faces and their bearing had the same seriousness.

'Harken to the wisdom that Bourne dispensing. Bourne know what he saying. That is why he is the political adviser to the Prime Minister. And to the whole party. If Bourne say the ship sinking, it sinking, in truth. And if Bourne, knowing that the ship sinking, and is holding-out a hand to you, to help in the rescuing of this ship, I feel that you should harken to Bourne. Listen to wisdom, Seabert.'

'Thank you, Brothers, thank you,' Alexander Bourne said. He was now like a man taken from the waves which had almost hugged him in a mortal embrace.

Seabert thought he looked like a preacher of the Church of

the Nazarene, after he had delivered a sermon of brimstone and sin.

'Thank you,' Mr Alexander Bourne said.

He took up his glass, and the three cocked-off fingers were more friendly.

'What you think *he* is doing inside there?'

Seabert looked at the office with the closed door.

'What you think it feel like for a man in *his* position as Prime Minister, to be begging a man that he-himself appoint, to do the party and the country, a favour?'

'Seabert, what your analysis is?'

Seabert looked again at the closed door. The loud laughter inside had stopped a long time ago. He could hear only the moving of a chair, and the shutting of metal drawers. Nathan had told him, before he was a party member, that it was inside this same office, and inside those same metal drawers, that thousands and thousands of dollars in hard cash were kept.

The drawers clapped shut. The chair moved again. Seabert heard voices talking in soft tones.

'Listen to me, Seabert. When this Guvvament fall, it going be pure cat-piss and pepper!'

Seabert had heard Sarge use these same words.

'And in order to prevent that happening, I want you to do this thing for me. As a favour. As a personal favour. Sarge have in his possession a certain book. A black book. We got to get that black book. Even if it mean killing Sarge.'

Something like a sudden exhalation of air came from Seabert.

The other two men just smiled.

Mr Alexander Bourne did not smile. His face was even, and neutral, and like a mask, like the face of a man who had just sentenced another man to death, but who has been accustomed to that kind of pronouncement.

'Even if it mean we got to kill Sarge.'

'Murder?' Seabert asked.

'Not murder, Seabert. Assassination.'

'But assassination is murder.'

'Murder is murder. Assassination is assassination.'

'But he would be dead!'

'As a fucking doornail!'

'Killed?'

'Yes. But in a different way. And for a different cause.'

Seabert felt trapped. He knew he was trapped. Was this what John Moore-Adams had told him was 'playing political football'?

He had visited Mr Adams to get a contribution to his campaign, and Mr Adams had listened patiently to him, and then had said, 'If you could get my boy his citizenship papers, so he could qualify for the Scholarship, if you would play political football, then. . . .'

Now, it all was beginning to fit into some pattern. But he was not intelligent enough to see the whole pattern.

'We got to get that book.'

He was about to ask what the book contained, but Alexander Bourne told him.

'That book have-in the political lives of all o' we. From Prime Minister down. A man could get kill, for having that kind of information. Could get his balls rip-out!'

Just then the door of the office, in which Seabert had heard the Prime Minister's voice, opened and a man came out. He looked important. He looked more important than any of them. Seabert knew the man.

The man came over to Mr Alexander Bourne, leaned over and whispered something into his ear. The other men in the room stood up, and became interested. Alexander Bourne immediately straightened up, used his large handkerchief again, and when he thought his face was cleaned, wiped his lips twice with it. He then followed the man into the office. The door was shut behind them.

Seabert sat limp. He did not know whether his first meeting with these important men had gone well. He thought of having to learn to change the gears of the Morris Minor. He remembered he had to drive through that always congested section of the city before he could get to the public library to pick up his daughter. He could not remember whether he had agreed to pick up Boy, too. He was peeved with his daughter. Nowadays, she was refusing to take the passenger bus, since he had come into his good political fortune. She was beginning to put on airs.

He remembered he had to buy some red snapper for his wife, for dinner. He started to make a mental list of things he had to do, and the list brought back the problems of driving the new car.

In the midst of this sorting of things to be done, Mr Alexander Bourne came back outside. He was a different man. Sterner, shaking and more visibly angry. Seabert could only guess what he had been told within the confidential walls of that office.

'Get that blasted book! If you know what is good for you, Seabert Mascoll Nathaniel Marshall, get that blasted book. You have two days to get it. Get that blasted book.'

'Well, look how long we standing up here, and I forget to order lunch. Christ this politics business giving me a bad case of ulcers, and gas,' a man said.

He did not break the tension, even if he had intended to.

'My political future is at stake.'

Mr Alexander Bourne looked at Seabert as he said this, and he made it appear as if it was Seabert who held the key and the responsibility for his future.

'But I won't be going-down by myself. A lot of people going-down with me.'

He held his glass of whisky and soda which had been replenished, with the three fingers, in the form of three brutal hooks, such as those that soldiers who have lost the use of their hands, have attached to their stumps. Seabert could feel the three steel hooks digging into his flesh.

'And I had-intend spending the night with a woman down in my constituency,' Mr Alexander Bourne said. 'And now, the blasted Skipper want me to visit Nathan. . . .'

The afternoon was still hot, when Nathan greeted him with two 'welcomes', at the front door. But Mr Alexander Bourne was not taken in by this hospitable pretence.

'Nathan, you always making sport with big people,' he taunted him.

There was no love between them. He knew that Nathan had prestige and influence in the village; and since Lionel's murder, Nathan had become an important man.

133

'Why you not helping in this election? And you have a bright son, who I understand going-up for the Scholarship. I know you like that boy. And what a nice thing it would be to see his picture in the papers, as the most brightest boy in the whole country!'

Nathan stopped smiling.

'Nathan, you know it is not right that you backing the oppositions, as I hearing.

At that moment, Nathan's wife came in from the kitchen.

'Well, mistress? How you? Everything all right? Your sister in Canal Zone, Panama, all right? The scholarship-boy all right? What a coincidence! I was just telling Nathan how I intend to make the Minister of Water Resources put running water in this whole district. Before the elections finish, before voting day even. And you walked in. Before this month end, you will see Guvvament trucks and lorries, Guvvament workers by the dozens down here working. I owes you that much.'

Nathan's wife placed the tray of food on the edge of the centre table, beside the family photographs. The photograph of Ella fell on its face.

Two bottles of rum, and a large bottle that once contained grapefruit juice, now filled with iced water. Chipped ice in a bowl; two large plates filled with corn beef seasoned in pepper and chopped raw onions; another bowl with a pile of brown, crispy, fried pork chops.

'Elections next two weeks, ain't it?'

He missed the point.

'What a politician your wife is! I wish I had the mistress in my corner.'

'Mr Bourne, why you tantalizing my soul for? I trusts in God.'

'Politics is the best God.'

'You blaspheming, man.'

'I didn't mean it so, mistress. I mean that after God, politics is the only thing you got.'

'I going pray for you, Mr Bourne. I going pray for you.'

And she left the men, and went back to the kitchen. But before she left, he promised her the water again. 'If it is the last thing I do, mistress, I giving you my word, you going-get water running all over this nice house, which I hear you intend to buy offa Mr Adams.'

She stopped dead, and looked at him, wondering how he knew.

'Well, yuh know that a politician got to keep his ears to the ground.'

She finally left, at this point.

'All I want from you, Nathan, in exchange for the water, is a lil X beside my name.'

'We will see.'

'That's good enough for me.'

But he was visibly disappointed. And he started to sweat. He shrugged his heavy woollen jacket into better fit, whipped out a large handkerchief and passed it over his face. He held his glass between two thick fingers, thumb and index finger. He tossed back the rum, and twisted up his face. The sting of the rum reflected on his face.

'Emmmm! Emmmm! I so-glad I visit you, today. Yuh know, only this morning I say to the Prime Minister, "Let me go and visit the people in my constituency. . . . They is the best in the country." You. The mistress. And Sarge. Best people in the whirl!'

He had thrown back another snap-glass of rum. His throat was thirsty. He was beginning to feel warm inside. 'Emmm! This is *fine* food. A fine wife you have, Nathan. And a fine son. Did I tell you already, that I been hearing how fine your son doing at the College? I even hear reports that he might get the Scholarship in Classics.'

He put his glass down. He wiped his face with the bedsheet of a hankerchief. He was ready to leave.

'A fine boy you have, Nathan. A fine boy!'

He got up to leave. Nathan walked him to the front door, wondering all the time, why he was praising his son so much.

'Now,' Mr Alexander Bourne said, on the threshold of the door, 'about this sad business. As I was telling the Prime Minister just before I rush down here, to see you, as I say to him, "Don't let we rush into things, and allow justice to be too quick. Just for this once, let we look at the political ins-and-outs." I talks to him, plain. Man to man. We is the same men.

135

He is the same man as me. This is my constituency, Nathan. And not even he-himself could get me re-elected down here. I owns down in here. I rules down in here. And I intend to see justice done down in here. Now, then. We two is men. The two o' we, gathered here this afternoon, is big men. Now. In regards to Sarge. And I know that Sarge is a personal friend of yours. But in regards of Sarge, I had a report placed on my desk this morning. That report say, Nathan, that Sarge is, well . . . maybe . . . well, you know what I mean, Nathan! The report is confidential. If I show you part of it, you will understand. I can't go round divulging things in Guvvament confidential files. But this is the position. Lionel was one of the hardest political workers we had. Lionel has bring-in, by himself, about two hundred votes for me in the last elections. I have loss a damn good worker by Lionel's death, Nathan. You would therefore understand my personal loss and bereavements.'

Nathan was not following him.

'Reports drop on my desk say that certain persons down here intend to defeat me and the Guvvament. But over my dead-body, Nathan. Over my dead-body. I had to tell the Prime Minister a piece o' my mind. I says to the Prime Minister, 'A man dead. It is true that he dead by misadventure. But he dead as hell, just the same.' Nathan, I have loss a party worker in Lionel. Now. In regards to certain things, and this is where Sarge come in. In regards to certain things, me and you can work out an arrangement whereby everybody involved will be happy. And I talking 'bout your son getting that Scholarship. Everybody can be happy. And I may as well tell you, Nathan, that I know that the Yankee-man up the hill trying to make trouble, if his son don't win over Boy. And the only problem he and his son have is that the son need Barbadian citizenship. I could fix-up the boy's citizenship. Just like that!'

Mr Alexander Bourne snapped his fingers, and gave Nathan a knowing wink.

'But,' he said, in a more sober and threatening voice, 'it would be a damn shame, wouldn't it, Nathan? To win a scholarship and have it take away, and given to the boy who come second. To forfeit a scholarship because you don't have a godfather in politics. It would be a damn shame. A godfather who have the power to file-away Henry Adams application for citizenship, and forget to sign it. A damn shame.'

The hint stiffened Nathan. Something like arthritis mixed with anger came over his body. Mr Alexander Bourne had one foot on the bottom step, and the other on the step above that. His eyes were turned away from Nathan. He was wiping his face with the large handkerchief.

Boy came through the gate, and seeing the two men, gave a little salute of courtesy. He was about to enter the house, when the representative said to him, 'I hear from reports, that you may be going-in for the Law, son. Your father was just telling me you have a chance for the big Scholarship.'

'Yes, sir.'

'And that Scholarship won't be bad, would it?'

'No, sir.'

'Good. I know your father will do the right thing to make-sure that you get what you deserve, under the circumstances.'

'Yes, sir.'

And Boy went inside. He wondered what foolishness his father was talking now, to put him in jeopardy.

'By the way, Nathan. We have Sarge down for Inspector o' Criminal Investigation. We know Sarge is a first-class detective. We know that. We don't want to be vindictive 'gainst no man. But we could always forget how good a man is. If that man vote against we. And we could as-easily give that promotion to a more lesser man. A man who vote for us. Understand? If we give a man a berry, that man have to play ball with us. Nathan, we even considering dropping the murder charge 'gainst Goalie, if we could guarantee peace and re-election. We considering all o' this, if we could guarantee that Seabert get a seat. And of course, if you use your influence and put a X beside my name! Lionel, poor foolish bastard, already dead and gone. And even if we play vindictive, it still can't bring-back the foolish son of a bitch to life! So, what you say, eh, Nathan?'

6

Clothes were sticking to the back. It was one hundred degrees in the shade. Where Boy was standing, with Henry Moore-Adams the Second and young Lascelles, under a tree, it was no less humid and hot.

It was four o'clock in the afternoon. The long black hearse, built in the days of funeral coaches, and when coaches were drawn by horses, was motorized now, was washed and greased with car polish, and freshened up for Lionel's last ride.

On this solemn journey, the hearse was decorated by flowers drawn in white delicate thin paint all over its glass panels. As Boy and his two friends watched it move over the roads, it looked like a fat black slug.

All the roads in the city were crowded. Jammed. Men and woman going home from work, or just going home, stopped; and some of them on bicycles rested one foot on the ground for balance, and they watched and waited until the procession passed them. Then they bobbed and weaved through the push of people, to overtake the procession, and stand and watch all over again.

Rain had fallen that morning. The road was clean. The air was clean. And the day was humid. It was almost impossible for Boy and Henry and young Lascelles to pass, so they decided to wait.

The mourners and some onlookers, who, like Boy could not continue home, walked in the procession.

'What a lovely funeral!' an old woman said; and made the sign of the Cross, two times, on her chest. 'Incidentally, who dead?'

'Lionel, the domino champion. He was a former gravedigger,' another woman told her.

'Well, I hope there is one leff-back, for his sake!'

The crowd overpowered her words, in case she had anything more to say, and soon she too disappeared from view.

Mr Alexander Bourne, Member of Parliament, was among the walking mourners. He was dressed in the same formal suit he had worn at his inauguration, ten years ago, when he was first elected from Sin-James East, to the House of Assembly. Beside him, walked his protégé, Seabert, in a new formal black suit, similar to the MP's. It was the piece of material he had promised to make into a suit for Sarge. He had added some glamorous touches to the suit to enhance its sombre appearance. The lapels and the tops of the pockets were trimmed in white.

Behind Mr Alexander Bourne walked Sarge, in official Police black serge, with brass and silver crossing his large chest and back. Sarge was not smiling. He was not mournful, either. Then, Nathan. In his black suit, mauve now through age and the mothballs which Boy had to put into it and already sweating under the armpits.

The Government had succeeded in organizing slick public relations to make the funeral effective and politically beneficial.

Every Cabinet minister was present. The Prime Minister himself led the double line of dignitaries; and the Government had decided that all the people at the funeral, especially the officials, were to get out of their cars about a mile from the main gate of the cemetery and walk through the streets.

'That way,' the Prime Minister had told them, at the executive meeting that morning, 'we will be showing our grief and our concern for the small man.'

They all laughed when he said this.

'And be-Christ, I don't want even to remind any of you bastards,' the Prime Minister went on, 'I do not want to say it more than one time. This Party is the party of the *small man*. It is a small-man party! And if any one of you here present, particularly one or two who want to be Prime Minister even before I resign, or dead, like Lionel, that stupid bastard . . . well, lemme tell you bitches, something, then! If any one o' you bastards in here now, do not understand why we walking that last mile *behind* Lionel's coffin, the stupid bitch who couldn't do nothing better than slam a blasted domino . . . well, ask the Member from the constituency of Westbury North! Ask him! He's getting more political licks down there, than what John

139

dream 'bout. This, therefore, gentlemen, is a *political funeral*. Lionel will be buried politically. So, we are walking that last mile outta pure politics. And be-Christ, when they drop Lionel's coffin inside that hole, after we walk-through the constituency of Westbury North, drench in sorrow, I want each and every one of you sons of bitches here-present to start crying. Weep. Cry. Weep like shite! There is going to be more votes swinging to our man, and to our Party, after this funeral, than what John write 'bout!'

And while the Prime Minister walked at the head of his Cabinet, followed by other party officials, all through the oppressive heat of the afternoon, the people shouted, 'Skipper! Skipper! *Skipper!*', in a crescendo of praise.

At one time, the Prime Minister nudged the MP for Westbury North, and whispered out of the left-hand corner of his mouth, with a wry smile on his face, 'What I tell you, this morning?'

The MP for Westbury North said, 'Remind me, Skipper, when we get back to party headquarters, to give you a report of a rumour I hear from a supporter who hear it from a reliable source. It is concerning the two members of the party who been trying to overthrow you. And another rumour is concerning Sarge.'

'We going-break their arse!'

The Prime Minister then took off his rimless spectacles. He mopped his high-brown face. And he smiled with the people cheering him.

'Skipper! Skipper! *Skipper!*'

His high brown skin was like polished rich leather. His tall body moved like a woman's, a dancer's, through the thickness of flesh exposed to the sun and the high smell of the crowd. He smelled their bodies and he smelled their perspiration; and their closeness to him offended his aristocratic sensibilities. He jerked his nostrils in disgust. And, immediately afterwards, he caught himself, and was smiling.

'Lick them at the polls, Skipper! Paint their arse in blows, on voting day! Mash-them-up.'

He put his spectacles back on and looked younger and more powerful.

140

The procession was now coming round the last corner before entering the main gate of the cemetery. There was a sidewalk in this stretch of the road, and the crowd grew larger, and space was tension, and the smells of the people and the smells of the Mayflower trees overhanging the cemetery, mixed themselves in one, strong, nauseating sensation.

'You walking with your gun?' the Prime Minister whispered out of the right-hand corner of his mouth to Mr Alexander Bourne. 'I don't like this crowd. I don't like these people. And I know that these blasted people don't really like me. You got your gun, just in case?'

'But Skipper! You know I does-sleep with my revolver in my hand!'

'I feel better, then.'

The main gate came to meet them. They had to force themselves through its narrower space. It took more than one hour for all the official mourners, and the people who had joined the cortège, to get inside the main gate.

The Government had instructed the Cemetery Board to close the gate immediately after the last person who looked like a 'real mourner' had got in. And this happened like clockwork. This Government was an efficient government. Everything worked. Political murders, firings from government posts, the slot-machines which the people branded 'one-hand bandits', and the misappropriation of government funds, all worked with a Mafia-like precision. Everything worked. Most unlike the Opposition Party.

The Prime Minister had personally ordered the members of his Security Force to pose as mourners and walk in the midst of the crowd. No chances were being taken. One hundred of the best; one hundred of the roughest; one hundred of the most loyal members of the Security Force had been assigned to this funeral.

Reporters and photographers were everywhere. The Government had already planned to put the funeral on the radio news that night, as the first item. Naturally, the Prime Minister would be on the front page of the morning newspaper. And the editor of *The Lighthouse*, the party organ, had been told to prepare a special edition and fill it with photographs of the funeral.

When enough of them had reached the side of the grave, the

Dean, dressed like damnation in black from head to foot; black covering his black body; with his spectacles of tortoise-shell shining in the dying light, began the service for the Burial of the Dead.

The Dean was already behaving, in his mind at least, as if he was the Lord Bishop of the country. He once uttered a wish about his aspirations loud enough, and in the well-chosen hearing of some Cabinet ministers. And the night he heard of Lionel's murder, he asked his wife, 'Now why it couldn't be the blasted Bishop? Instead of that fool?'

His wife said, 'As far's I know, the Lord Bishop does not play dominoes.'

The Dean liked large ceremonies. Official and with spit and polish. Military and social events brought out the best of his civility and propriety. On this occasion, he would use a voice most suited to the sombreness and the sadness of the afternoon.

The stickiness of the weather did not bother him, dressed as he was, in his heavy clerical black.

He began by speaking of love; of family; of something he called 'the family of love'; and 'the family of the people and politicians'; of politics and of power. Lastly, he mentioned the dead. But he stressed something which he called 'the politics of love'.

The Prime Minister knew already what the Dean would say in the eulogy. For the Prime Minister had told him what to say.

'*I am the resurrection and the life, said the Lord: he that believeth in me, though he were dead, yet shall he live. . . .*'

The Dean spoke the words as if they were his own poetry, and he moved his tongue over them and made them sound like honey.

'The Dean could preach *too* sweet!' Mr Alexander Bourne said. 'Too sweet, in truth!'

And at this point, the Prime Minister drew his handkerchief from his breast pocket, took off his rimless spectacles, and wiped his eyes. A sandfly had got into one. He held his head down, giving the impression and the posture of sadness. And the people saw him, and thought he was weeping for the dead.

'*I know that my Redeemer liveth, and that he shall stand. . . .*'

142

These words made Lionel's family start to cry. His woman, from whom he had two children, and with whom he had lived, was crying. His other woman, from whom he had one son, and with whom he did not live, she was crying. His three sisters, one of whom had come in from Booklyn, New York, by boat; his mother and father; and all the members of the Barbados Domino Players' Society, all dressed in black, with handkerchiefs of white dots on black silk jutting from their pockets, they were all crying.

But the loudest, most body-shaking crying, came from the woman with whom Lionel had lived.

She burst into an earth-rending weeping, raising her voice when the Dean emphasized a portion of the Scriptures, and she lowered it when he was almost whispering about 'brotherly love'. Her voice out-reached all the other voices, and climbed to the tops of the almond trees, in its sharp sadness. It was higher, clearer, and more unsettling than the shimmering dying light on the casuarina trees surrounding them.

Mr Alexander Bourne saw a photographer point his lens in his direction, and quickly started to wipe his sweating face with a large blue and white polka-dotted handkerchief. And he started to weep. The flash bulb exploded like a large firefly, before he could take the handkerchief away from his face.

Lionel's woman jumped into the air.

She threw her long silk blue dress above her thighs, in the gesture of grief. Her legs were luscious and thick. Mr Alexander Bourne noticed them. Some other men looked, liked what they saw, but put it out of their minds, for the time being. They understood.

They understood that Lionel, alas, no longer had all this beautiful black flesh within his grasp, within his hand, as he once used to hold the seven devastating domino seeds.

She was a woman of some class, of good body and looks, breeding and thighs; and Mr Alexander Bourne started to think of slamming, of slamming a domino; and could no longer concentrate on the sadness of the moment.

He moved over, and rested a comforting hand on her soft shoulder. And she screamed.

143

She screamed again. And the Dean had to pause in his reading of the Order for the Burial of the Dead. And then a hymn was sung.

Boy thought of his mother.

Safe home, safe home in port!
Rent cordage, shatter'd deck. . . .

'Hymn 609,' he told young Lascelles, who would appreciate it.

'Remind me,' the Prime Minister told his aide, Mr Alexander Bourne, while the people were singing, 'to call in the union boss of the Harbour Workers Union, when we get back to the office. I am going to get him to break-up that blasted strike.' He wiped his eyes. 'Sarge here?' His aide nodded. 'I want a tail put on Sarge. From today. You can't trust nobody, nowadays. Particularly, the Police!'

The singing went on, punctuated by the weeping and the lamenting, and finally by the hitting of the thick black soil on the brown coffin. The undertaker, the largest and most expensive 'duppy agent' in the country, and a member of the Government party, took off the silver-painted handles and other decorations from the coffin before it was lowered into the dark crevice. The mould pounded on the shined mahogany box, just as Lionel himself used to pound a 'key card', in a championship domino game.

As the mould fell, less loudly now as the crevice in the earth filled up as Lionel's box was being covered, the screaming and screeling and the wailing came to an end.

It was strange how unnoticeable it came. There was now only the moaning from the family, a sound like the painful, almost suppressed groan of a toothache. An occasional white handkerchief was taken out by a politician, and placed respectfully at the eyes.

The Prime Minister whispered to his aide, 'We got to set up a television station soon. State-owned, of course. All this *nice* feeling, this afternoon, should be captured with a coloured television camera. It would make nice news.'

144

The choir boys of the Cathedral, who had marched at the head of the procession, even in front of the row of the Prime Minister and his Cabinet, now began to sing the hymn without which no funeral ceremony in the country could end. 'Abide with Me.'

It had the same popular appeal as 'God Save The King'. The bass singers and the altos made poetry with the parts. The people sang as if they were in competition, and they tried to drown the voices of the choir, with their untrained and improvised tenors and altos. They sang this hymn as if they were at a wedding.

'Abide with Me' became, in the way they rendered it, like a national Sunday anthem. The people knew they had good reason to sing it. Without reservation. So, they lifted their voices to the tops of the almond trees and the casuarina trees, and shook the earth with a deep feeling.

> *. . . Shine through the gloom and point me to the skies*
> *Heaven's morning breaks, and earth's vain shadows flee*
> *In life. . . .*

And they paused at this phrase, for emphasis, but Boy who was at the edge of the funeral party thought they paused as if their own lives were in question, as they seemed to have caught the full meaning of 'life' in the short phrase.

> *. . . in death . . .*

And here too, they paused again, a gradual diminution of sadness was touched upon.

> *O Lord . . .*

Boy thought they were about to shout now, and compel God to listen, at least to listen to their miseries.

> *. . . abide with me!*

For days afterwards, the people who lived near the cemetery, and those from the village who had gone to the funeral as witnesses, and those in the Government, and in politics, said, 'What a *lovely* funeral Lionel had!'

And more than anything else, they remembered the singing of 'Abide with Me'. And especially the way the choir and the people sang the last line in the last verse.

'We send-off Lionel to his final resting place with one of the loveliest funerals for the year! And with such a pretty song! "Abide with me, Lord, abide with me. . . ." '

Mr Alexander Bourne wiped his face, and sang two more lines of the hymn.

'And that blasted coffin cost the Party two hundred dollars. The dearest coffin in the history of political democracy in this country. But we going-get back every penny, though!'

A deal involving Seabert, Mr Alexander Bourne, John Moore-Adams and Sarge was being discussed.

'Politicians is crooks. All o' them. Blasted snakes, if yuh know what I mean!'

Sarge said it so often, it was becoming like a chorus.

The date of the election was to be five days after the funeral. And the Government wanted the black book with the list, which they knew Sarge had. Sarge was now hearing from certain sources that his telephone was tapped. He heard he was being followed. And he heard that his good friend, Nathan, was being watched. Boy knew nothing of these schemes.

But Nathan became scared. He was scared for himself, and for his son.

Sarge was forced to look at the deal to see whether it was good for his family. He had two sons attending a secondary school. He had lots of women friends, and he felt that Mr Alexander Bourne would blackmail him on this.

'One of the women I been seeing belongst to the Harbour Workers Union. I hear the Guvvament breaking up that strike. You know Alexander Bourne is such a bastard, he bound to expose me, man,' Sarge said.

'We is men, man,' Seabert consoled him. 'More basic than being politicians, we is men.'

Seabert had brought the deal from party headquarters straight to Manny Batson's rum shop.

'This is the deal,' Seabert said, with a puffed-chest import-ance. 'We will give you . . . by we, I mean the Guvvament will give you leave with pay. Outta the country, of course. Beginning the day before voting day.'

The men were speechless.

'I remember,' Seabert went on, 'that years ago, you was talking 'bout going up to London-England, to do Law.'

'It would be the first time in all the history of this blasted country,' Nathan said, 'that a ordinary policeman ever qualify as barrister-at-law.'

'Think of the future, Sarge,' Seabert said. 'You may even be the first black Chief Justice.'

'He can't be the *first!*' Nathan said. 'He will be the second.'

The men were about to jump on Nathan's apparent foolish remark, when he held up his hand, and got their attention. He remembered what Boy had told him.

'The *first* Chief Justice of this great country who was black, was a former slave, by the name of Sir Connerd Reeves!'

'Conrad Reeves? Everybody knows that!' Seabert said, although he had forgotten the great man, among his countless clippings and photographs.

'I like that,' Sarge said. 'I like being first, all the time.'

'I know how ambitious you is, Sarge. If there was a different Guvvament in power, five years ago you could be Inspector o' Police.'

'They got we by the balls,' Nathan said. 'So, we got to play political football.'

'Nathan got a point,' Sarge said. 'But if yuh know what I mean, I would say that a man could promise a man a vote, but not even Godalmighty could make that man mark a X 'gainst that man's name, when voting day come. Seabert, you want this seat in Sin-James East? Well, tell we hummuch you are willing to pay for the seat?'

'As a unboughtable man myself, how much you willing to pay for this seat?'

Manny Batson looked Seabert full in the eye as he spoke.

'Nathan and me is the only two real bystanders in this deal. But they rope we in, nevertheless. They already start playing vindictive with me. Only this morning I start hearing rumours to the effects that the Guvvament going-close down my premises. They want to smoke-me-out. I is a small business-man. I don't have no reserve stock o' goods. Not one shite do I have in reserves. And I been selling rum and salt fish for twenty-something years. The Guvvament got that power over me. The Member o' Parlment, Godblindhim, I mean Alexander Bourne, is coming for an answer soon. I sensible-enough to realize that Bourne and the Guvvament playing from a flatform of power and pull. I calls it power and pull. Sarge, they got you by the balls.'

'So, what we can do?' Nathan wanted to know.

'Play-along. If only for the time being. And, Seabert, if you don't mind, we got to play-along with you, too. You is more one o' we, as an inhabitant o' this village, than you is one o' them, being a politician.'

'I been thinking so, too,' Seabert said.

'One thing 'bout this particular democracy we got. You could force a man to listen to you. You could force a man to go to the polls. You could buy him and seduce him with the biggest lorry-load o' corn beef and biscuits. Salt fish and rum. But be-Jesus-Christ, you can't hold that man's finger and mek him write X, be-Jesus-Christ, against *anybody's* name! Not if he don't want to mark that *X*. You see where I coming from?'

They all nodded.

Sarge buttoned up the four buttons of his grey undershirt. Nathan smiled, relieved. He was thinking of Boy. The examination for the Scholarship was a few weeks away.

It was suddenly quiet. The sea was at high tide.

'Well, Seabert can deliver the answer to Alexander Bourne, then. There is politicians and politicians. And some of the best don't run for office. Right?'

They shook hands. It was a conspiracy. They could hear the sea. And they could hear the large black car the moment it drew up in front of the rum shop. Mr Alexander Bourne was in the back seat. The chauffeur was standing beside the bonnet, talking to a woman. Seabert went to the car and talked to Alexander Bourne. The back room was cooler now. There was light in the room. Mr Alexander Bourne climbed the single step ahead of Seabert, and walked like a man reprieved from an expected sentence which he knew was going to be long, into the back room.

'I just saw your boy with a handful o' big books, Nathan,' he said. 'I sure would hate that boy not to get the Scholarship.'

Sarge smiled. Nathan did not.

148

Manny Batson had brought in a platter of pork chops. Mr Alexander Bourne put his hand into the platter and lifted one, the biggest he could see, to his mouth. Grease appeared at both corners of his mouth and he used his large white handkerchief to wipe it away. He washed down the pork chop with a snap of rum.

'Manny boy, if we play political football, I-myself will make-sure that it is possible for you to have more of these lovely pork chops for your customers. I-myself will make-sure that you never is in short supply. You will have reserves like any of the big merchants in the city.'

The men watched him as he talked and ate.

'Well.' He stopped chewing. His jaw was like a balloon. The mashed-up pork chop was still not swallowed. 'Well, have we reach consensus? We have a consensus, as we says at executive meetings?' The men just watched him. 'Nathan?'

'Consensus.'

'And Sarge?'

'Consensus reach.'

Mr Alexander Bourne breathed deeply. He swallowed the minced-up pork chop. 'Emmm!' he said, to clear his throat. 'Manny, where you stand?'

'Consensus.'

'Coppersettick!' Seabert said, and beamed.

'Well, look nuh,' Mr Alexander Bourne said, 'let we drink on it. Let we drink a little something, as man. Seabert Mascoll Nathaniel Marshall, Esquire, the next MP for Sin-James East, whiching as you know is butting and bounding on my constituency, is *my* man! So, let we drink to the next MP for Sin-James East! Hip-pip!'

'Hooray!'

'Pi-pi-pip!'

'Hooray!'

'I have never feel so good, in a long time,' Mr Alexander Bourne said, holding the snap-glass between index finger and big thumb. 'I have never feel so good in all my political career, as I feel this Thursday evening, drinking 'mongst friends and political allies. And I going-tell you-all something, now!' He refilled his snap-glass, took a sip, and said, 'Nathan, your son

149

don't have one blasted problem in regards to that Scholarship if
you come on board. *When*. Not, if. Seal and sign? Seal and sign!
The Scholarship is his! And Sarge, the minute you hand-over
that black book, rightthatveryminute! Rightthatveryminute,
we handing you a first-class cabin ticket on a Canadian lady-
boat, and you going-up to London-England and read Law! I
have never feel so great! Hi-pi-pi-pi-pip!'

'Hooray!'

Everything that had wheels, everything that could move,
whether it was a donkey cart or a dilapidated car, was
conscripted by the politicians and their supporters and thrown
into the election campaign by the two main parties. Some
politicians who insisted that they were 'independent' men, who
belonged to what they called 'grass-roots' political movements,
and who had no more than three hundred supporting members
amongst them, these independent candidates had to cut and
contrive their resources of transportation as best they could.

But it was the Government Party which raked up everything
on wheels, in sight. Their supporters went into garages and
paid motor mechanics to resurrect piles of tin and rubber, and
put engines into them, and got them on the road, in order to
spread a new political gospel designed to get them back in
power.

Their slogan was LICKS, LICKS LIKE PIGEON-PEAS. Every
household served pigeon peas and rice and baked pork, on
Sundays. The slogan caught on like an epidemic.

'When we get-back-in,' the Prime Minister told a strategy
meeting for candidates, at a hide-away beach house, 'when we
regain power for the second time, *anybody* at all, who didn't
vote for us, going-see *something!* Their arse going-be hot! If they
didn't vote for us, they *dead!* And if they're not dead, they're
not going to eat. So, they may as well be dead.'

Things on wheels moved all over the country, in the city, in
back alleys, even in those areas where the few tourists lay and
sunned and sinned. No area where more than five persons lived
was spared from the political meetings and the indoctrination of
the Government. Their last political message, spread from all
the platforms in the country, was HELP FOR THE SMALL MAN.

But the party got most of its money from the big-business class and the plantation owners.

The best calypsonians, the best singers in the country, were cajoled to compose 'hot tunes' on the spot, on the spur of the moment. These songs were recorded in unprofessional haste, and they went through the land, blaring from loudspeakers. Everybody knew the political songs by heart. The children felt the country was enjoying a long school holiday. There was festivity and music and dancing in the streets. Boy was engaged at the height of this easy living, with studying for the Scholarship. And there was much rum drinking.

The rum shops and the shops that sold 'goods' throughout the land were suddenly stocked with foodstuff. Nobody knew where it came from. Only one month before the election date was announced, the Minister of Consumer Food went on radio and read off a list of 'scarce items'. He made it sound like a list of the dead at sea, on land and in the air, which the BBC World Service read every night during the War.

'Corn beef scarce. The price is raise by twenty per-cent. Soap scarce. Soap-prices raise by fifteen per-cent. Cement scarce. Cement prices, because of shortages and because of the recent hurricane in the Carbean, and because of Cuba. . . .'

'That is what he actually said? "Because o' Cuba?" '

'. . . we can't expect no more building in the construction industry, nor no development in this country. Not quite yet.'

And now, in the heat of campaigning, men and women waited like piranhas in a starved pool of shallow gifts, these men and women who were the village politicians.

These men and women filled the rum shops throughout the village, and stood on the steps of the shops and cursed and shouted and decided ahead of voting day, which party would form the Government. Those who disagreed with them, with the prevailing opinion, had their family history exposed in public, in the vilest, most vitriolic, and sometimes in the most humorous detail. Secrets of sex, petty crime and of avariciousness were exposed to the entire village.

Those who yearned for this gossip, those who wanted to put somebody 'in his place', all they had to do was attend a political meeting and listen to the politicians who behaved like holy-rollers, like revivalists on the platforms. Or they would congregate the morning after, at the public standpipe, and fill their curiosity as they filled their buckets with the slowly-running clear fresh water. A lot of people were being put into their places at election time. It was a national pastime, like the singing of hymns on Sundays.

The shops were filled with food. Corn beef went down in price. Most of it was given away by the shopkeepers themselves. The politicians whom they supported paid the bill. The two big political parties got hold of the largest of these small rum-shop owners, and paid them and their political pimps and 'yard-fowls' lots of money; they, in turn, gave away tins of imported corn beef. *Fray Bentos*. That was the best brand. Some pimps and 'yard-fowls', who could not be put into their places, ordered Scotch whisky to show how important they were, instead of rum.

In these last hectic days of campaigning, whisky became the national drink. Men drank rum for three and three-quarter years, and praised their God in their drunkenness, and would think of no other liquor strong enough to bring out the devils in the body and in the mind. But by the last quarter of the fourth year, approaching the time of election campaigning, it had to be Scotch whisky.

'Man, we drink whisky like pure water, offa Seabert the politician, last night!' a man in Manny Batson's rum shop said. 'And we haven't yet pushed a blasted hand in a blasted pocket to pay for none! A real freeness!'

And the man tottered off to another freeness, to another rum shop, frequented and sponsored by the candidate he knew he would vote for.

'A political freeness!' his friend had agreed. And hand on drunken shoulder, they had faded into the night.

Round-necked shirts with short sleeves, with the slogan HELP FOR THE SMALL MAN, dyed red in the colour of the Government, suddenly appeared in the village. And little three-paged books with SMALL MAN written on them, were scattered in the roads, in the streets, in the avenues and in the alleys from the windows of the rescued vehicles that travelled throughout the country like crabs on the scavenged beach. Men who could drive, men who didn't have drivers' 'licents', made big money, good money, transporting politics.

The opposition party accused the Government of accepting aid from the Amurcans and the Canadians. They accused them of not loving the small man. They accused them of the reverse.

One well-known, popular politician of the opposition, said from a platform, 'The Guvvament have, to wit, imported, brought-in all these shirts and pamphlets from Amurca. Canada senning-in and senning-down money by the plane-load. And thereby, this murdering Guvvament have put the small man, and the small-man businessman outta jobs, and into starvation and into hardships. My information tells me, ladies and gentlemen, that this Guvvament is allowing foreign intervention to the tune of thirteen thousand dollars a day in foreign currency!'

A heckler shouted back from the dark fringe of the huge crowd, 'And why you-all don't thief some, too?'

The crowd exploded in jeers.

The Government party accused the opposition of having their campaign materials printed in Britain. 'The opposition is nothing more than Churchillian socialists!' the Prime Minister said one night.

And a heckler at that meeting screamed, 'And your Guvvament got hammers and sickles in your headquarters offices!'

That was the end of the speech. Bottles and rock-stones came from all directions, like waves in a storm. Men and women scampered. Children shrieked. Boy ran and hid under a parked lorry. The platform was ripped apart. And when the police arrived at the scene, it looked as if a storm had passed over the grass-piece. The police had been drinking rum in a bar nearby. They were not ambitious to save the Prime Minister who had called the police 'bastards'.

The Prime Minister ordered an investigation to look into 'police abnormalities, infelicities, and irregularities'. He threatened the next day to dismiss the Commissioner of Police. Sarge watched and laughed.

7

The campaign was in its final day. People started to talk in whispers. Fear replaced the feeling of 'freeness'. The campaign literature, the corn beef, the free rum, the freenesses and the noise and the singing took on a new form.

Reprisals now took the country in a tight grip, and by storm; and transformed it for the day of voting into a whispering state of spite. People in jobs sponsored and given to them by politicians walked about like mummies. Others feared they would be fired. Some civil servants were already seconded to dead-end positions; some demoted; some wrote to cousins in Panama and in Amurca, for help and for sponsorship; and for visas to emigrate. And fights and violence and the appearance of rumours and guns and knives became the talk of the village, in the remaining time.

Just as Nathan stepped out of his house around eight o'clock one night, to go to the rum shop, his wife said to him, 'Be careful, man. Something *bad* going-happen, Nathan. Be careful.'

The examination room was hot. And humid. Deathlike and uncomfortable. All the windows in the hall at the College were open. And still, there was no breeze.

Boy looked out the window that faced and framed the playing field. The College's star batsman, a boy of sixteen years, was at the practice nets. His whites were blinding in the afternoon sun. Boy watched him make two strokes. The first one went through the covers. And the second one went towards point. They were correct, sharp, savage and keen as a surgeon's knife.

To get to England and Oxford, or Cambridge, he had to win the Scholarship: that is to say, come first in the entire island. England was still on his mind, although he had promised his uncle to go to Canada, because his uncle had promised Canada and university fees.

'No Thorne begs the stinking bitches in any Guvvament for money to pay for education!'

Yes . . . the only way he could leave for England, in spite of his uncle, to read Law at Oxford, was by winning this Scholarship. The five-dollar money orders his aunt in the Canal Zone had been sending every month could not, even if they were collected for twelve months, with compound interest, pay for the passage to England. If he refused to go to Canada, would his uncle pay for England?

He had overheard what Mr Alexander Bourne had told his father. He had understood the threat. He was old enough to know the threats of politicians. Mr Bourne's words now became mixed with his translation of the Distinction Latin Unseen. He became temporarily unsettled. He had to cross out the last sentence he wrote on his examination paper.

Boy glanced at young Lascelles sitting four desks away, and at Henry at the end of the same row. Both of them looked confident.

Henry was now talking about studying at the Massachusetts Institute of Technology. Henry was always using high-sounding names. All the places he wanted to go to had imposing names, which he equated with their high-sounding education.

'Massachusetts Institute of Technology?' young Lascelles asked. 'Sounds more like a prison, an institution, to me.'

'I'm really glad I wasn't born in this stupid country!' Henry told him.

'Henry is an Amurcan,' young Lascelles had said one day. 'A bright Amurcan amongst very bright black Englishmen.'

The breeze came through the open windows like a heavy leaden oppression. Shirts were opened at the neck. Ties pulled down. And loosened, away from the parched necks. And in the silence of this trembling concentration, only the scratching of fountain pens was heard. And an occasional cough.

Boy looked out of the window to see the red ball come over the trees on the edge of the field, and break the pane in the large glass window. The ball rolled into the examination room. The boys roared with applause. And no sooner had the ball stopped on the hard polished floor, near the bottom of the platform, than the bell rang.

Time had come. One life had come to a scratching halt. . . .
Just as the ball had rallied to a stop on the clean floor.

'*Time!*' the Invigilator announced.

8

ELECT SEABERT MASCOLL NATHANIEL MARSHALL
A SMALL MAN LIKE YOU.

This was his poster nailed on to the rum shop.

Manny Batson had capitulated. There was a mug-shot of
Seabert in the middle of the poster. His mouth was wide open.
And his eyes looked fierce. In his hand was a rolled-up
newspaper. He had forgotten to smile. Since he entered
politics, he stopped smiling. The newspaper, Boy felt, was
placed in his hands by the party's photographer, to give him an
educated appearance. And the photograph did him more justice
for handsomeness, than he had in real life.

Seabert loved his posters. Everywhere he went, he gave one
to whoever would take it. The posters covered the rum shop
like wallpaper. And in his own tailor shop, in which he had put
a 'prentice to run things', while he was campaigning, almost
one wall was covered by his new political personality and
presence.

Boy thought he was a lazy campaigner. More than once, Mr
Alexander Bourne, Seabert's mentor, had to punish him with
remonstrations in front of the men, in the rum shop.

'Seabert, you's sitting down on your arse, selling coals to
Newcastle!'.

It is late. A clock somewhere in the almost deserted rum shop
has just struck four times. And in a few more hours, Seabert's
fate will have been sealed.

'When I get in,' he tells them, finishing his hopes in that short
sentence of fierce syntax, 'when I get in'.

And he brandishes a poster in Sarge's face. He does not feel he has converted the converted. For he is more comfortable talking to Sarge and Nathan and Manny Batson and people he knows, than going into people's backyards and telling them about running water and 'lectricity.

His daughter Patricia canvassed for him night and day. Amurca, a new Singer sewing machine and perhaps a husband beckoned and seemed to propel her legs, and add strength to her normally weak constitution.

And Nathan, who was not sure that the deal involving his son, and the purchase of the house from John Moore-Adams would come off, all of which Mr Alexander Bourne reminded him *would*, Nathan promised day and night to work for Seabert; and day and night, as he left the house for the rum shop, and to *talk* about helping to elect Seabert, his wife told him, 'Something *bad* is going to happen. Be careful, Nathan.'

Sarge was convinced now that he was being followed from the day after the funeral. He was in a constant predicament of jitters and nervous allegiance. He did not know what to do. Everywhere he went, whether he was on duty directing traffic on the small black and white box in the city, or off-duty, drinking rum in Manny's shop, he felt he was being shadowed by a Security Force man. Sarge planned and plotted.

'He will get a stiff cut arse from me. Whoever he is! And whenever I catch him!'

But the Security Force man was never caught. And the day seemed unwilling to come that would deliver Sarge from his judgement. And now, it was early morning, voting day.

Boy noticed that although the tempo of things had stepped up, it was still thick. The opposition party had geared itself for a mortal fight. It was survival, or death. Its campaign literature appeared side by side of the Government's, overnight; and within an hour of its appearance, it miraculously disappeared. No one knew what had happened to it.

Boy was home when he heard the Prime Minister's voice on the radio. He felt his voice had a tinge of laughter in it.

'My Government does not,' he said, 'will not, and never shall condone vandalism. My Government is not a vindictive Government.'

157

The same words were listened to in the rum shop, and a loud cheer broke out. Seabert was the one who cheered loudest, caught as he was converting the converted.

'My Government has not, will not, and never shall cause *any* man, in particular a *small man*. . . .'

A louder roar went up in the shop.

And then all of a sudden, something happened.

Great, deep-chested laughter leaked through to the entire country, through the Rediffusion radio speakers. They all could hear and recognize the Prime Minister's voice saying, 'These kiss-me-arse poor people that we have in this country must really think I am an arse not to hang Goalie for killing one of my supporters. . . .'

And just as suddenly, the full blare of 'God Save the King' came on. But the people had already heard. Boy could not believe it. His mother, who had been rocking and listening, was frozen in the chair.

The Prime Minister's voice smote them dumb. They could not believe he would talk to them so. They did not believe he hated them so. And some of the men in the rum shop, through shock, argued that it was not his voice. It was sabotage, they said.

The next day, the general manager of the radio station was fired. The programme manager, the interviewer, the script assistant and the technical operator were placed on one month's leave, without pay.

'I always knew he was a snake!' Sarge said.

'Sabotage,' Seabert said. 'Them blasted radio announcers should be shot. Or fired!'

This was the time for being common. And crude. And plain. And the representative of their village of Sin-James West, Mr Alexander Bourne, carried this feeling of 'commonness' everywhere he went, on this last day.

'Call me *Bournie*. I is a small man, like you. A *personna non greater*, like any of you, at that! Bournie to you, Sarge. As man!'

And whenever he met Sarge, he would say, 'Sarge, I am in your hands. You have me hand-cuff. My whole political future is in your two hands, Sarge. We have a deal. As man!'

Within one hour of the Prime Minister's radio broadcast, Mr Alexander Bourne, caught literally with his pants down, in the home of one of his women, promptly considered it to be political savvy to pass through his constituency, meaning to pass by the rum shop and to see for himself how much damage had been done by the prime ministerial snicker.

Alexander Bourne knew that the rum shop was the hub of awareness in things other than politics.

The woman's house was up the hill, near where John Moore-Adams lived. He had got his chauffeur to drop him off, and he had sent the tired, overworked man back to head-quarters, to be on guard, and also to be able to pin down the chauffeur in case of emergency. He also wanted to get him out of the way.

Such an emergency had arisen. The chauffeur had just returned to the woman's house, with an urgent message from the Prime Minister and a file. And as he was driving Mr Alexander Bourne down the hill, they saw Sarge entering the rum shop.

'I have something confidential to show you, Sarge.'

Sarge automatically went on his guard.

Unknown to Sarge and to Mr Alexander Bourne, the Prime Minister, realizing the broadcast error, had decided to do something brave, something rash, reckless, to try to repair the unfortunate slip. He sent a file to Alexander Bourne. The Prime Minister emptied the contents of the red folder. The folder was empty. CONFIDENTIAL: EYES ONLY was marked on it. He knew Alexander Bourne. And he knew the bureaucratic ways of the Police. And he knew that of all his political colleagues, he could trust Alexander Bourne's political savvy. He was aware of the man's ambition, his greed, and his love of power. So, he sent the empty file with a message.

But Mr Alexander Bourne knew, even before the chauffeur arrived, catching him in the middle of coming, that he had to go down to the rum shop, and test the waters himself.

'This is pure dynamite, Sarge! And confidential as hell.'

He saw his chance to kill two birds with one file; and he managed to get Sarge's full attention, with little difficulty.

'Three men. Only three men in the whole blasted Guvvament

have ever seen this file. The PM, the Governor, and your humble servant. I intend to show you this piece o' dynamite. This is a eyes-only document.'

He put his arm round Sarge, and led him to the large, black Humber Hawk, his official car. The chauffeur was taking a nod, with his head resting on the open window. Alexander Bourne reached inside, beside the exhausted man, and took out a large black briefcase. He snapped the locks open with a great flourish, and took out the red file folder.

Sarge's eyes rested on the red, then on the official stamp, and finally, on CONFIDENTIAL: EYES ONLY. He became stiff, and was beside himself with excitement. He himself knew the damage to careers that such files contained. Alexander Bourne had stuffed pieces of black stationery paper, and hastily torn pieces of newspaper pages from his briefcase, into the file. In his own handwriting, he had written on the cover of the file, 'Sargeant Joseph Crawford's. AKA, Sarge, promotion to Inspector of Police Criminal Investigation Department, CID.'

The light outside the shop was bad. But not bad enough for Sarge's eyes to see in one red flash, that he had been given back his rank and that the threat of a forced holiday had apparently been forgotten.

Alexander Bourne wet his large thumb and second finger, before he turned the pages. He held his other hand over the true subject of the file, and he covered the contents page. He showed Sarge only his name. Sarge was impressed. And the moment the MP thought Sarge saw his name, he snapped the file shut.

He put it back into the briefcase, and locked it. He put the key into his waistcoat pocket.

'I just demonstrate to you who your real friends is. As man!'

'And let me say now, to your face, Bournie man, and man-to-man, that I had you wrong. I had you wrong wrong wrong.'

'I looks after my people. I-myself, Alexander Bourne, is a man of the people. All that I asking you, Sarge, is to put that little X in the right place, when you vote for Seabert. And that is the right place.'

He moved away from the car. The chauffeur was snoring.

'And when you in the right mood, man, you could always

hand-over that little black book to me, man. No hurry. And no fuss.'

Sarge was convinced, and happy. Alexander Bourne walked with his arm round Sarge's shoulder, and led him into the back room. Nathan and Seabert were holding court. Nathan had been drinking heavily, and falling asleep between snaps, and Seabert was rehearsing his maiden speech.

'I see, my learned friend,' Alexander Bourne said to Seabert, 'that you are still amongst the converted!'

Corn beef and biscuits were on a plate; and two large bottles, one with water and the other with rum on the table.

'Sarge just seen the light. Sarge just seen his name in print.'

'As man!' Sarge said.

And he smiled. He had something on Seabert and on Nathan and on Manny.

Mr Alexander Bourne smiled to himself. It was so easy for a politician with savvy to fool even a top detective. But he became uncontrite, and wiped away the smile within, when he realized that he had made a career of fooling people. All he had done was to show them a red file.

The true subject of the file he had just shown to Sarge, bore the subject: *'Government discussions with various farmers engaged in raising chickens, ducks and fowls.' To be dealt with later* was written below that.

9

The shadows were crisp and well-formed. The leaves on the mahogany trees and the casuarina trees were cleaned by the formation of dew. The air had a freshness that was similar to an early morning bath in the sea. And the sea was calm, the waves at peace, and what movement there was was like a thin skin peeled back across the vast surface.

Only further out where some fishing boats were conquering the scarceness of fish, Nathan amongst them, was there any semblance of a ripple. The sun was already out. But its heat had not yet descended upon the people.

Boy was at the beach. He had arrived so early that he was in time to see his father throw the seine net into the waking waves, to catch a few sprats. And the sprats apparently still sleeping, Nathan decided to drop that annoyance, and jump into his boat. Boy helped him push *Labour Blest* into the deeper water.

Boy was one of those gallant pioneers who sought the glimpse of first crabs returning from their nightly whoring and scratching, on the vacuumed beach, where the sand was shining and wet at this hour and looked like pearl, and where the few donkeys in the village were being bathed by their owners. It was still too early in the morning to shout, as small boys and girls always did just before they rushed into the oncoming waves.

There were hardly any waves. Just a wholesale moving of the body of water, in and out.

And when he came out of the sea, and walked the short distance home, the road was already full of people. But it was quiet. Too quiet to be normal. No one was talking. No one was quarrelling. No one was relating the tales of the previous night. No one was talking about the election. It was voting day. And still, there was this strange feeling, this contentment, as if it was Sunday.

It was voting day. Boy got ready for College and left. And before he left, Rediffusion was playing hymns and sacred music. But the moment he was away from the village, the sun came out in full blast.

John Moore-Adams parked his large American car in front of Nathan's house. He blew his horn loud and long, in the first seven notes of a popular song. Nathan recognized the notes. It was the way people blew their horns in the village.

John Moore-Adams was in a bad mood. He blew the car horn again.

Beep! bee-bee-bee-beep! Beep-beep!

'That blasted Yankee!'

Nathan walked slowly, insolently through the darkened front-house, out on to the cement steps of the verandah, swung the two halves of the door open, continued to be noisy as if he already owned the house, and stood at the front gate. The shining, large Amurcan car was parked right before him. He could not move, even if he wanted to. This blasted ugly car, Nathan said to himself; why can't he drive a nice little English car, like everybody else?

The shine on the car matched the broad grin on John Moore-Adams' face.

'I say, Nate! Got a cold beer in the frig?'

Beer was not popular in the village. Nathan hated his request for beer, and his Amurcan accent.

'I come to talk to you, boy.'

Nathan hated even more his habit of calling him 'boy'. No one, in all his life, ever called a man, boy. Certainly not like that.

'Come in, Mr Adams. Come in.'

'Lemme park this automobile properly. Christ, Nate, you see all the confusion this elections bringing to this peaceable neighbourhood? Every goddamn night, automobiles passing my property, and won't let me catch my goddamn rest. Goddamn. All these niggers running all over the place, playing politicians.'

He parked the car a little further away from the gate, but no more properly. He then revved up the engine as if he was about to race off; turned the ignition off, and slid out from behind the wheel. The wheel was on the wrong side, Nathan noticed. On the left side. The automobile carried the caution, LEFT HAN DRIV. A D was now missing along with the E.

'How ya like the automobile? Cost me fifty bucks this morning, already. Took she in to get the air-conditioning fixed. One o' those niggers tried to fix it. The niggers in this place who pretend they know mechanics! Nate, the best goddamn mechanics I left back in the States, in Amerrica.'

When John Moore-Adams stood up, Nathan realized what a huge man he was. He was about six feet five. And he must have weighed two hundred and sixty pounds. Nathan thought of Joe Louis. But John Moore-Adams was not handsome.

'You got a beer in the ice-box?'

All these strange words, Nathan thought.

'I must say Nate, you keeps this place like it's your own. Can't complain about you lowering my property value. No siree!'

Nathan could not decide whether he liked John Moore-Adams' Amurcan clothes. They were soft and clean and lightweight. Nathan could smell his aftershave lotion. It seemed

as if John Moore-Adams had bathed in it. In a better time of
mood and relationship, on one of his trips from Amurca, he had
given Nathan a large bottle of aftershave. Mennen. Nathan
liked the sound of the name. And he enjoyed that smell for
months. And when the bottle was empty, he poured Limacol
into it, and kept the bottle when there was no more Limacol.
The bottle still stood in his bedroom.

'Nate, boy? When last you heard from your wife's sister?
Goddamn! This place's kept finer than I thought. How long you
been living here? Don't tell me. I know. Can't expect me to live
in this house and the house up the hill at the same time, can ya?
No, siree. This goddamn humidity.'

The villagers called it 'the heat'.

'Worse goddamn humidity than the one I left back in
Brooklyn, States-side. 'Specially during the summer.'

'Well, good morning, Mr Adams!'

It was Nathan's wife, greeting the landlord, as if she was
singing a joyous hymn. In her heart, she was seeing Johnny, the
man with gold in his teeth and on eight out of ten fingers. She
continued to smile at this large man standing before her,
demanding a cold beer, as if her home was a restaurant, or a rum
shop. But she had class. And vengeance. And the nastiness
which superior birth and genteel upbringing can supply in
situations like this.

She was prepared for him. In her hands was a mahogany
serving tray with the map of the country cut out in the middle,
in cedar. On the tray, which she held like a national treasure,
were two beers in two large glasses. The bottles from which she
had poured the beer remained on the tray. She knew what she
was doing. For she had, by this casual and unnecessary gesture,
made the gesture itself into a more calculating statement than it
appeared. The beer was Tennants. Imported English beer.

Froth hugged the rims of the glasses. The glasses had
Guinness Stout printed on them.

She was telling Mr Adams known to her only as Johnny, that
Nathan might be poor, might be a tenant of his, but that he had
class. This was her point. He was her landlord, only for the time
being.

'Have one, Mr Adams.'

164

She said it as a bred and born Thorne would have said it.
'Good morning, ma'am.'
Mr Adams was the only person who called her 'ma'am'.
It must be another one of his strange Amurcan customs, she always said. But she liked the 'ma'am'.
He held the glass she offered him to his lips, and when he took it away, the glass was empty. The froth from the beer was now a white moustache. He cleaned it with a multi-coloured handkerchief. He wiped the sweatband of his white straw hat, wiped his forehead with the handkerchief, and then gave her back the glass. 'Ahhhh! Nothing beats this humidity like a cold beer!'
'Another one, Mr Adams? You like Tennants imported beer?'
'Don't mind if I do, ma'am.'
She left him, shaking her head at Mr Adams' strangeness.
'A goddamn fine woman, Nate!' he said, when she was out of earshot. 'Sometimes, I feel I need one of these fine Bajan women to keep my bed warm, nights. But between me and you, Nate, I don't trust them further than I can goddamn throw them. With one exception. And she's in the Canal Zone, in Panama. She was such a goddamn fine woman! But these women here, all they want is your goddamn money. But I'll be goddamn, Nate, boy. I worked goddamn hard to 'cumulate the property I have. And it costs bucks to send my boy to the College. How's your boy?'
'You came to talk about political matters? Well, let we talk in here.'
He offered him one of the Berbice chairs in the dark fronthouse. When he sat down, Mr Adams' chair cried out. It had never borne such weight before.
'Level with me, Nate. What's your opinion of all this goddamn political stuff? I hope you're not mixed up in politics? Worst thing for a black man. All this political stuff. I'm goddamn glad I loss the nomination to Seabert. Back in Amerrica we coloured people stay *far* from all this goddamn political stuff. Best policy for a coloured man to have. Live and let live. Hear no evil, see no goddamn evil, speak *nothin'*. Not a goddamn thing!'
Nathan's wife brought more beer. She excused herself and went into the backyard where she was washing.
John Moore-Adams took off his straw hat, placed it gingerly down on an empty chair, loosened his light-coloured tie,

unbuttoned two buttons on his white shirt, and unbuttoned his white jacket. His trousers were white. And the seams in them looked like razor-blades. He dressed always like a man of means. And he was a man of means. A big man in the village. Gold glittered on four fingers of both hands, and on his wrist. He wore the biggest gold watch Nathan had ever seen. When he smiled, which he seldom did, gold glittered between his teeth.

He seemed always to be impatient about time. Time he had. Time he had on his hand. And time he wasted. Wherever he was, he was always flinging his left hand near his face, and looking for his watch. To look at it better, he sometimes pushed back his shirt-sleeve. Now, after he looked at it, he seemed to have forgotten that he had done so. And he looked at it again.

Nathan found his antics intriguing. He himself never owned a wrist watch. He was a fisherman. He told the time by the sun, by day; and at night, if it was necessary, by the BBC radio news, and by the buses passing in front of his house. But the noise from the nearby rum shop was his best barometer of time.

John Moore-Adams looked at his watch again.

'What you know about Sarge? Sarge lived in Amerrica for a time. Ya know that, don't ya? But what kind o' man you know Sarge to be, Nate?'

'Sarge?'

Nathan took out his cigarettes. He didn't offer one to Mr Adams. Mr Adams was a Jehovah Witness. Beer and cigars were his only human failings, he said. He said he drank beer on Saturdays and Sundays.

'You ask me about Sarge? Well, Sarge been a sergeant in these parts for more than ten years. When Sarge was first transfer down here, he was a corporal. We see the progress that Sarge make as the progress that the village make. Sarge is part of the village. But you asking me a political question, isn't it? So, you expecting a political answer. Well, let me see. . . .'

'Chew on this, in the meantime. That goddamn nigger, Bourne, came to my place with a cock-and-bull story concerning a deal about my son and the Scholarship. He will see to it, if I support Seabert. Support Seabert?'

'But Seabert is a leader in this village!'

'Seabert is a goddam tailor! And a bad one at that!'

'He still have leadership qualities, Mr Adams. A man have leadership qualities to lead the people of this village, if that man can drink a lotta rum, and have a lotta women. And if he have a big prick in his pants. *This* is leadership in this village.'

Nathan grabbed his trousers at the fly, in a tight fist, for a brief dramatic moment. '*This* is leadership in this village.'

And immediately afterwards, he regretted that he had given the demonstration.

'So, why my son can't get the Scholarship, with my playing political football? Because he wasn't really born here?'

'Far's I know, Mr Adams, the Scholarship was set up for people born here by the Englishmen who rule over this place, even before me and you was born. It is like history, or tradition.'

'Well, I'll be goddamn. I was born here. And that's good enough to make my son born here, too. Ya know, Nate. I left this place exactly because of this foolishness. Nate, do you forget I was a gardener? I paid my dues, Nate. A man can't be no goddamn man, if he don't pay his dues. And I will shoot any politician, be he the Prime Minister, Bourne, Seabert, any-goddamn-one o' them, if they make my boy pay dues he don't deserve to pay.'

He looked at his watch with a grand flourish of his hand. He was angry. He sipped his beer.

'This brings me back to Sarge. I'll be goddamn if I had to depend on the poor-arse niggers in this village, to buy me a beer or a hot dog.'

Nathan wondered why he used the word, 'hot dog'. There were no hot dogs in the village.

'I'm proud to be an Amerrican. I am a Barbadian by birth. But my goddamn heart and allegiance is Amerrican. Those goddamn Stars-and-Strikes! Nate, I'm gonna tell ya. If tomorrow, this country was at war with Amerrica, I'll be killing more goddamn Barbadian niggers than what you could shake a stick at! And I'm gonna tell you something else. I am a Mason. Been a goddamn Mason since I lived in Amerrica. And Masons is people who stick together. Hence, Sarge. I backed Sarge's application to be a Mason. And between me and you and the doorpost, if any politician, Bourne or any of them, go through with their plan to assassinate Sarge, all hell will break loose in this village!'

167

Nathan was speechless. He almost dropped his glass of beer. He coughed to clear his throat of the cigarette smoke.

'Assassinate, Mr Adams?'

'Where've you been?'

'*Assassinate?*'

'Shit, Nate. Don't play dumb with me.'

He smiled. Gold glimmered.

'This is why I don't meddle in the politics of this goddamn poor-arse place. Any man who meddles in politics, and don't know how to play political football, and don't know what to expect from politics, is a goddamn fool. In politics, you have to kill you goddamn mother to stay in power. That is politics. A rough goddamn game.'

'But . . . but, in my very hearing, I hear Mr Bourne promise to. . . .'

'Assassinate, Nate.'

'. . . make Sarge an Inspector of. . . .'

'You's a goddamn chump, Nathan.'

'But, Mr Bourne. . . .'

'Should be shot, Nathan. Should be shot! That nigger should be shot!'

He flourished his wrist again. Nathan hoped he was about to leave. But he settled himself down with his unfinished beer.

'And nobody told you that that nigger went to the Headmaster of the College to ask that your boy should be pushed aside for the Scholarship?'

'Jesus Christ, *no!* If I had a gun!'

'And you sitting down here on your black arse expecting pennies from heaven, and from Mr Bourne?'

'Mr Adams, I been begging this Guvvament for years now, to lend me some money to repair my fishing boats. You think the Guvvament would notice me? I only get involve in these elections because of Seabert. And Mr Bourne. Mr Bourne promise me, sitting in the very same chair you sitting in now, and in front of my wife, that when he get re-elected, I will have the loan for the fishing boats. But now, you telling me a different story. You telling me I can't trust even my mother.'

'Take that murderer, Goalie. He's still living in caves. . . .'

'But how you know all these things, Mr Adams?'

'Nate, when a man lived in Amerrica, he learns a few things. One of them things is information. If you have information, not one goddamn soul, living or dead, could touch you. Information is power, Nate.'

'But-but. . . .'

'A Mason is a man who gotta know things. 'Smatter of fact, I'll tell ya what I'll do for you, Nathan. One o' these nights, I'm gonna take you. And if ya like what ya see, then you can make up your goddamn mind. Ain't no goddamn politician gonna give you nothing for nothing. Instead o' you sitting down in your living-room, by your hearth in the evening, drinking a cold beer, you're running over the place, attending political meetings, and backing a nigger who's got a knife up your arse. And another one up your boy's arse! Nate, wake up, boy.'

Nathan was now completely peeved at the chastising. And the word, *boy*, grated him. And so too did the word *nigger*.

'But I didn't know.'

'Is in your goddamn place to *know*.'

'I don't know how to thank you, Mr Adams.'

'Get your goddamn hands on some money, Nate! and come and see me. And start things rolling about purchasing this goddamn old house off my hands, Nate. Or lemme give it to Moo-Moo's mother to live in!'

'You mean that, Mr Adams?'

'When I arrived, I had made up my goddamn mind to give you notice to vacate, Nate. But during our little chit-chat, and as I watch these photos on your centre table, I see my first love. Ella. Nate, I'm still in love with Ella. Ella's photo brought back memories. Sad memories. And good memories. It is them memories that make me change my mind about you. In Amerrica, and in the Masons, I've learned a few things, Nate.'

But John Moore-Adams was thinking also that Nathan was stupid, and therefore loveable and trustworthy.

'I intend to back my boy to my last dollar. And pack his arse off to Amerrica to an Amerrican university. Win the Scholarship, or lose! People in this village will talk about Oxford and Cambridge. But look at it this way, Nate. Oxford and Cambridge have train the goddamn niggers who're running 'bout here, keeping us in a new kind o' slavery. So, why should

169

I pay good money to send my boy to a place like that? To have him return back here, and behave like a goddamn white nigger to his own poor-arse coloured people?'

'I see your point.'

'Well, get some money, Nate. And stop all this horse-shit 'bout politics. I'm gonna tell you something else, too. I got me two of the nicest guns money could buy. Got them in Amerrica. I keeps them both loaded. Under my pillow. I taught my boy to use them, too. Just in case. Any-goddamn-person, from headmaster down to politician, Nate, I will pepper his arse with buck-shot.'

'Buck-shot?'

Nathan has never heard the term.

'The night that nigger, Bourne came to my place, I put his arse to siddown. I went to my frig and I took out a bottle of ice water. And I placed a big forty-ounce o' the best Scotch, the very best, on my centre table. And I tell him drink. Drink. You shouldda seen that nigger's face! His eyes couldn't leave the bottle o' Chivas Regal. Then, I walked inside my bedroom. I brush-way my two pillows. And I took up my two guns, and chose the best one of the two. My goddamn revolver. The biggest of the two. And I walked back in there, with that nigger. I placed two glasses, crystal glasses I picked up in Amerrica, on the table. Beside the revolver. And do you know what I say to that bastard, Nate?'

'I can't guess, Mr Adams.'

'Well, I'll tell ya. I says to Lex, "All the niggers in this village may call you Mr Alexander Bourne, and some may address you as Mr MP. But to me you isn't nothing but a goddamn crook. You's in my goddamn house, now. And I will call you Lex. So, Lex, let me hear what this bullshit is that you want to tell me." '

He smiled for the second time during his long stay. Nathan saw the gold.

'That son of a bitch got up and say he had a meeting at party headquarters. "No, no, no, Lex. Sit your arse down" I says. "Siddown and let me hear what bullshit you come in my goddamn house to tell me." '

'But, Mr Adams. . . .'

170

'And something else, Nate. Call me John. From today. No more o' this colonial bullshit in regards to Mr Adams. You know as well as hell, Nate, that I am the man who breed your sister-in-law, Ella, and got her pregnant, and cause her to have an abortion. So, don't gimme this shit. I owns the house you living in. But I don't goddamn own *you*. No man. *No man* can't own another man. Nobody can't own you, Nate. Unless you let them. Not even the goddamn Prime Minister, that red-skin son of a bitch!'

'All right, John.'

'*Good.*'

'Thank you, Mr John . . . I mean, thank you, John.'

'All goddamn deals *off.*'

Nathan twirled the glass of beer in his hand.

'Have another beer, John?'

'No, Nate. I'm on my way to vote this goddamn Guvvament out o' power. If it's the last thing I do.'

He got up to leave. He filled the verandah with his power and size. His clothes seemed to brighten the verandah. And his aftershave lotion changed the old wormy, bookish odour of the verandah to a fresh, grand smell. Nathan thought of the Mennen bottle he had filled with Limacol. He called out to his wife to say goodbye to Mr Adams. When she came, wiping the soap-suds into her apron, Mr Adams smiled, for the third time in his long visit.

'Ma'am, I've had me a *fine* time!'

'Me and John been talking,' Nathan said.

She did not know about whom her husband was speaking.

'John here. . . .'

'Oh!' she said, 'you mean Mr Adams?'

'Been telling me I should take this old house off his hands. Purchase. And possession.'

'Oh?' she said, and smiled.

'I already wrote to your sister, ma'am. To tell her. And ma'am. . . .'

He went towards her, and placed his arm round her soft body, and rubbed his sweet-smelling aftershave lotioned face on both her cheeks. It was something he had picked up in Amerrica, he said.

'The only decent way to greet friends. And ma'am, I wish to personally congratulate you, on the success of your son. If he win the Scholarship, and beat the nigger I got up there for a son, so be it. I congratulate you, ma'am, in regards to your new home!'

John Moore-Adams placed his white straw hat daintily on his head, at a wicked, cocky angle. He wiped his face clean, pulled his tie up, and buttoned his shirt and jacket. When he felt he was ready, tidy and smelling clean and looking like a black American tourist, complete in image, except for the camera strung over his shoulder, he danced down the steps.

'Well, ma'am. Well, Nate. I'm on my way. To vote those bastards *out*!'

10

The only other time, before this morning, that there were so many people, such a large crowd in the city, cramming all space, all alleys, the main roads and the back streets, like sardines on the few sidewalks, and on the side lanes, in all the history of the country, was during the Riots.

On that morning in 1937, years ago, before Boy was born, there was shouting and gunfire and shooting and screaming and bottles thrown, and people beaten up by the police and killed by the police and the Volunteer Force. Blood ran in the gutters then. And none of the poor black people, caught in the cross fire, knew what was going on. All they knew was what they had heard. 'There's a riot!' Nobody knew what had caused it. Nobody knew why they were rioting.

But on this morning! This bright morning, with the skies bluer than ever, and the smell of the sea coming across the road, and the smell of the flowers, on this day after the election, at about eight o'clock, the multitude of people in the roads, in the alleys, on boats in the Harbour, on house-tops, and sitting in cars drinking, they all knew. They knew why they were there.

The Government had fallen.

Alexander Bourne had lost his seat.

Seabert Mascoll Nathaniel Marshall had lost his deposit. And soon would, according to John Moore-Adams, lose his house, his wife, his daughter, and his tailor shop.

The Government had been defeated.

Nathan was already drunk.

Sarge was sitting in a chair, in the rum shop, all buttons loosened on his Inspector's uniform of khaki, his Sam Brown belt on the floor with the sand and the sawdust and the dead bees and dead flies, slopping, slopped and sloshed.

Manny Batson was saying all the time, to no one in particular, for no one was listening, they were all drunk, 'I is an unboughtable man. I is an unboughtable man.'

Nathan's wife was in her backyard, hanging out clothes and singing 'Ride on, Ride on in Majesty'. And when the words slipped her memory, she improvised new ones.

From eighteen seats out of twenty-four in the House of Assembly, the Government was reduced to two.

'Be-Jesus-Christ!' Sarge said, as he named the two seats. 'The Prime Minister get-back his seat. And the man who walk beside the Prime Minister at Lionel's funeral, the MP for Westbury South. He retain his seat.'

The funeral, and the public relations surrounding it, had apparently been good for that MP.

In the rejoicing and the confusion, and in the new breath of release and freedom in the land, no one paid much attention to Goalie the murderer.

Goalie was shot dead by a policeman. He was seen leaving a gully on the plantation property, near John Moore-Adams' house. For one day, the villagers said that John Moore-Adams had squealed. But in the euphoria of the voting, they forgot about Goalie, about Mr Adams and about Lionel.

'We free! We free!' the people screamed. 'We free!'

Three times. As if for emphasis. And Mr Adams told Nathan, as they drove in the large Amurcan car, 'Free at last! Free at last!'

Two times. But his Amurcan accent understandably made up for the difference.

Nathan added 'Thank God almighty, we free at last!'

II

Moo-Moo's mother's husband came in suddenly, on a boat, the day of the voting, and without notice, visited his home, to find Mr John Moore-Adams in bed, comfortable and customarily with his wife; and after he thought of his choices, he beat her very near death and ran away and went to another part of the country to live, to rest his anger, to lick his wounds, until his ship was ready to leave.

So, Mr John Moore-Adams' cries of 'Free at last! Free at last!', had the double irony of a double-barrelled meaning.

Nobody could find Moo-Moo's mother's husband. And his wife had to cover her shame. And Sarge, who had been assigned to the case, became too caught up in the celebration of victory to worry too much about the investigation. It could wait. And tempers would melt. And Moo-Moo's mother's wemms and welts would heal. And she would drop the charges, and begin to sing again and laugh loudly.

Those who had supported the opposition party, and those who had not, came out dressed in the colours of the victors. Red, yellow and blue. Corn beef and biscuits. Rum and Scotch whisky appeared out of hiding. The people in the village walked and danced in the middle of the roads, taunting cars. And they sat on cars. Cars blew their horns to clear a path as much as to celebrate the stunning victory.

A few policemen tried without much enthusiasm to direct traffic, and to hide their enjoyment and approval at the defeat of the Government.

For the police had been angry. The threats to Sarge's life, and his demotion, had shivered through the ranks; and a cancer of

discontent had developed. But now, all their personal dif-
ferences were forgotten.

They had been convinced, and they said so amongst
themselves, that the Government had been involved in all the
unsolved murders in the country. And police sergeants from
the city who knew Sarge said openly, even before the deadening
defeat at the polls, that the Prime Minister himself had been
involved in the laying of the plots for Sarge's assassination. The
police were glad that the Government fell.

So, the people stood talking in the roads. They cheered and
laughed and screamed for joy when the long procession of
victorious politicians, with the Prime Minister elect, came
towards them, arm linked in arm, sweating in the hot sun, and
singing 'For He's a Jolly Good Fellow', and brandishing
house-brooms.

'Sweep the fuckers out!' a drunken man said, apparently not
sober even before the voting.

The broom was the symbol of the opposition party during the
campaign.

It was the first time in living memory that so many people,
most of whom were from the lower classes, had gathered in the
roads, in the city, in the country districts, to celebrate anything.
And it was the first time they could tell you why they were doing
it, in the middle of the road, in such numbers.

It was the first time Boy had seen this spectacle.

'We have to lock-up the Prime Minister, for murdering
Goalie.'

'And for murdering Lionel, too.'

'And for tampering with the small man.'

'But can a Prime Minister be lock-up?'

'And for making things scarce, when they was not scarce.'

'And for fooling we for ten years.'

'And we got to lock-up Bournie!'

'For what?'

'What *for?*'

'Because, because . . . he *lost!*'

'This country is build on British justice, so we got to lock up
the former Prime Minister!'

12

The rum shop got a new name and a new look. Manny Batson had 'come into some money'. And he put a coat of white paint all over the outside of the shop. New blinds. New shelves which were full. And stocked with the staples of the country's new prosperity. Tins of Rankin biscuits; all the local brands of rum and falernum; and thousands of tins of corn beef. The best. *Fray Bentos*. On the front, spanning the shop, like the outstretched arms of a wrestler, from one end to the other, was a sign, BROOKLYN CAFETERIA, MR MANNY BATSON, ESQUIRE, PROPRIATOR.

Boy saw the sign and he pointed out the mistake in the spelling of 'proprietor'. Manny called over to Seabert Mascoll Nathaniel Marshall, political candidate, formerly; now, simply Seabert the tailor, to paint over the wrong letter, and put in the correct one. Seabert had painted signs when tailoring was not making money. But he was a weak speller.

Boy had told his father, Nathan, about the mistake first. And Nathan walked over, with a coached pride, tapped Manny on his shoulder, and said, 'I going-bet you a bottle of rum, Manny, that I can find a mistake in your new sign.'

'Blind you, Nathan! You think you are a College-boy? Seabert, the once-honourable representative for Sin-James East, paint this sign. The sign spell right.'

Nathan had the correct spelling Boy had given him in his pocket.

'Seabert!' Manny shouted over, 'man, come over to my premises, and tell me 'bout this sign.'

'You like the sign, Nathan?'

'Nathan like the sign. I like the sign. But the sign spell wrong. Nathan say you make a mistake.'

'What mistake? You see a mistake in that sign, Nathan?'

'A bottle o' rum.'

'Man, kiss my arse! You think you could spell better than me?'

'A bottle of rum, Mr Former MP. I bet you a bottle of rum I see a mistake in your sign. And another bottle of rum that I could spell the word right.'

Seabert looked at Manny. Many men were behaving with this uppitiness, Seabert knew, since the election results. Manny looked at Seabert. Then Manny remembered he had just installed a telephone.

'Lemme call the newspaper. The newspaper would know.'

'Before you call, which word you going-ask them to spell? Which is the wrong word?' Seabert asked.

'That is the bet, Seabert.'

'Well, if I don't know the rass-hole word. . . .'

Seabert was losing his temper easily these days. Defeat and the loss of his deposit, plus the loss of the car the party had given him, rested heavily on his nerves.

'If I don't know the kiss-me-arse word you have in mind, how the hell Manny could get the right spelling?'

'A third bottle to find the word, then, Mr Member o' Parlment!'

'You, you-you! Yuh see you? You, God-blind-you, since you and that Yankee-man is friends, you playing a lotta shite 'bout-here, Nathan!'

Seabert and Manny, with the help of two customers, who had come into the rum shop, looked and argued about the sign. And through the process of elimination, they discovered, without Nathan's assistance, that PROPRIATOR was the word.

'You printed the word pretty, though!' one of the customers said.

'Seabert is the prettiest, best painter in the world!' Manny said. 'But he can't spell one shite!'

'And yuh don't need Esquire after Mister, once yuh use Mister first,' Nathan told Seabert.

And when the sign was corrected, Manny insisting that he wanted *Mr* and *Esquire* with his name, and they were drinking snaps in the Private Quarters, renamed for the Back Room, Seabert told Nathan, 'Thanks, man. You save my future political career, in case I running in politics next time. It would look bad, to see me, a former candidate in a national elections, the prospected MP for Sin-James East, can't spell "proprietor". Now, if I had-get elected, you know I wouldda take care of your. . . .'

Nathan remembered John Moore-Adams' caution about politicians' promises; and he merely shook his head, and drank another snap. He drew the three bottles he had won closer to him. He might even take one to his new friend, John Moore-Adams, John to him, nowadays.

He might even keep one for Boy, to take with him overseas, in case. . . .

John was recommending him for the Masons. He had also promised to lend him a book, *Jim Crow in the United States*. Boy would have to find time to read it for him. But he didn't know: his son was thinking of overseas.

Mr Adams didn't know that Nathan could not read or write. But what the hell, Nathan thought, he'd take the book, and walk through the village with it under his arm; display it even in the Brooklyn Cafeteria; and when time allowed, get Boy to read certain passages to him, more than once, so that he might memorize them, and argue with Seabert, who had already taken down most of his pictures and photographs of his famous political figures of the world. The tailor shop was now bare. The only reminder from times past was the campaign poster, VOTE FOR SEABERT MASCOLL NATHANIEL MARSHALL, A SMALL MAN LIKE YOU.

And Nathan hoped that the *Jim Crow* book had in many pictures. . . .

13

Even in defeat and with his political life in a shambles, his chauffeur-driven Humber Hawk taken away, his financial position levelled like a field of sugar cane that was recently harvested and left almost bare, except for the useless 'trash' and cane-ruts, Mr Alexander Bourne was a formidable enemy. He was now using a hired car from Dean's Garages & Stables.

He was now a private citizen. And he was facing litigation in the Courts, with Inspector Joseph Crawford of the Criminal Investigation Department, alias Sarge, as the Police prosecutor for the Crown.

Sarge had not coughed up the little black book, in which Alexander Bourne's fate was printed and soon to be sealed. Other politicians' fates were among the dog-eared pages. Those persons whose lives had a meaning beneath the former panoply of politics and power, those persons who had lived lives as if the former Government would always be in power, those persons who had dared the law and had dared the morality of the country, those persons, silent, hidden, chinks within the woodwork of a political system that stifled the small man, while pretending it loved him, all these persons now found themselves before the Courts, in an aftermath of political house-cleaning.

'It is pure spite!'

Mr Alexander Bourne claimed this, when the first summons arrived at his large home. It was the first of three to follow.

'It is pure political spite. If we had get-back-in, be-Christ. . . .'

And his nervousness and his seriousness, brought on by the situation, prevented him from making further comment.

But he was still a powerful man. And he had to do something about the sharp cutlass being held over his head, by Sarge. Not by the police. Not by the Crown. Not even by the new Attorney-General, now a black man like himself. But by Sarge. It was Sarge. Sarge, Sarge, Sarge!

'This blasted Inspector Sarge!'

And he knew he would use his power, whatever of it that was left, to save himself from answering the charges, to wit: 'Misappropriation of Government Funds' according to some Section of the Criminal Code; the 'Non-payment of Taxes for ten years', according to another Section of a different Criminal Code . . . to save his house, his household, his wife who was hinting about leaving him, to save his skin, for the country did not tolerate political losers, who became unmentionable, then unmentioned, then forgotten, then despised . . . and the Prime Minister, one of the two from the old brigade who had been re-elected, and who had returned to his Law practice, safe and sound among briefs and cases for the rich merchants in the city, and the plantation owners, the Prime Minister had given him *one* piece of good advice.

The afternoon Alexander Bourne saw him, the former Prime Minister was dressed in barrister's silks.

'I will give you one piece o' good advice, for your own good. Bournie, boy, *brek for yourself!*'

The first thing Sarge should have noticed was that his bicycle was facing north. In the wrong direction. As a right-handed man, he had always leaned his bicycle against a house, or against a boulder, facing south.

And when he had left John Moore-Adams' house, he knew he had drunk too much Chivas Regal. His legs were unsteady.

The second thing he should have noticed, as a detective, was that the back tyre was softer than when he had arrived, three hours before. He had a bicycle pump, but he was too drunk to think of using it. So, when he rode off, he could feel the gravel of the road, in the ride, under his seat.

He did not turn on his headlamp. He would wait until he reached a safe distance from the house, before switching on the generator to the front tyre.

It was all downhill. He would free-wheel, and muffle the ticking of the three-speed gears.

The cool night air started to clear his head. He was feeling better. The new khaki uniform of the Inspector fitted him well, and close, and the pips on his shoulders made him feel brave, and therefore careless.

The night was dark. The houses on both sides of the hill were buried in darkness, and in fields of sugar cane. The air was soft and the smell of the flowers and the roses, and in particular, the Lady-of-the-Night, was high. This was one thing he always liked about living in this part of the country. The smell of the night. And the sound of the sea, when he reached the lower road, the fine-teeth of the comb that demarcated the village; and the soft crackling of the berries under his bicycle tyres, berries fallen from the overhanging trees. . . .

Coming down was easy. He applied the brakes, just a little, to make his travelling more quiet and more even. Like a detective, like a thief.

Sarge was proud of being a detective. He liked the stealth. Many nights, dark like this one, Sarge had crept up on suspects and on some who were not suspects, and before they knew it, his pee-cured bull-pistle viciously ripped confession and co-operation, and guilt, out of their backs. He was a firm policeman to criminals. To some, he was even friendly. Like Brandford, the rapist. Brandford was now in Glendairy Prison, serving five years. Most of them liked him. But he knew he always had enemies among them.

He passed the first cross in the road on the hill. And he felt safer, and soberer. He turned on his light. He put the bicycle into low speed. Just as he relaxed, just as he started to hum 'A Tisket a Tasket', and revel in the sweet memories of Ella Fitzgerald singing this song, the lights of a parked car were turned on.

Immediately, he became alert. The car was behind him. He measured the width of the road. But he was not paying attention. He should have seen the car earlier on, even in the darkness, parked under a tree, as he came down the hill.

He reached a stretch of road that had no passageways to lead to the houses built on the ridge. Only steep steps cut out of the limestone. The road was like a canal, made out of natural rock. The road looked like a river of cool, black tar. The ridge was about four or five feet high. He could not escape by jumping off the road. There was nowhere to go. Meanwhile, the car was getting closer.

He remembered he was a detective. All the skills of self-preservation and protection that he had learned in Amurca, on special courses, now rushed through his mind: last year, at the Annual Police Manly Arts Contest, he had won the first prize. Mr Alexander Bourne, MP, had presented him with his prize, a silver-painted silver cup. If only he wasn't dressed in his new khaki uniform, with the Sam Brown belt. If only he hadn't refused to wear mufti. But he was caught now, in a tight, new, unaccustomed uniform.

The car picked up speed. And it came at him. He had just pulled his revolver from his armpit, where he kept his holster.

When the car hit him, he was thrown into the middle of the road, against the embankment. The two men got out and stood over him. One of them took Sarge's revolver out of his right hand. The other picked up his officer's cap.

They carried these back to the car, which was idling in the middle of the road. They worked fast. Not a word passed between them.

They threw his bicycle into the trunk of the car. They lifted Sarge from the road. Blood was splattered on the uniform. They threw Sarge into the trunk, with the bicycle. And they closed the trunk. The car was a hired car from Dean's Garages & Stables.

The car raced to the first break in the embankment, a small inlet scarcely large enough for the large car. It turned round and went back up the hill. As it reached a house, a short distance from the road, the driver turned off the lights, and drove across the grass-piece, in darkness.

The house was a large, black silhouette against the sky. Fields of young sugar canes were blowing in the wind. And some distance from them a dog whined.

The car stopped. The men got out. And they waited to see if the dog would whine again, if the dog was too close, if they were safe.

And in this dogged silence, they carried Sarge along a track between two fields, hearing only the soft crackling of the trash from the canes, through the green darkness, then through the lightness of the dark night, until they reached the well.

Before they threw Sarge in, one man searched his four pockets in the tunic. But he could not find what he was looking for. And he searched the other two pockets in the trousers.

You could not tell how great was the disappointment. For the man did not express it. The only noise was the growling of the dog, moments away, and the brushing of the canes, blades against blades, and then the wait, and then the untellable longer wait until the weight struck the water, far far far down into the well. And then the silence. And then the soft footfalls on the thick grass, and then the brushing of hands in the manner of a job well done.

And in all this time, not one word was broken. Not a gesture of regret or of guilt.

14

The local newspaper carried three photographs. One was of young Lascelles, who came second. The second one was of Henry Moore-Adams the Second, who came third.

At the top of the page, in a photograph which showed him grinning, teeth white in a natural smile; broad face, short brilliantined hair, with the married man's parting in the middle, a shirt that looked whiter even than the pages of the newspaper, and school tie and blazer, was the portrait of Boy – Thorne, Michael William Wilberforce, winner of the Barbados Scholarship in Classics.

The biographical note said he had scored the highest marks recorded in the history of the Barbados Scholarship.

'Thorne, MWW, comes from a breed of Classical scholars and from a country which boasts the highest literacy rate in the world,' the newspaper proclaimed.

There was also a picture of John Moore-Adams, dressed in the same suit he had worn when he had the talk with Nathan, long ago. It showed him gesticulating with both hands, in anger, while he held a straw hat in one demonstrating hand.

Nathan could not read what was printed below the photograph; but he imagined that Mr Adams was saying, 'You-all niggers in this poor-arse goddamn place. . . .'

The newspaper was superlative in its praise for the two young scholars, Boy and Henry, from the village. But no less praise was bestowed on the head of young Lascelles, 'a young man, the son of a distinguished jurist, an English expatriate, but one who holds this small country in the highest esteem, a true son of the soil.'

Everybody in the village was now talking about Boy. Everybody was now talking about education and the most brilliant boy ever born in the village.

'It is the first time,' the newspaper went on, 'in our long history of high academic achievement, that a naturalized son of this soil has ever held such high academic honours.'

Boy could not decide if the reference was to young Lascelles, or to Henry Moore-Adams the Second.

His mother however, was not so uncertain. She recognized the name Thorne. It was printed in large type. And without help, she read the name. The message was brought home to her. Her son had blessed her name. A name which she held with pride, but which, because of the background of the name, and the first holders of the name, had been left among the tall weeds, amongst the fields of sugar and yams in the country district of Sin-Joseph. But now, it was a name of worth. And public worth at that.

She encouraged fantasies of dynastic dimensions, built dreams of greatness, and submerged herself in a warm tub of family love.

She held the newspaper in both hands. The pages were closed. And were resting on her breasts. And from time to time, she would open the pages and stare at her son's photograph, and say nothing at all. She knew she would never throw this newspaper away.

Nathan reached over and touched her on her shoulder. He held his hand there. Then he let his hand drop from her shoulder and touch her breasts. She held her hand over his. And he was aware, at this moment, of a great tremor of joy, on her sagging breast. But he could still remember and feel the stiff round memory of those breasts, when they were round and firm, when she was the age of Moo-Moo's mother. She was the 'best looking red-skin woman' in the village.

'Stop your lawlessness, man!'

But a look of deep, long-lasting love came to her eyes. His hand was still firm on her soft breast. She was almost fifty-five. And she was still young in her body. He wished she did not cover her body under so many clothes. And he wished. . . .

'Look, woman, you is still the sweetest, best woman I ever take to bed!'

'But Nathan. Suppose your son hear you with all this lawlessness? And at *your* age?'

She put her hand under her skirt. Nathan's body jumped in anticipation. But all she did was pull out a purse, made of the same material as her dress. Her wallet. In it she kept all her money.

'Take this.'

It was a twenty-dollar bill.

'And before you come home tonight from the Brooklyn Cafeteria, I want you to buy me a nip-bottle of five-star, VSOP Hennessey brandy, please.'

She took out another twenty-dollar bill.

'And you hold on 'pon this.'

She smiled very sweetly, as she gave him the money. And he felt the urge throughout his body. She smiled so very sweetly, and her smile was so much a reflection of the young girl he had known years ago on her father's land, that he forgot to ask her where she got all this money.

'Five outta this is for Boy. You could keep the change. I know times hard with you. But a man have to have change rackling-'bout in his pockets, otherwise, he isn't a man.'

'Girl! Look, girl!'

And that was all he said; all he needed to say, in the heavy sensual moment of their long life together.

'And whenever you get back, I will have your pillow from your room, and your pyjamas underneath your pillow, and that pillow will be beside me, in my bedroom.'

It would be the first time in years that he would feel her body beside his in bed. The front-house where they were sitting took on a soft dimness; he could smell the Bournes Bay Rum she used on her body as perfume; he could smell the flowers round the house, and he could hear the sea.

15

The knocking on the door was soft, but clear.

Tap! ta-ta-ta-tap! Tap-tap!

If John Moore-Adams wasn't sitting beside him, Nathan would have sworn that it was *he*, John Moore himself, who was outside knocking.

It was his code. The same way he blew his car horn. To Nathan, this knocking sounded very strange. Like something that Masons did.

Mr Adams got up, without being perturbed, and went to the door. The knocking was repeated before he reached the door.

Boy and John Moore-Adams the Second (Boy began calling him that after the feature story in the newspaper) were in the large living-room at the front of the large house. Patricia, Grace and Moo-Moo were there, too, and were dancing.

They were invited because Mr Adams was 'packing this goddamn boy to Amerrica, in a week or two, goddammit!' And John Moore-Adams the Second had himself announced to them that he was entering the Massachusetts Institute (not Institution!) of Technology, to study mathematics.

The latest Amurcan dance music was being played loudly. Nathan could not understand how the knocking was heard above all this noise.

It must be how these Mason-men knocked, and called one another.

For the past two months, John Moore-Adams had been telling Nathan some of the mysteries of the Masons. They intrigued him. And frightened him. There were so many explanations and mysterious solutions to the simplest things that happened in everyday life.

He was scared to join this fraternity. But he knew it could protect him. He already thought his son's success in the Scholarship examination had something to do with his cautious closeness with the Masons. Mr Adams told him so.

The Masons might even make him a powerful man.

Mr Adams came back from the door, passed through the room and went to open a side door. As the door was opened, Nathan heard him laugh.

'*Goddamn!*'

A woman came into view. For a split second, Nathan thought it was Moo-Moo's mother. Her husband was still hiding in the country district. And the villagers were saying that any day now, this cruel man was sure to come and kill Mr Adams.

But when the person turned, it was Seabert.

'Would ya look at this goddamn nigger!'

'Oh Christ! I thought you was Moo-Moo mother, Seabert!'

Mr Adams' face turned severe at the mention of her name. Immediately, his countenance relaxed, and he began to make feigned grabs at Seabert's imitation breasts, laughing loudly as he grabbed.

'Sarge used to dress so, when he was tracking down criminals. Remember that, Seabert?'

'Yuh can't be too careful, in this place, if you have a background in politics,' Seabert said.

'But would ya look at this bastard!'

'Can't let yuh left hand know. . . .'

And Seabert ran his hand from his neck over the zipper, and ripped the dress into half, and exposed his normal clothes. When he stepped out of the dress, and it was at his feet, he balled it up most undaintily, and threw it on a chair. Then he sat down.

They all laughed.

'Lemme close the door of this den,' John Moore-Adams said.

Nathan had never heard a room called by that name before. The only dens he heard about were places where they kept animals, like lions. But he was fascinated by all these things that Amurcans did. Educated people had such strange ways! Boy, his own son, called the verandah a 'study'. But he understood that. Boy studied there. But why should a place where men sat and talked and drank, and discussed women and life, be called a den?

Boy too, was intrigued by the 'den'. The nearest comparison was with Seabert's former gallery of pictures and photographs and newspaper clippings. This 'den' was covered with framed photographs of black men. They were all Amurcans. There were two black women among the men. John Moore-Adams told Boy the women were Sojourner Truth, and Harriett Tubman.

There was a wall of shelves filled with books. It was a book from one of these shelves, Boy realized, that the book *Jim Crow* had come.

Seabert looked more comfortable and relaxed, too much at ease for Nathan, in this 'den'. Nathan wondered if Seabert had one of these 'dens' in his home.

On a table in the centre of the 'den', and which was covered with a multi-coloured piece of cloth, was a half-gallon bottle of Chivas Regal. On the cloth was painted the Empire State Building and the faces of all the Amurcan presidents.

'You niggers see the kind o' stuff *we* used to drink States-side, Nate?' Seabert said, claiming a strange association with things big, and talking as if he was an Amurcan, now that he was in this 'den'. 'States-side, you sees the best! And you drinks the goddamn best!'

Nathan felt Seabert was talking very strange tonight.

'You eats the very best. And you fucks the very best!'

Nathan had never heard him use all these 'you eats', 'you drinks' and 'you fucks'. And Seabert never used such profanities.

'You Amurcans really talk funny, in truth,' Nathan said. 'Uh mean, everybody in this village does-say "you foops". No other word, but "foop". This is the way Masons does-talk? I like it, though. Perhaps, I should try and talk this way, this Amurcan way.'

'Have a shot, Seabert.'

'Don't mind if ah do, John.'

'Nate here and me, we been chomping on a few ideas. I guess ya heard that my boy leaving for college in the states? First thing next week.'

John Moore-Adams' pride covered his large face. The 'den' was humid, and perspiration covered his face, too.

'So, what's happening, Seabert, now that you's a former politician?'

Nathan waited to hear him give some details about his

political career, perhaps, even hear some gossip about Moo-
Moo's mother's husband.

'*Cum-see! Cum-sah!*'

That was all Seabert said.

The children were in the living room, dancing to the loud
Amurcan music.

John Moore-Adams poured two bottles of beer into a large
mug. The mug had USA printed on it. Beneath USA was a flag
of the United States of Amurca. Nathan was sitting below
another, bigger Amurcan flag. This one was pinned on to the
wall. John Moore-Adams was beneath the smaller flag. Nathan
watched the majestic colours, and ran his eyes over the waves of
stripes, until his eyes blurred and became cloudy, when he tried
to count the stars on the flag. John Moore-Adams noticed his
interest, and smiled proudly.

'Home of the goddamn free! Freer than this country,'
Seabert said.

'Land of the goddamn brave!' John Moore-Adams said.

Seabert unbuttoned his shirt, and took a .38 revolver from its
holster. He placed it on the chair beside his dress.

'Not *there*, man!' John Moore-Adams scolded him. 'Have
more respect for your *piece*.'

He took Seabert's revolver from the chair, unclipped the
safety catch, did something with the clip, and spun the barrel.

Nathan was getting a bit scared, being so close to these two
Amurcans.

John Moore-Adams put the revolver to his head, and pulled
the trigger.

Click!

He was smiling, just as he had smiled that morning in
Nathan's house.

Click!

The children in the living room was dancing and laughing.
For that moment of their glee, the Amurcan tune on the
record-player could not be heard. When their laughter died
down, Nathan heard another *click!* and he could hear the tune,
'Evening Shadows Make Me Blue'.

'The *best* dance-pieces in the world come from Amurca!' It
was his son speaking. He had never heard Boy express this kind

of knowledge before. Strange how he had raised him all these years and had never heard him make this kind of comment. In a few weeks, he would be gone from the country, perhaps for ever.

Click!

'You not drinking, Nate? You listening to the kids? Leave the kids to themselves. They're doing their thing.'

The smile came back to his face. He drank half his beer, and smacked his lips. He held the revolver dangling in his hand, as if he had forgotten it there. He was bored with his game of Russian Roulette.

'A lotta shit's gonna break-out here,' Seabert said, 'now that Sarge dead.'

It was strange how they had forgotten Sarge.

'For Sarge,' John Moore-Adams said, dropping a few drops of beer on the floor of the 'den'.

'To Sarge,' the other two men said, and dropped a few drops of their Chivas Regal on the glazed surface of the linoleum. Sarge was in this way remembered in the correct ritual of the village.

John Moore-Adams went into his kitchen and brought out a ham. He had a bottle with green things in it. He picked out one with a fork, and chomped on it with glee. Before he smiled, his expression turned sour.

'Pickles!' he announced. 'The Jews have given goddamn pickles to western civilization!'

Nobody knew what he was talking about. He then returned to the kitchen, and brought out the biggest turkey any of them had seen. He got an electric knife for carving and sawed the turkey into large, unprofessional pieces. He did the same thing to the ham. Nathan was amazed at the thickness of the slices. They were cut as Nathan himself chopped up wood: no regard to size and servings. What was chopped was what came off under the blade of the chopper.

When John Moore-Adams took platters into the living-room, along with the mini-electric saw, a cheer from the children went up.

'I really didn't know they was out to get Sarge,' Seabert said. 'The nigger shouldda protected himself better. He was a

190

detective *and* a goddamn Mason. Sarge shouldda known that
the first law of western civilization is cover your arse.'

Seabert stopped tearing at the turkey. He pushed his hand
under one armpit, and left it there for a moment. He began
eating again. His revolver was safe under his arm.

'Oh! John I forgot to tell you why I came dressed in a dress.
The rumour is that . . . you know who? . . . was seen in the
village late last night. So, I came to warn you. As man! Not that
that stupid seaman could touch a man like you.'

'Let the *mother* come!' John Moore-Adams said. He held a
large piece of turkey between his teeth. Gold in his teeth flashed
like lightning, and when he removed his hand which was
holding the turkey, Nathan thought he heard the flesh tear and
rip. 'Let the *mother* come!'

'I sorry I didn't tell you the minute I got here,' Seabert said.

'Let the *mother* come!'

There was a knocking at the front door. The men stopped
eating. John Moore-Adams moved towards his bedroom.
Seabert placed his hand under his armpit. He was not scratching
it. Nathan saw the gun in John Moore-Adams' hand, when he
came out. Nobody moved. A cheer went up in the living-room. It
was Moo-Moo's mother. From where he sat, Nathan could smell
her perfume. John Moore-Adams settled back down, got drinks
and stuffing from the turkey and took them into the living-room.
Nathan heard him say, 'The men're in the den'.

When he came back with her, and her thin cotton dress was
crushed at her waist just where his hand held her, and Nathan
could see the outline of her thighs, and smell the full force of her
perfume, he thought of his wife, and he knew why this woman's
husband would want to kill any man who interfered, or touch this
sweet, soft, black body. John Moore-Adams held her in a loving
close embrace, and Nathan knew that he too knew what he held
in his arm. She had deep blue rings round her eyes. Her
husband's anger must have been harsh.

'I been just telling these niggers,' he began; and before he
could continue, Moo-Moo's mother burst out into a deep-
throated laughter, as if she had heard the end of what he was
about to say, as if it was one of her dirty jokes. 'I been telling these
niggers here about western civilization. And how the food

they're eating, ham and turkey and Jewish pickles is the supper we eats in Amerrica on Thanksgiving. This is a Thanksgiving Supper, tonight.'

Boy appeared behind them, in the middle of the doorway, watching. Nathan saw him and wondered why he found big people's company more interesting than that of the children. He stood watching Moo-Moo's mother until she sat down. And then he disappeared.

'John, boy,' Nathan said, stretching and yawning, 'now that you got company, I think I going down the hill. Tomorrow is Sunday.'

'You tekking Communion?' Moo-Moo's mother asked, and immediately, she laughed aloud. As if it was a joke, which it was.

'Tomorrow is Sunday. And the wife taking me to church.'

'Abyssinia!' Seabert said.

'Take this goddamn thing with ya, nigger!'

So, Seabert took up the dress, balled it up, and placed it under his arms.

'And don't forget,' he told John Moore-Adams.

'I got *everything* I need!'

He slapped his breast where his gun was; and he slapped Moo-Moo's mother's bottom, where his sensuality was.

'Send Boy home when you want to turn in,' Nathan said. He was already moving towards the door, with Seabert. But Seabert paused.

'One for the road!'

And the three men and the woman filled their glasses, and held their heads back, and swallowed the liquor in one gulp.

'To Sarge!' John Moore-Adams said, and threw his glass against the wall, where it shattered. The men were amazed; but the explosion was for a good cause, for a good man, for good memory.

'I'm gonna toss those niggers out, right now, so me and my woman can be alone, *all by our lonesome!*'

When John Moore-Adams said this, Nathan and Seabert were already moving down the steep steps, away from the house, seeking the path that led to the road.

They looked back and could hear the woman's loud laughter,

and the loud Amurcan music and they could see the house on fire with electricity, standing by itself on the top of the hill, bright and noisy as the plantation's cane factory in the heat of the harvest season, grinding sugar canes.

'If I was a more younger man,' Nathan was saying, 'Seabert, I tell you this, between me and you. But if I was a more younger man, I don't mind telling you, but I won't mind tekking a piece offa Moo-Moo mother.'

'*You* would foop she, Nathan?'

'If I was a younger man.'

'You could still try, though.'

'Let we snap one before we turn-in for the night,' Nathan suggested. 'The Brooklyn still open.'

Seabert told Manny Batson about Nathan's fantasies. Manny Batson just laughed and laughed. He was glad for the company, for he was sleeping in the Private Quarters, since business was slow. He rearranged the three chairs on which he had been sleeping round a table. It was after two in the morning. He scraped his feet as he walked, and Nathan and Seabert could hear his footsteps like sandpaper over wallaba wood.

'Between sleep-and-wake, I could swear I was talking to that woman's husband. My two eyes was half-open, but I swear I heard that man telling me something. . . .'

Manny seemed to forget what he wanted to say; and he went instead to get the drinks. He dropped the bottle of rum on the bare, clean, hard table. He dropped the bottle with iced water on the table with such force as to break it. The three short, thick snap-glasses sounded like blanks when Manny placed them on the table.

'The merchant ship leffing first thing, bright and early in the morning. You hear?'

Manny Batson was talking as if he was still asleep. Neither Nathan nor Seabert worried to answer.

'It now sink-in. Just before I fall off, and I must o' been sleeping two or three hours now. Second sleep, yuh know? But the meaning just hit me. Your boy. Nathan, I mean Boy. It now hit me that we have a Prime Minister in our midst. He not too young. And he got the brains. He have the family. He have the looks. The only quality I don't know if he have, is whether he likes enough woman. You have to like woman, know woman, foop woman, and have woman like you, to be Prime Minister o' this blasted country. In other words, a grass roots man.'

'That is not what grass-roots mean,' Seabert said. 'Grass-roots mean the people. Socialism.'

'To you, it mean that. But talking strict politics, and especially the politics of this country, grass-roots mean *one thing*. It means *down on your back in a grass-piece!*'

The flash came as quickly and lasted as long as a light bulb that is blown.

'You see the lightning?' Nathan asked.

There was another flash.

'But the weather didn't say storms, nor even rain.'

The flash seemed to be just behind the rum shop. Through the window, they could see the movement against the skies. The skies were the colour of a sunrise.

'A fire?' Manny Batson asked. 'A cane fire?'

'Seabert said he heard the husband was in the area, tonight,' Nathan said. He did not know why he said that.

It was then that they heard the explosion. Nathan had long ruled out a storm. It was his fisherman's instincts. No rain was falling. And men did not dynamite fish in the sea at this hour.

The three of them ran outside, and stood in the road, and looked up the hill. The entire hill was on fire. It seemed to them that the entire section of the island, above their heads, was on fire. No cane fire had burned so savagely, had made so much noise, had raged as if it wanted to engulf the entire population.

Others ran out of their houses, and joined them. Still others, further along the road, like lazy waves, ebbed from dark front doors and came and stood in the middle of the road.

Seabert saw Patricia looking through the window of his house. And soon after that, Boy dressed in pyjamas, came and stood below Patricia's window. Seabert and Nathan shook their heads and said nothing.

'Jesus Christ almighty!' Manny Batson said. He was pointing the index finger on his left hand up the hill, in a manner of warning. 'Jesus Christ! *That* is what I didn't remember to tell you-all. That is what I didn't remember.'

Two

SNOW

16

Nathan was dressed in his black suit. His wife was in white. On her head was her hat, worn like a crown. All round its brim were plastic painted fruits. The shoes she was wearing this hot morning she had worn on Sarge's wedding day. More recently, to his funeral, held exactly three days ago. The shoes were tight on her feet.

She and Nathan were standing at the door of the Departures Lounge of the new airport. It was the first time they had visited the airport.

She had bathed twice the day before: the first time, at five in the morning, which was her usual time; and later, at nine o'clock in the evening, in preparation for her husband. She had rubbed her body with Bournes Bay Rum; she had plaited her hair in two long strands, had oiled it with coconut oil, and freshened it with a few drops of Bournes, she had sipped the Hennessey; and she had timed its effect upon her body with the hour of her husband's arrival. She had timed that arrival for midnight. Midnight was a special hour. The worst things happened at midnight. And the best things happened at midnight. And midnight was safe. Boy would be sleeping.

And then, after she had waited, the explosion came, and drove her back into a kind of widowhood. She accepted it, for it was God telling her about the sins of the flesh. If her husband did not agree with God, she said to God, that same night before she eventually went to sleep, then he can find a young girl. She was satisfied in the continuation of her widowhood.

So, this morning was a happy morning. Happier than it was sad. And she came to regard Boy's departure as a permanent separation. The best persons she loved were now separated from her. Sister and son.

She knew Boy was going to Trinity College in Toronto, for four years. She merely knew the name. It was just a name. And

197

she had heard the names of so many cities since he won the Scholarship, that she concluded they were only names. They did not touch her daily life. Trinity College in Toronto was therefore the same to her as the Canal Zone in Panama. They were 'away'. And they had taken the best two persons in her life away.

She had been spending quite a lot of time, for the past few days, crying. Her life seemed recently to be a life of tears. She had cried for Lionel. She had cried for Goalie. She had cried for Sarge. She had cried last night for John Moore-Adams. And she had cried for Moo-Moo's mother. And for Henry. She had cried for sinners and for saints. She did not see any difference in them. And all the way to the airport, in the hired car, she had cried for Boy. And some of her tears were for Moo-Moo, whom she had taken in to live with her.

Everyone from the village, almost, was at the airport. They had rented cars, had pooled their resources, and were now standing at the wire, with their faces pressed on the warm metal, and marked by the shape of the mesh.

All social and political rivalries had been forgotten. The village was fresh again, like the clearness of a morning after a night of rain. It was knitted back into a family of love.

Some brought water coconuts. Some brought baked coconut bread. Some brought Limacol, and Canadian Healing Oil, and Bournes Bay Rum.

'How the hell you expect my son to take all these things to Canada?' Nathan asked them. He was joking. He was choked with pride. 'He can't take all.'

And some had brought the local village 'sweeties'.

Moo-Moo was red in the eye, with sorrow and with sadness.

'I feel my heart breaking,' she told Boy. 'I already had a broken heart, when you had to leave. And after the explosion, I have another broken heart. But I know you are going to write me and tell me about Toronto and Trinity College.'

She had brought a book to give to Boy. *The Sonnets of Shakespeare*. On the fly leaf she had written: *To the Man I love*.

Seabert watched the plane rise slowly, and then turn, and come back in the same direction, but at a higher altitude. As he watched it, standing at the wire fence, with Nathan pressed against his body, and Boy's mother beside him, he looked up and found Boy when the plane passed for the last time.

Boy too was looking as it passed. And he began to worry about himself.

What direction was this plane taking him? What direction was his plane going to take, or follow? And what direction would it take when it left the outline of the island beginning to be buried in the deep blue sea? The sea and the land became one blur. And the land was not only buried: it was the burial ground of three persons he loved: John Moore-Adams; John Moore-Adams the Second; and Moo-Moo's mother.

17

Boy recognized no face, knew no face, could make no comparison from among all the faces he met on Bloor Street, on Yonge Street and Spadina Avenue, with any of the faces he had grown up seeing in Barbados; and he seemed to be swimming among these faces, in waves, in the early morning when waves are small; but when these waves met him and touched his body, and then his neck, then his chin, his mouth, inside his mouth, burning and then blinding his eyes with their inhospitable saltiness, and covered his head; and his head was underneath, drowning; when he was beneath the waves, fluttering; underground, invisible; and the more he walked these same three streets, the more he felt he was sinking, for still there was no face he met that he knew: he was angry at himself for voluntarily coming to this vastness, this dislocation, this strangeness which surrounded him on all sides, just as he felt imprisoned within the walls of Trinity College.

Boy could not tell himself that he was taking walks. To him, walks are the stretching of the legs along known paths, and seeing known faces, touching known sidewalks, kicking known dogs that are dogs. In this city, he merely touched the pavements of Harbord Street going west to Spadina, south to College, east along College to Queen's Park where he faced the forbidding and foreboding parliament building.

Boy was ambitious enough to want to climb these parliament building steps in Toronto, but he knew he could not, since they were white: there is winter in the land that is covering this wet white day that finds him in a streetcar on his way to no destination, even though he will disembark at Yonge Street.

A black woman is at the back of the streetcar. She is the first black woman he has seen. She is the only black woman in the streetcar. All round her the seats are empty, including half of the seat on which she sits, and there are men and women standing round her, quaranteeing her, surrounding her, protecting her. They are all white.

The black woman gets off at Bay, and immediately, the men and women rush for the seat the black woman had occupied, and a white woman plops fatigued into the black woman's vacated seat and a boy into the one next to it. She was a leper. The seat is now uncolonied, and unquarantined by white bottoms.

The black woman's departure makes him think of home. Sometimes, in the school bus returning to his village, in the heat of the day, amongst the heavy smells of fish-sellers, and in the thickness of the after-vomit of the man who hissed abuses with rum in his voice, sometimes in these circumstances, Boy wished he himself could be quarantined alone on a seat. But Barbados was too crowded to be unfriendly. And in Barbados, every face is known, whether it is your mother's, or your enemy's.

And the tragic journey that brought him to this vast whiteness came back to him with thick nostalgia. . . . The Police Band had struck up *God Save The King*. The trees and the buildings and the people shivered with joy. The sun was hot. Dead, black cockles from the night before, and resting in spots on the shimmering white of the walks that led from the classrooms to the Great Hall, were crushed beneath the heels of the Guard of Honour. It was a sound like the crackling of parched peanuts.

The Guard of Honour was a small detachment of the Police

Force. Sarge was at the head of the line. There were three lines. Up and down, in and out of these lines, walked the Governor of the country; and beside him marched the officer in charge of the detachment, and the Governor's ADC. Behind them, walking like recent recruits, marched the Headmaster of the College and Mr John Barrington Lascelles, King's Counsel, chairman of the board of governors of the College.

As these men walked and marched, the already dead cockles on the pavement exploded in a soft cry of anguish; and when they had moved along, pools of squashed bodies, brown paste, were left amongst the gravel on the pavement.

Sarge had a spike of silver that punched through the top of his helmet. It shone like silver. The sun made stars of it. You could hardly look at it without being blinded. Around Sarge's chin was a strap of silver. His white tunic was so clean, so starched, so firm and so white, that that too almost sparkled in the sun.

The Governor was dressed in white. From neck to ankles. His helmet was white, with a thick band of blue satin around the crown, and his silver chin-strap made him look like a bridled horse. He was a short man. Shorter than the head-master. He wore round tortoise-shell spectacles, and the glass and the brass buttons and the silver and the chin-strap made him look cruel and powerful and far away, in his disapproving excellent Excellency. He walked with a limp. They said he got it in the Boer War. On his head, on his helmet, instead of the silver spike which Sarge and the other policemen wore, he had plumes. But from the distance, where Boy had been standing with the other prize winners, it looked as if the Governor had a rooster that was crowing on his head. . . . On this street car, which he had travelled from one end of a men's clothing store to the end of a window of glass with tartan scarves in it, he had thought happily of an afternoon that began at one o'clock and that stretched to five, more than five years ago. He felt warmer in the cold, standing, hulk of metal and smelly leather and clangs. . . . 'Goddamn! Travel and travelling,' said John Moore-Adams. 'Travel and travelling is a son of a bitch! You're in for a goddamn experience, boy. I have travel from Miamah whiching is in Florida, right through the Florida Keys, straight as a goddamn arrow up through the Southern States where the racism is as thick as a goddamn dark night in Barbados, through the Mid-Wess, well. . . .' Boy wondered how he would look wearing a tartan scarf. Red, black, blue with a touch of white? Did it have white in its intricate pattern? . . . 'Lemme 'numerate the goddamn states I have pass through, then. Florida, Alabama-*goddamn*, Mississippah, the longest name in the goddamn States, Louisianne, Arkan*saw*, Missourah, Il-*linoise*, Indianah, Oheeo, Pennsylvania, and when I reach New-York-New-York, goddamn, and was met at the train station by my side-kick, all that nigger could ask me was, "John, how's the goddamn trip?". I couldn't speak a goddamn word! My tongue was tied-up, I was suffering from speechless-ness from not speaking a goddamn word during that goddamn journey. Not one nigger, white or black, in all that time, in all them goddamn states had the common decency to speak to me. Goddamn! That's something you'll learn when you reach Toronto. I don't know Toronto. Only bears and goddamn polo-bears lives there. And far's I understand, Toronto and Canada have a white-only policy. But I'll be goddamn if you don't find yourself travelling for hours and days, and not one goddamn nigger, white or black sitting beside you, would ever open his goddamn mouth to say, "How?" '. . . . Boy had come through all of this unscathed, although there was a temporary loss of speech. On his arrival, he had not spoken with anyone, no one had spoken with him; only to him; and he felt this unspeakable and unimaginable loss of speech and of exhilara-tion and absence of the exchanging of ideas to be as cold as the street car.

His uncle also gave him advice, and eight hundred Canadian dollars, as pocket money.

'As a going-away gift, as a blasted keep-sake, just in case,' his uncle had told him, as they sat in the balcony of Goddards drinking rum and water. 'And the stinking bitches, those sons o' bitches, and when you meet them on a bus, or in the tube, or a street car, all they intend to say to you in the way o' conversation is "Fine weather we're having, what?". Those stinking bitches who come down here from England, and Canada and see *life*, for the first time in their life! You may be making a mistake by going to such a young country, a ex-colony. But England,

where the real stinking bitches come from, may be the same as
Canada. Six o' one, and half-dozen o' the next!'

All this is memory. Brought back to him by the appearance
and the disappearance of the black woman on the streetcar that
afternoon, in the wet white road.

He can hardly see more than ten feet before him. The snow is
wet, and is like a thick white blind before him. Although he
cannot see clearly, barely distinguishing only frayed outlines of
people and things, still he feels protected by this white fuzziness.

There was suddenly talk at the College about Suez. Nasser.
Egypt. This crazy man. Imagine. Just imagine. To think of it!

'Gentlemen of College,' the Head of College began. Cups and
saucers were placed quietly as cheap china can be quiet, on the
large, scarred, history-eaten dining tables. There were clearings
of the throat, just as members of the upper classes do when they
want to make a devastating point to an inferior.

'Ahem! Ah-hem!' went through the room like bullets aimed
for the heart.

'Gentlemen,' he said.

Boy heard the word stressed, and knew that the stress was an
unnecessary reminder that they were all upper crust, not only of
the College, but of the best families.

'Gentlemen, today is a dark day in the history of the British
Empire. Nasser has seized the Suez. The Suez is British
property. Suez belongs to the English. Our grandfathers made
it. Our grandfathers built it. Indeed, our grandfathers civilized
it. And the entire continent in which it lies. We have called you
here, to this meeting, to get your unanimous support in the
drafting and the writing of a Statement of Condemnation of
Nasser. This Statement of Condemnation will be sent to the
British High Commissioner in Ottawa. We have been assured
that our Statement will be passed on to the very highest levels in
the British Government. This College, built on the strong
foundations of loyalty and allegiance to the British Crown, can do
no less than express in the very strongest terms, its disgust and its
resentment of the dastardly act perpetrated by Nasser. Do I have
unanimous agreement?'

Boy watched as unanimous agreement was given even before
he swallowed the last drop of the cold instant coffee.

He was a part of the 'we'. We. He was once again in loyal allegiance to the British Crown. He was stunned when the meeting broke into this patriotic song.

Rule! Brit-tanniah!
Brit-tanniah rule the waves!
For Brit-tuns, ne-ver-ne-ver
Ne-ver shall be slaves!

He was standing, during this appeal for loyalty, and the singing, beside a tall princely African from Ghana who had told him he was born in poverty, but had retained enough Latin and Greek to be made into a 'national student' and embark on his twentieth year, on a kind of twentieth century middle passage, with fees paid, books, room, board, clothes, cigarettes, Scotch whisky, and French-letters paid for, out of the national treasury. This African, clothed in his own speechlessness remained silent, during the speech and during the singing.

18

His first letter arrived.

'Dear Boy,

'Every evening when the fellows meet in my tailor shop, and start talking about international politics which is all they talks about these days, I looks at the old photographs and pictures you use to look at, and which I have put back up after I left politics, and whenever I look at the picture of Marcus Garvey and the one of the Great Nkrumah of Ghana, I always think of you. I hope you are doing well with your studies and that soon you will be coming back home. Since you leave, a lot of things have happen. We found out about the disappearance of your friend, Sarge. Sarge was found in a dry well, killed. The police are up in arms. Everybody is saying that a certain person, a person who was a politician, is the person responsible. I can't call no names, because you never know who will read this letter before it get to you. If you think that things was strange in the last elections when I was a candidate, well things are more serious now. Telephone calls are listened to by a woman in the Exchange who have political leadings, and you cannot even trust your own daughter or son, not to mention wife or woman. I have left the political criminals with who I was associated in the last elections, and I joined the party in power now. But I do not intend to run again. I join the party in power out of sheer politics and philosophy. You know I was a man who believe in the common man, and in the plight of the common man. But I know that I do not have the education and the learning that leadership qualities demands, and that is why I writing this letter. They ask me to write you. I can't name names. But they feel that your background and your learning and the experience you getting up there in Canada will be good for the party, and for the common man of this country. I ajjure you to think about this. And join the party. As a matter of fact, I already put down your name as a member. I enclose a application form for the same membership. If you don't want to join, send back the form not full out. If you want to join, good.

'The Mistress, your Mother, and Nathan fine. But I wish you would write them. I could help them out with reading your letter, even if it is confidential. You know me. My daughter get vex one morning, and left for Amurca. She write her cousin and got fixed up, and she is in Brooklyn today. Moo-Moo is in the Civil Service, working in the Law Courts. The village quiet. The country quiet. The Carbean quiet. Everything quiet. And it is this quiet that got me real scared, that something terrible in store for us. Politicians is politicians. No difference.

'I mention Sarge, the late Sarge. There is a rumour going round here that Nathan your father told somebody where to find Sarge body, and that Nathan was pointing his finger at a certain person, a certain person who was a political person, and that it is Nathan, so the rumour says, who is the instrument of making the police find out what happened to Sarge. They are now watching Nathan. Nathan is in danger. That is why I ask you to write your old people, to make them feel safe and happy. Mr Lassills the white man from England is prosecuting for the police in regards to Sarge, and any time now we will hear the verdict and the scandal.

'Last night we had a big argument about who is the greatest man out of Nkrumah and Nasser. I tell the fellows I going write you for an answer, because you are in a big country and news from a big country is more bigger news than the news and the newsmongerers in this blasted small place.

'Your friend,
'Affectionally,
'Seabert.'

Boy's room at the College always made him feel he was in a cell. It is a square room. It has a bed. And a bedspread. The bedspread has the cultural pattern of Scotland. His mother called her off-spring Scottish people. But he cannot relate to the stripes and the reds and the plaids. It has a book case. It has a table. And a desk. It has a notice board made out of something like hardened sponge.

He tied Seabert's letter with a red ribbon. The ribbon is from a gift he received one Christmas, his first cold Christmas, from the Friendly Relations with Overseas Students, called FROSH. The gift was a box of Cadbury chocolates.

He was walking back to the College one Thursday when he met four women. Their disregard for Canadian fashion and colour scheme told him they were West Indians.

'You think he is one o' them students?'

'One o' them Wess-indian students?'

'He could be a coloured porter, too.'

The four of them were wearing coats too large for them. One was in red. Boy thought of communism, and of a time when recent graduates from the London School of Economics returned home wearing red ties, and were immediately branded communists. One was in green. Her complexion was black and the green was ironical and comic; and he remembered the first St Patrick's Day, when a student said, 'Where's your green?' He had no green. Had never worn green. The third woman was in white. She was his complexion. The white against her pale body made her look pale and sickly. The fourth woman wore dark brown fur.

Their heads were covered in hats made of wool. Long woollen scarves with tassels at the end, with horizontal stripes which looked like tubes, were wrapped around their necks in such a way that the cold wind blowing against them made their eyes run water.

Boy is standing now before a glass-case of toothbrushes, flowers encased in stubby tubes of glass, like private collections of sea water and coral stone; greeting cards for mothers, fathers, boy friends and girl friends; and some for those already dead; and bright red boxes in the shape of hearts; and replicas of buildings he had seen in textbooks of geography, all reminding him of the Empire State Building, which he had seen in John Moore-Adams' house in Barbados; and other buildings of marvellous heights, all in Amurca; and one post card with *Niagara Falls Canada* on it: the single reminder of the land on which he is standing, seeing all these *wonders* of the world, all situated in Amurca.

Boy feels trapped. Under the sea. Like a fish. Out of its proper depth of water. On the beach at home, he would dive under the surface of the water, clearer than this wall of glass, and with a wooden box that had a bottom of glass, see the minutiae and the flotsam, the jetsam, the grains of sand, the dead fish, and the skeletons of man-eating beasts of the sea, and of fishermen, which could be mistaken for precious jewels and other stones and corals which tourists grab from the deep and then elevate in worth and value, vulgarity and sentimentality; and he could look through his 'glass-box' and see the magnification of dead things which the water made moving, and forget in this transformation, that he had earlier crunched them underfoot, kicked them out of his path, and gave them a value they deserved.

'The city is clean,' he had written to Seabert, soon after he arrived. 'The streets are always clean. They are so clean that I have never rested my eyes on a used package of cigarettes on the sidewalk. There are no used French-letters. No dead animals. Nothing I have seen here gives me the impression that living people live in this city. I wonder where the garbage is kept. The city is clean and white as an attitude.'

He is standing now, one inch from the radiator in his room, the radiator which gives off warm air only, and which makes a hissing noise that gives the impression that the air is really warmer, and is heat. He turns on the early morning classical concert on his radio and listens to the CBC's broadcast of Beethoven's Third Symphony. He is close to the window pane, but the more he concentrates on the four figures below in the white graveyard of the cold quadrangle, the more his vision becomes blurred, so that he is now looking through a cloud caused by his own vapour; but the four figures can still be seen, throwing snowballs at each other, and rejoicing with yells in that activity, and in the bull's-eye of a perfect throw, and amused at themselves for having invented this mature and adult version of a child's diversion. Boy feels there is another, more rational cause: they are amused that they, all four of them, are able to divert their attention and soothe their anxiety from the impending final examinations in three weeks' time.

He is incapable of this kind of diversion. He will sit in the examination room, not knowing anyone. There is no diversion for him. He cannot skate on the ice; he cannot play ice hockey; he cannot ski; he cannot climb mountains; he cannot dig a small hole in the ice and drop a line through it and wait in that cold dispensation with the patience of the Eskimo; he cannot divert himself in any manner common to this country in this winter of sports. But he does not regard them as sports. The Third Symphony reaches that part which he always said was written for hot blood, for people from the tropics; and each time he hears this passage, he tries with reason and with no evidence, to lay claim to Beethoven, and make him a man from his kind of hot climate. Beethoven is black, he concluded.

Boy has a colour print of Beethoven which shows him as a light-complexioned man, like a West Indian. But it cannot be just this, because many West Indians do not listen to classical music, do not compose classical music, are not taught, generally, an appreciation of classical music, not with the bellowing of Amurcan popular music in their ears from birth. He is glad for his own appreciation which was trained through the diligence of an Englishman who was choir-master and organist and homosexual, at the Anglican Church in the village. Boy escaped him.

The four figures in the quadrangle are still throwing snowballs. A snowball touches his window like a kiss from lips

that have been exposed to the wind that blows like the arctic at
the corner of Bloor and Avenue Road; and for a moment, he can
see nothing but the stylized snowflake of the crash of the
snowball. And soon after that moment, his warmer blood,
helped by the hissing radiator, clears the vision, and the four
figures are rolled into a heap of scrimmage, on the whitened
grass of the quadrangle.

. . . The parade, that day in Barbados, was over, and the
inspection was over. The parents were all colours under the
sun. And they were dressed in as many colours. The women,
mostly mothers among them, were large and healthy-looking;
and most of them looked as if they were pregnant. They all wore
hats of various sizes. Some of the hats the mothers wore were
like stunted towers, with no brims. Their dresses were new,
were shiny, were silk and shark-skin; were high at the neck; no
breastline and no breasts were visible; and these dresses
covered hefty arms like shining sheaves, and ventured below
the knees. Only the few foreign women, the wives of senior civil
servants of the Colonial Office, and of hotel managers, wore
cotton frocks. Their dresses just reached two inches above the
knees. It was the terrible heat and humidity of the island, they
said. And they wore sandals. The Headmaster's wife wore low-
heeled shoes which exposed her toes. And no nylons to cover
the thick hair on her legs. All her toes, including the big toes,
were painted red. On the fringe of the thick coloured crowd,
and joining reluctantly, as it was heading towards the Great
Hall, but mainly because they were tasting rum and gingers,
and stuffing three corn-beef sandwiches at a time into their
mouths, before the sandwiches were officially served, were
John Moore-Adams, the tailor Seabert, and Nathan, his father.
They looked out of place. And stiff in formal clothes. None of
them was accustomed to the formality of the College, and it
made them look stiff, and Nathan's and Seabert's old suits
looked like formal clothes which they were not accustomed to
wearing to such functions of stiff formality. *Their* own formal
functions were funerals and weddings and services-of-songs,
and Christmas and Easter. Beside John Moore-Adams, the two
of them, uncomfortable, but well padded and greased by the

corn-beef sandwiches with edges trimmed and wilted lettuce protruding, were severe in their brown three-piece suits, black serge turning green, and a light-grey shark-skin get-up, worn, tailored, and pressed by the tailor himself.

These three men were the biggest in his village. The fourth was Sarge. . . . The four figures below are still rolling in their melting glee, and playing with balls of snow. He can see them better now. The Third Symphony is ended. And the hissing radiator is less noisy and his breath has cleared his vision and he can identify each of his four colleagues; and soon afterwards he hears four pairs of feet slapping the linoleum of the hallway, in hard pounding determination; and then four pairs of feet are being scraped, and then he hears one pair as it stomps the small space in front of the door that is beside his room; and when the door is opened, and one last stomping of feet is wiping out the previous short exhilaration of diversion from the long night that the young man will spend, with a bent back and bent neck and sore shoulders over the texts of economic theory, the moment the last stomp is planted firmly on the bare cold floor inside the threshold, there is a loud bang of the door he shuts. It is a declaration that he has voluntarily put an end to that frolic. The bang of the door shakes him in his own room, and immediately the world is quiet, silent almost, and it becomes large and lonely and he feels he is alone in all the world. And he is.

He soon hears the springs of the mattress next door, beside the desk, the sudden squeal of the metal, and the temperamental bouncing of the body on the mattress, in search of a trough of comfort large enough to fit the fatigue of the body exhausted by the throwing of the balls of snow. The springs cry out again. And this is followed by a heavy blow to the mattress, as if a boxer is punching his frustration and his determination out of the heavy bag. The springs again. And then, a quiet shifting of a body, lighter now through the approach of rest. And now, all he can hear is the hissing of the radiator in his own room, and the banging and clanking of pipes and engines and furnaces in the deeper belly of the College. He thinks he can hear the wind. But there is no wind. There is never any wind in this country at this time. He thinks he can hear the stars moving.

He listens closely. There is someone talking. He listens, and it is the torment of the man next door; and he puts his ear to his window; and the speech and the voice move along, and he presses his ear to the side of his room. 'I can't make it,' he hears. 'I can't make these exams. Holy Christ!'

At this point in the self-deprecating, aimless talk adjoining him, Boy realizes that he has been listening to a monologue of suicide. . . . '*Jees!*'

He puts on his heavy navy-blue cashmere winter coat, worn by his uncle in Oxford; and puts his rubber boots over his black wellingtons. He leaves his door unlocked.

From here, down the four steps into the quadrangle, he is closer to the full groan of the guts of the College giving off turned-down heat at this time of night; across the quadrangle where there are no traces of snowballs, only fresh snow which has devoured the pleasure the four students were having; and with a cold hand against the heavy door which years ago a taxi driver bringing him to this college could not push open, due to fortress-like security, he makes the hinges announce his intrusion into the sepulchre of the night. The night porter is startled from his bed which is the panel of the switchboard; eyes red, confusion and embarrassment that he has been caught with his head and hands down.

'Taking a walk, sir?'

Before Boy touches the other, smaller, heavy door, the porter is down amongst the cords and switches and knobs and levers on the over-crowded board which is now his bed. He leaves him there, and goes out into the pure whiteness of the terrible night, thick and dangerous and overgrown, impassable and un-charted, monotonous as a jungle which you travel at your peril. He sees the snow and the cold and the night in this way: a jungle.

The music of Beethoven is still in his head, and he carries it the same way a foreigner carries things from his past, as bench-marks, to let himself know that he still exists as he was before, in a new but inhospitable land; and also to people his head against the foreigners of the night and of the land, he enters conversation with himself, just as the student beside him was talking himself into suicide.

These conversations Boy has with himself allow him to keep

in touch with what he used to know, with that former sanity, with friends who will bring no new danger. And if the distraction can take his mind off his present predicament: to stay in Toronto, or to return to Barbados, then perhaps, what he has set out to find, will come to fruition at that spot which he, and only he, can determine as the terminus of this absurd venturing forth into this unknown snowing night.

He knows that this is the walk of an idiot, but that it is the basis of the founding of empires. Disatisfaction, insomnia, greed, rudderlessness and pride and malevolence make adventurers of men. He read that somewhere, in Canada.

They want him back home in Barbados soon, to enter politics and waste his education on the common man; and no one among them has asked if he has the inclination and the moral and ethical preparation for such a task. Three of them have used strong and wrong arguments: arguments of love, to make him love politics.

The strongest came from Young Lascelles:

'Dear MWWT, In the two and almost three years that you've been up in Northamerica, I have completed my studies in Law and am proud to inform you that as of today, I am a qualified Solicitor.

'If you go on to the Inns of Court, as you said you would, you would have to take briefs from me. If you came back now, after your BA in Economics, and are articled with my father and myself (I am a junior partner), you will make bundles of money from the first day.

'People are saying you are some kind of political saviour of our country. Think about it. There may be gold in the streets of Canada and America, but down here in Barbados, if you are a Solicitor, money grows on coconut trees!

'Affectionately yours,

'John Barrington Lascelles, the Second (!) – as our old, late friend, Henry would say.

'P.S. By the way, your old man and your old lady are both well.

'P.P.S. Shall I have the stationers provide the letterhead, Lascelles, Lascelles and Thorne? That certain person of the white suit and cork hat, your rich uncle, has funds in our firm. This is confidential.'

He enters the archway under the clocktower on the main campus.

'I will have to do it,' he tells himself.

Walking under the archway, he is impressed that the tower under which he stands in his new white jungle is the same kind of masonry as the Clock Tower in his College in Barbados.

'I can't imagine myself on a platform, speaking to the common man!'

The snow is falling into his eyes, so he cannot see straight ahead. He begins to see dozens of faces coming at him through the thick whiteness; and the faces look black, against the jungle of snow; and as he walks over ground which only five or six months ago was green and cut to the same monotonous level, and watered by the same revolving spout with the same measurement of water, he sees these faces turn into the faces of the crowd in Barbados, expecting knowledge: he can see Sarge's face, and Lionel's and Manny Batson's, the rum shop owner; other faces could be Seabert's, John Moore-Adams', Moo-Moo's mother – God rest their souls! – and Moo-Moo's, Nathan's, Goalie's and Brandford's.

He is heading towards the boundary of the campus now, and he must keep his eyes on the ground, for the snow is blinding him, in the same way as he supposed the undergrowth in a different jungle blinds fast progress, and demands the use of sharp cutlasses, and the determination of harder steel.

Guiding him over this uncharted thick snow are footprints which men before him have made, and beside the footprints are red points, dots that have been disconnected from a compass. He must look down. And looking down, he sees the drops of red. And he must decide if they are made from paint, or from blood. And so, he follows their direction, footprints and drops, and then voices ahead of him shorten the distance of feet and blood. The feet and the blood become thicker. The voices are screaming, and chastising; and they are accompanied by heavy noises; bulk against metal, like the pounding of a drum that is struck by a careless and unmusical hand, with a sound disregard of known rhythm.

The voices come out of the unseeing whiteness of his new jungle, and he is upon them, two figures clenched in an unfair

213

closeness. One of them holds the other by the throat, near the head, and is pounding the head and all of the body he can grab in his hold, against the cold car whose colour and model Boy cannot make out; and the woman is screaming. But her screams become lower each time her head is rammed against the car. And the man breathes more deeply with satisfaction, at the impact which he seems to relish, for it is driving some sense into her body.

'Please! Please! Please,' she moans, sensibly.

Each word comes after the piston of the man's hand lands, and before the piston again drives her flat against the white car.

'Please!'

A short silence. And then the blow.

'I'm appealing to you!'

Another blow.

'Please!'

And this blow seems to be his acknowledgement of her pleading. She recovers some resistance, prepares her insensible body for the next brutal assault upon her beauty; she is probably a woman of lovely hips and thighs and legs and breasts; beautiful to look at, otherwise there would not be this jealousy of blows, and she would not now be smashed against a car.

Boy has now reached a spot in his journey from which he dares not continue; and so he turns back, and can still hear, 'Please!'; and then can only imagine that he is hearing it, as he walks a clean path, the only footprints his, if he should look behind him; the snow clean as the streets of the city in normal times of day; the blood already melted and having lost its significance; and then, one last 'Please', said in a whisper at his distance from the scene, as if the 'please' is really a gratified, final acknowledgement that the deed, whatever it was, whatever its cause, is at last properly punished.

Boy must find his own way now, without assistance of any kind.

Three

TRIUMPH

19

The first thing he took off was his jacket. He threw it on the overhead rack. It was warm. Then he took off his waistcoat. But before he stuffed it in the pocket of the seat, he removed the gold pocket watch, a gift from his uncle, three years ago. It was as if his blood was being bathed in the sea. Then, he took off the College tie, and folded it into half, and then in quarters; and he looked with some soft sentiment at the red bishop's mitres on the black background, and eventually, he placed the tie beside the waistcoat. His body now felt as if a strong snap of rum had hit him, at the pit of his stomach, and he had suddenly felt his entire body surrender, with a spasm, to the enervating drink. He loosened four shirt buttons, from the neck to the middle of the chest, exposing the gold chain round his neck. It was tropical and joy; peace and excitement.

The plane came out of a patch of clouds, and the skies screamed in a deep blue welcome; the air inside the plane was hot, but felt as if he was sitting in the verandah of the old house, witnessing daybreak, and feeling the breeze from the sea massage his body. At this point, he had had two rums and water. The sun played on the tip of the wing. The faces on his left when he glanced in that direction, were broad and soft and smiling. He had just picked up a woman's magazine that had fallen into the aisle.

'Oh, thank you. Thank you very much, young man. And are you returning home?'

Boy smiled, and answered her question.

He was thinking of the sea and of *Labour Blest*, moving from the crowded beach, on a Sunday morning, when his father Nathan took him for a 'spin in the blasted boat, boy!' He was sailing on a soft cushion of water and air and clouds and he knew every dimension, every manoeuvre, every nuance of the journey, although he knew nothing about navigation. But he was in a friendliness of spirit and of environment.

It was the second time he had read Seabert's letter, the last one he received, the one the night porter had forgotten, and off which he had seduced the resplendent exotic bird on the postage stamp.

Seabert had addressed his letter: *To Mr M. W. W. Thorne, Esquire, BA (Toronto), Political Leader of the Democratic Party of Barbados, Trinity College, Hoskin Avenue, Canada.*

'My dear Boy,

'Something I have to tell you. You have a political career here. Keep it dark. Bourne the former representative got five years. And the day before he was to begin serving sentence, he put a gun to his fucking head.

'I am not suppose to tell you this, but your mother is poorly. Nathan your father, say not to write and tell you, because he want you to come back here as a qualify man.

'But when you can, come home. Everybody waiting for you. Politically speaking, the former prime minister is now the richest man in the country, and there is some people who come into my tailor shop saying he is the best leader we ever had, because he get rich from politics.

'But we waiting on you. Come. Seabert.'

The black wellingtons on his feet were giving him a cramp. And their closeness began to make him feel that his feet were lost, cut off, were not there. He took them off, and pushed them under the seat in front of him. The soothing air, coming from somewhere in the plane, gave him the free sensation of being barefooted.

He thought of his mother, and the long journey he had taken with her, many years ago. He thought of the Saturday night 'socials' he used to attend, when he refused to dance, and sat instead near the bandstand and listen to every riff every improvisation of Percy Greene's Orchestra playing waltzes and fox-trots. The music came back, strong and thick as blood, like a shot of the strongest rum, like a religion of certain opiate strength and conviction, and he was once again in the glory of the repetitive pounding of steel pans and bass guitars.

And in this mood, reflecting the happy times he was about to face in a few hours, he dozed off. . . .

20

It was like a wedding. Faces were pressed against the wire fence that separated the greeters from the people arriving. And Boy recognized each face. Or almost all, for some he had never seen in this setting of extreme, unrestrained ecstasy and joy. He was home.

It was a hot day. Hotter than the morning of his departure.

His uncle was resplendent in white. Seabert was dressed in the same suit he had worn to Lionel's funeral. Manny Batson was there, waving the country's flag. Nathan welcomed his son in the same black suit in which he had walked beside Seabert, on another occasion. Nathan looked older than the suit.

It was just as Boy, in a gesture of extreme foolishness (something he had picked up in Canada), had risen from the hot, dirty, and dusty tarmac, placing a kiss of benediction and of style, beside himself to be home, that the power of the welcome hit him. He was more joyful to be back in Barbados than for the hero's welcome he was receiving. He did not think of himself as a hero. And certainly not as a big man. But the people said he was.

Patricia was there. She opened her mouth and screamed, 'Skipper! Skipper!' And that political welcome, that politically segregating term of power and influence, set his mind back to many other times when the words were shouted at another man.

Moo-Moo remained at the wire fence, her soft cheeks pressed into the harsh metal as if she was doing a penance of silent joy.

Boy's uncle took charge of the proceedings. He embraced Boy, throwing both strong arms round him, with such force and with such stickiness that Boy could smell his perspiration and feel blood from his body entering his own. His uncle did not use aftershave lotion.

'Skipper! Skipper!'

It was a cheer that deadened the air. It was a cheer that brought Boy back to life with such force that tears streamed from his eyes. He was shaking. He was bareheaded. No jacket, no tie, and when the cheer went up again, a man screamed, 'The comma-man! The comma-man!'

Boy looked down, and realized that he had come home wearing only socks.

'The comma-man touch!'

'Skipper! Skipper!'

James Clarke, the shopkeeper and his mother's friend, was there.

'The brains come back!' he shouted, and waved. 'The brains back home.'

Boy's uncle led him to a large black car, and as they drove off, Boy saw Young Lascelles, dressed in a woollen three-piece, black felt hat, and umbrella rolled up, sitting in the back seat of the old black Humber Hawk, waving like royalty. . . .

'You have any idea,' his uncle said, driving and looking sideways at him, and making him feel extremely nervous about the narrow roads, whose smallness he had forgotten, and the threat of a fatal accident. 'You know who you is? You have any idea who you is? You have any idea who you is, the minute you step-off that blasted plane?'

Where was his mother? The excitement had caused him to accept the faces at the wire fence; but now that he was moving again, on a journey which he both knew and did not know, he wondered about his mother.

'Have you *any* idea? Boy, do you know who the arse you is?'

'Meet you down in the village!'

It was Seabert passing in a rented car. Nathan was beside Seabert. And in the back seat were Patricia, Moo-Moo and Manny Batson.

Boy could see the tears in his father's eyes as the car sped past. He thought of his mother again.

'Ch'ist, boy! This is a day! You understand what happening to you? Today is a day come true. You have any idea, at all? Do you know, for instance, that in this blasted island, right here in Barbados, in the early history, that there was some white indenture servants who refuse to put up with the shite that the

English stinking bitches was feeding them with? In particular the white indenture servants, call them slaves, man! In particular them that come from Scotland? Man, they resist like shite! They resist the hard conditions, and at least two times, one was in the year 1633, or early in 1634 that they lay some plans for the stinking bitches?'

The large black car was like a beetle crawling through the valleys of green sugar cane fields, swallowed and partly hidden from sight. Boy could see nothing but moving canes, like crowded teeth bunched together, all symmetrical, rushing at him, while he was not moving; or moving very slowly, like a beetle that had eaten too much.

'Know where you come from, boy! Men like Seabert and Manny Batson, and the man that kill Johnny Adams, is men after my own heart. Tough men. Men o' principles. Men who can't be bought. I not mentioning Nathan, because Nathan is your blasted father. So, at least he's mention in that respects. But these white indenture servants that I was telling you about, those blasted revolutionary people was always close to the slaves, meaning people like Seabert and Manny Batson. And Nathan. 'Cause under the stinking bitches, indenture servant and slave receive the same bull-pistle lash in their arse, boy! It was much of a muchness. They had a common experience. They didn't trust no Englishman. Animosities breed allegiance, and it was only time before the two groups join-in to throw a lash at the oppressor. But why I lecturing you, and you just come down from university?'

In the valley of the green fields, it was easy for Boy to imagine the land in 1633. The plantation house on his left hand, washed in pink paint, with green eye-lids for the shutters on its numerous windows, sleepy at this time of the bright afternoon, stood shamefacedly amongst trees green with health and burdened by fruits. Breadfruit trees. In 1633, this plantation house had been there. Built even years before. And the indentured servants and slaves of that time are the men and women that dot the landscape that changes from dark green to that undefinable colour of withered cush-cush grass, and dried stalks of the same sugar cane.

'As you know, or should know, life for the slaves was a bitch,

boy! Incidentally. The fellow that put a stick o' dynamite under
Johnny Adams house, they say he hiding in a cave. Caves, Jesus
Christ! Caves! Even in the times I telling you about. There was
caves that serve the same purpose. In particular where we
originate from. Caves of all size and dimensions. Scattered all
over the Scotland District. Sin-Thomas and Sin-Joseph is where
the caves was that hid those revolutionary bastards, my forebears
and your forebears. A proud race o' bastards, boy! That is what I
mean, when I ask you, as I been asking you since we left the
airport, if you know who you is? All the things ever done in this
blasted island, in regards to freeing people, or raising-up people
from the various forms o' slavery, was done or 'riginated by
people from Sin-Thomas and Sin-Joseph. And them two par-
ishes is where you come from. I mean, you don't have to believe
me. Go in the public library, or the museum any morning, and see
um in black and white.'

Boy thought of Sheila, on her weekly trek to take out books
about adventure and mystery.

'So, don't feel you *special*. Don't feel you is some kind o'
chosen person. That it is a mistake, or a accident that the
blasted people in this country sent for you, and encourage you
to come back here, to tek up a political career. Don't think
they didn't had no other choice! Ch'ist, there is choices like
pigeon-peas. And don't tell me no shite that you too young. Or
that you don't have no political experience. Ch'ist, Her
Majesty Queen Elizabeth the First was thirteen or fourteen,
be-Ch'ist, she wasn't even seeing her menses, when she was
put on the throne o' England to rule, be-Ch'ist, the colonies,
the dominions and the empire. Including we down here in
Barbados. If Elizabeth could do it, you as a Thorne can do it,
too!'

The car came down the hill, stripped of its coat of green
protection, for the sugar canes had been reaped all in his area
where Boy was now. He saw the plantation house in the
distance, amongst spires of blue beckoning smoke that signal-
led food cooking, and shaking behind the mahogany trees and
the casuarina trees that looked like gigantic paint brushes
rubbing the colour of the sunset and shading the pink wash
from uninterrupted stares.

Boy recognized the pasture where the boys played cricket on Sundays during matins and Sunday school, and were called 'ungodly heathens' by the old women of the village. He recognized the house where Moo-Moo's mother lived and where he used to play *London's Bridge Is Falling Down*. He saw the gully sloping towards the sea which was a thin blue line in the golden distance, and the gully where he had hunted mongoose and monkeys, when he lived in the chattel house nearby. On his right, is a pile of limestone, and mortar and burnt wood, the remains of windows and doors, and the long steep untouched coral stone steps that lead from the structure which is now a memorial, a monument, and which years before was the biggest house in the village. John Moore-Adams would be pleased to know that the village could not forget him, Boy thinks, and would be reeling with laughter that he had to be remembered, even through a pile of debris.

A sudden pain entered Boy's guts, like the pain that comes from a fright or from a heartache.

The large black car is skirting the village, from the hillside.

'One o' the first things you should know,' his uncle is saying, 'is that it was a deliberate plan to exclude and shut-out people in this part o' the world, from the political system in the big countries, like Canada and England. I think they does call them metropolitcan centres. You will learn that when it comes to certain people, a policy or a plan is nothing more than a trick. The first trickster was Columbus. Columbus kill people like me and you, like Seabert and Nathan. I think it was the King o' Spain that ask Columbus why he killing off poor decent people, and all Columbus could say was that yuh can't use the same standards to judge Europeans as to judge Wessindians. The next stinking bitch was a man name Christopher Codrington. We just pass a big college dedicated to his memory, the bastard. But um was he who tell England that the whole Carbean should be a gar'son. Can you imagine that? The whole Wessindies a gar'son. The third bastard was a man name Fenelon. You know and I know that 'bout-here we know nothing 'bout French. Jesus Ch'ist, we can't even pronounce a good French wine by name. Fenelon wanted to keep we in ignorance, like sheeps and pigs and animals. Like beasts. And the fourth, was the one they sent to Trinidad, a man by the name o' Lord Harris. I wonder if Harsun College named after that bitch! I used to think that this same Lord Harris was a calypsonian like the Trinidadian fellow who came to be known as Lord Kitchener. But I was wrong. And it was only after I stayed up late one night, trying to make sense concerning my present and my past that I come-across Lord Harris. Lord Harris advocate that we should be treated like children. Like the coolies from Africa and India. There is no need for me to mention the one they send to Jamaica, a man by the name o' Lord Eyre. Well, he was the biggest stinking bitch outta all o' them. . . .'

Boy did not hear all that his uncle was saying, the landscape which the words were painting with blood and terror, was bright and green, speckled by the tricks the sun was playing on the trees and on the houses and on the white gravel road.

The car was moving through a lane which was really a driveway. It was longer than a lane, and belonged to one person, one house, one estate, one plantation. It was like a snake, moving on the side of a pond filled with water lilies, and then, with a soft tack of a sailboat, on the side of a line of casuarina trees, and finally, when it straightened itself out, and Boy could see in the distance, travelling over this arrow of white road, the pink-washed three-storey structure stood as strong and as powerfully built as the wicket gate in the fortress-like main door of Trinity College; but this house, and this vista was warm with its welcome.

'*This* is who you are!'

Boy could see men and women in the fields, animals and birds and chickens on the lawn in front the house, and as the car circled the paved area in front of the four pillars and the four doors, Boy saw the woman, standing on the bottom of three steps painted red, dressed in white with the pleats as distinct as if they were part of the design, her feet shining in the late afternoon sun, and on her head the white head-tie that made her look part-Indian.

The tears of joy and the sudden pain in his guts from the unexpected sight clouded his eyes and made him oblivious to the other cars that drew up behind him. It was his mother.